FREAKS of NATURE

Wendy Brotherlin

Spencer Hill Press

Contact: Spencer Hill Press, PO Box 243, Marlborough, CT, 06447, USA

Please visit our website at www.spencerhillpress.com

First Edition: May 2014

Brotherlin, Wendy, 1967

Freaks of Nature : a novel / by Wendy Brotherlin - 1st ed. p. cm.

Summary:Seven psionic teenagers travel by jet to an unknown location, all of them in trouble with the authorities for escaping their assigned government detainment facilities.

The author acknowledges the copyrighted or trademarked status and trademark owners of the following wordmarks mentioned in this fiction: Barbie, Chanel, Cheerios,ChristianLouboutin, Godiva, Pooh, Starbucks, Superman,Taser

Cover design by Lisa Amowitz

Interior artwork by Mike Corriero © 2014

by Wendy Brotherlin

Interior layout by Jennifer Carson

ISBN978-1633920-06-4 Paperback

ISBN 978-1-63392-007-1 Ebook

Printed in the United States of America

For my parents, who always encouraged me to follow my dreams

The unnatural—that too is natural.
–Goethe

Prologue

THE global Ebola-X pandemic of 2022 lasted five months, two weeks, and six days before a cure could be found. People died.

A *lot* of people died.

For the survivors, there were side effects from the vaccine.

One in particular, really. *The one that changed everything.*

Women gave birth to babies born with intense blue eyes. Eyes that swirled with vibrant color due to the abundant indigo blood vessels that ran outward from the pupil and throughout the sclera.

The eyes were as arresting as an exploding supernova. *Starburst eyes*, people called them.

As the babies grew, there were other signs of mutation.

Disturbing, potentially dangerous signs.

The public was alarmed, despite this mutation being found in a very small percentage of the population—one in twenty thousand births.

These children had astounding mental abilities. They became known as *psions.*

But such unbridled power could not be trusted to mere children.

The government stepped in. Laws were passed. The starburst children were separated from their families and sent to special boarding institutions. Institutions that appeared far more like prisons than schools.

That's when those incredible starburst eyes began to signify something altogether different for the baseline *homo sapiens* and the *psion* alike…

Fear.

Chapter One

DEVON McWilliams gripped his broken arm firmly to his side as he made his way down the steep slope of a towering butte. The badlands of North Dakota, with their inhospitable terrain and deathly cold nights, were the last place on earth he wanted to be on the brittle cusp of spring. His legs ached from exhaustion, but sheer terror pressed him onward. He struggled to make it to the rendezvous point before the authorities closed in. To complete this nightmare, Devon had stupidly made his escape from the North Central Psi Facility without a coat. It was a totally lame move he'd regretted the instant he leapt to freedom, but there was nothing to do about it now. He had to keep moving. He was exposed up here and the temperature was dropping quickly.

Devon's eyes swept over the rock-strewn wasteland that surrounded him. A storm gathered in the distance, and lightning flashed ominously within billowing black clouds. A thunderstorm tonight would make his desperate situation downright dire. Heavy rainfall would mean the flooding of hundreds of dry riverbeds within minutes. With daylight waning, he would have to keep the storm in mind as he searched for a safe place to rest.

"That's why they call it the *badlands*, stupid," Devon grumbled. "And not a flipping plant in sight."

Of all the idiotic psychic abilities to have, talking to plants rated right up there with navel gazing and gelatin juggling—neither of which were a particularly useful or *dangerous* talent to possess. But it was his calling. His *special* gift.

In other words, Devon's psionic powers made him the laughing stock of the entire North Central Psi Facility. Even the facility scientists had seemed to think Devon's powers were a joke. After his initial testing, during which there had been much snickering, Devon had never once been recalled for further training. Apparently, those in power had no use for his abilities, other than tending to the headmistress's creeping charlies.

There wasn't a single person at North Central who would have believed that a loser like "Plant Boy" McWilliams would be the first-ever psion to successfully escape from their fortified facility.

Better yet, he'd only gotten this far across the badlands because of the plants he had stumbled across. It was his rotten luck that he'd made a bad decision, listening to a pair of disoriented yuccas awakening from their winter slumber instead of the whiny hood phlox. The yuccas' directions had led him to this particularly perilious butte, where Devon had found an utter lack of helpful vegetation.

A few feet away, he spotted a scraggly-looking clump of little bluestem growing along the edge of the trail. But Devon knew better than to ask the grass family anything. They produced an endless psionic shriek at being touched, or trod upon, which happened, like, *all the time!* No, he'd just have to wait until he got down off this butte before he asked for directions.

Movement deep in the canyon drew his attention to a hawk soaring soundlessly over a patch of prairie grass, hunting for its dinner. The hawk didn't appear the least bit concerned by the approaching storm as it lazily circled below Devon, making its way closer to the canyon floor. Perhaps it had spied a fat field mouse, or a prairie dog pup wandering too far from its home.

Home.

The word alone caused Devon to choke back raw emotions that he didn't have time to deal with. It had been eighteen months since he had last seen his family. He hadn't wanted to leave home, but there had always been extreme pressure from the government and local officials for Devon to attend a national psi facility. Nobody seemed to care that Devon wasn't a danger to anyone. Then, two years ago, the powers that be threatened to revoke his father's medical license, and that's when Devon pleaded with his parents to let him go. What he hadn't known at the time was that the North Central Psi Facility would be hell on earth for a kid who talked to plants.

As he swallowed his rage and sadness, he ripped his gaze too quickly from the canyon floor and promptly slid on a patch of loose rock. He reeled, stumbling backward, and the pain from his arm rocketed through his body. White spots burst before his eyes, obscuring his vision. Teetering on the brink of disaster, he managed to regain his balance mere inches from the cliff's edge by plopping on his butt.

Breathing hard, Devon pinned his throbbing arm to his chest as he got a good look at the seventy-foot drop to the boulder-strewn ground below. He gulped hard. There would have been no surviving that fall.

Mindful of the drop, Devon slowly rose and turned back toward the trail. Before he could take a step, the ground beneath his feet gave way.

He cried out as he slid straight down the butte's face only to land squarely on another ledge eight feet below.

A bolt of pain shot from his injured arm like he'd grabbed a live wire, and his vision swam. He thought for sure he was going to hurl, or pass out and tumble to his death.

Cursing, Devon spit dirt from his mouth and leaned his forehead against the cool rock face as he fought to control his breathing. His legs trembled with the effort of keeping him upright on the tiny lip of rock. His limbs turned to lead, and his movements introduced him to an unparalleled level of exhausted torment. But he wasn't about to give up. Not when he had come all this way on his own. He'd give just about anything to have his friend, Colton Weaver, here with him now.

Badass Colton. The coolest, most levelheaded and self-possessed kid at the North Central Psi Facility. His roommate. Well, *dead roommate* now—dead because of their botched escape. Dead because of the deafening burst of gunfire that had torn his friend apart—the blood blossoming across Colton's chest—his look of utter surprise—

Devon moaned. He couldn't think about this right now! His lack of survival training meant that he had to remain focused and get his ass back on that animal trail if he wished to survive the night. Time was running out.

Looking up, Devon saw that the trail was definitely within reach. All he needed was to find a decent foothold.

Beads of sweat dotted his brow, and Devon grunted with each jostle of his arm. He was pretty sure that he had broken both of the bones in his forearm. He just hoped that, once he met up with the Psionic Underground Network, they could fix it.

By the time his sneakers had found a sturdy rock outcropping to balance on, Devon was squinting into the gray of twilight. It was getting harder to see, and as the shadows grew, so did his fear. If the psi facility's guards caught him now, he knew that he would never be allowed to see his family again.

"No, not gonna happen," he said to himself through clenched teeth.

With his good arm, Devon reached blindly above his head, searching for a firm handhold. He mistakenly grabbed a little bluestem. The psychic screech blasted through his brain, sending him reeling. He released his grip on the thin brown grass, but in his haste he lost his foothold and shot down the canyon wall with all the grace of a flailing water buffalo.

He screamed as the ground rushed up to meet him. Jagged rocks and sharp brush tore at his flesh and clothing. This was it—the end of Devon McWilliams, the boy who could talk to plants—for all the good *that* ever did him.

Devon's descent was cut short by the outstretched limbs of a juniper tree, which violently plucked him from the canyon wall with the strength and resilience only a cliff-dwelling member of the cypress family could manage. Devon slammed into the gnarled trunk face-first and an explosion of stars filled his vision.

Curse words tumbled from Devon's lips as he slid down the juniper's slanting trunk, his face painfully scraping against the rough bark. He managed to stop his descent using his legs and one good arm, and gripped the tiny little tree for all he was worth. His heart pounded against his ribcage with adrenaline-charged ferocity until he was quite certain that it would burst.

The wind…it carries the scent of spring…and so shall I carry you…

"That's certainly kind of you," he said to the juniper, using the most respectful tone he could muster, while at the same time trying not to gasp in pain. "But I can't stay long. I have, uh…friends to meet."

Devon frowned at his own stupid lie as he clung to the tiny juniper thirty feet above the ground. Still reeling from the fall, he struggled to get his bearings. It was dreadfully cold up there. The icy wind burned his skin, especially along the right side of his face, where he had collided with the tree.

The tree that had just saved his life.

Life! Life! Water and sun are life! Turn your face to the sun, young one, and you too shall shine!

"Mmm-hmm," Devon mumbled as he fought to calm a sudden wave of nausea. It wasn't unpleasant talking to trees, because their voices held the soothing, deep richness of the earth. Flowers, on the other hand, were like talking to a gaggle of know-it-all great-aunts—no matter what one said, they were always right and they would never shut up about it.

And then there were the shrubs, which were a bit trickier to communicate with. Shrubs, it seemed, never had much to say. Devon had to work hard to get a shrub to open up. They were so doggone slow to trust anyone. However, his efforts were almost always rewarded with astute and accurate information. Shrubs didn't miss a thing. They were, it seemed, the polar opposite of the useless grasses, which merely screamed all the time. That's why Devon stuck to sidewalks and paved roads and avoided flower shops.The cries of freshly cut flowers were as irritating as the whine of a dentist's drill inside his head. The sensation made him wince just to think about. Botanical gardens were out of the question too, as he had found out two months ago when he and a shapely blonde waterwielder named Shelby were asked to find the reasons behind a failing wetlands exhibit. The sheer presence of so many different varieties of plant life completely overwhelmed him.

In short, he'd passed out. Cold.

That's not the best way to impress girls at fifteen.

Or, like, ever.

"Shelby Weizerman sure wasn't impressed," Devon muttered under his breath. He was starting to feel better. Scanning the rocky surface below, he located a deep crevasse cut into the rock face about five feet away that gently sloped down to the canyon floor. It was a pathway to safety.

Shell-bee Wise-man... Does she drink of the sun? Does she dip her roots in the cool mountain pools of knowledge?

"Probably not," Devon said to the tree as he fingered a newly formed leaf bud on a branch. "But she sure was hot."

Aaahhhh, the juniper sighed as if in understanding. *The sun... Divinity.*

Devon grinned. Talking to trees was like talking to his crazy cousin Pete when he went off his meds—profound one minute, spouting nonsense the next. Still, there was comfort in hearing another's voice. Even if it was all in his head.

He had spoken to a cluster of leopard lilies shortly after he had emerged from the facility's back gate. They had kindly pointed out to him which direction to run. Yesterday, a rather scraggly-looking choke cherry shrub had told him where to find water, and a copse of cottonwood trees had stood sentry over him last night. He had fallen asleep to their deep voices humming, in chorus, an elaborate tune set to a beat driven by the wind. As the cottonwoods swayed, their voices moved and turned in complex runs that at once contrasted and blended in magnificent ways. It was the kind of music that stirred Devon's soul and, at the same time, produced a lingering sadness. No one else on the planet would ever hear it but him. Nor was he able to recreate it for others. It was a blessing and a curse. It reinforced the fact that Devon was different. And that difference made him lonely.

The juniper started humming, its deep psychic baritone rising and falling to the pulse of the chilly canyon wind. It was utterly beautiful and incredibly forlorn at the same time.

"I must leave you," Devon said, stroking the tree's bark with his good hand. "Thank you…for everything."

Stay the night... My branches will cradle you... Have no fear...

Devon nodded. Trees had such big hearts, but they hadn't quite the same concept of cold as humans did. "Nevertheless, my friend, I must depart." He patted the bark, and to his surprise, the entire tree erupted with buds. Exhaustion was impairing his mental discipline. His power was getting away from him.

He slid off the juniper's trunk and stepped onto a rocky outcropping below. His arm hurt like hell, but if he had clung to that tree a moment longer, he would have caused it to fully bloom. If that happened this early in spring, the juniper would surely perish.

Devon wasn't about to be responsible for any more death.

Half-sliding, half-walking, he managed to clumsily navigate the five feet to the crevice. His entire body ached from the beating it had taken over the last two days, and he'd torn holes in not only his sweater and jeans but along the sides of his sneakers as well. He had gotten used to the feeling of tiny rocks rolling around in his shoes, but the minute he dropped down into the crevice, to his consternation, he discovered *sand.*

"Oh, you gotta be kidding me!" he cried as his feet sank into the crevice floor. Sand poured into his shoes, and Devon found himself flailing to keep his balance. Moving his broken arm had been the wrong thing to do, and the ensuing pain was enough to send him crashing into the wall.

He reached out his good hand in an effort to steady himself, and a sharp rock snagged his sweater. It was just what he needed to stop his momentum. He grabbed the side of the wall and steadied himself before pulling his sweater free from the rock. The sky above was now a deep indigo. He had only minutes before the last of the sunlight was gone for the day.

Ignoring the sand in his shoes and the throbbing pain that terrorized his body with every beat of his heart, Devon felt his way along the crevice. He thought that he must appear every inch the madman with his greasy brown hair matted to his scalp, his wild starburst-blue eyes, and his lips curled back in a feral grimace. He held out his good arm before him as he stumbled toward the opening.

Devon freaked as a tacky silk covered his face and filled his mouth. He cried out while spitting and clawing at the spiderweb covering his face. Staggering blindly out of the crevice, he tripped and landed in a heap on the hard canyon floor. His good arm had broken his fall, but the jolt to his body had him seeing stars again. He groaned as nausea crashed over him in waves.

This time, he did puke…all over a spindly-limbed skunkbush.

Warm rain? The little bush sounded confused.

Devon whimpered. His arm ached so badly that he couldn't move. He could hardly draw air into his lungs.

Oh! The rain has stopped so soon!

Devon was in too much pain to reply to the skunkbush. The sun had set and the cold wind blew with devastating authority over the canyon floor. It wouldn't take long for him to freeze to death if he stopped moving.

"Must get going," he groaned, and that's when he heard the prairie grass *scream.*

"Oh, no," Devon gasped. Frantic, he tried to get to his feet, but he was simply too exhausted. All he could manage was to roll over onto his knees.

"He's over here!" a man's voice shouted. High-powered spotlights clicked on, leaving Devon blinded by the glare.

He shielded his eyes with his good arm and peered into the brightness. Unfortunately, he saw neither his Psionic Underground contact, nor the North Central Psi Facility guards. What Devon saw was much worse than that.

A platoon of armed men, looking like sleek high-tech ninjas in their black fatigues and lightweight armor, surrounded him. Dark helmets with their mirrored visors pulled down made the men virtually identical, right down to their big-ass guns and itchy trigger fingers.

The government had called in the *military* to retrieve him. That was definitely not good news. They weren't planning on taking him back to school.

Where they'd take him, Devon would never return.

Washington, DC.

"You Devon McWilliams?" a gruff voice asked. "Psionic ward of the North Central Facility, student number 7-5-2-6-8-2-6-9?"

Devon hesitated. He blinked into the bright lights as he slowly sat back on his heels. Everyone surrounding him was an adult. That meant they were baselines—not one of them had psionic powers. That's why they seemed so damn indecent in their weapon selections. They had no idea what "Plant Boy" might do to them.

That thought by itself would have been laughable, if the situation hadn't been quite so perilous.

Devon looked directly at the soldier who had addressed him. "Uh, yes, sir. I'm Devon McWilliams."

The Taser probes bit through his sweater and into his chest with the ferocity of two angry rattlesnakes. Devon flew backwards and hit the ground hard as fifty thousand volts ripped though him. The pain was lightning-hot and bone-deep; all the while, he flopped around in the dirt like a hooked trout.

When the electrocution ceased, Devon slammed to the ground headfirst beside the skunkbush—his face managing to land smack-dab in his own pool of vomit.

Consciousness fading, he could hear the soldiers' footfalls approaching as they tightened their ring around him. Life as he knew it was over. He was now a prisoner of the US government. He would never see his family again.

But worst of all, he had failed his one and only friend…

And that made Devon McWilliams the ultimate loser.

Chapter Two

DEVON'S pain-wracked body, twitching and throbbing, brought him to consciousness before his eyes even opened. Everything ached—his chest, his arms—especially his broken left arm—his lips, even his hair! And to top it off, something stank—*bad!* Like he was trapped in a vomit-filled porta-potty or something.

Wait…was he sitting up?

Devon's eyes flew open. Before he had the chance to properly take in his surroundings, he was pulling against restraints he couldn't quite comprehend in his effort to flee.

"What the hell!" he cried. His wrists and forearms were encased in metal bands and shackled to thick chains connected to the armrests of his chair. His pelvis was anchored firmly to his seat by a wide steel bar that fit snugly across his lap. Even his ankles were securely fastened to something below. When Devon realized that he absolutely could not move of his own accord, he suddenly remembered that he was now a prisoner of the United States government.

"Oh, no way! Not even!" Devon shouted. He bucked against the pelvis restraint, totally flipping out. He'd always been a "good kid." As a psion, would he be forced to wear prison orange or a different, no-less-horrible color? Devon didn't want to find out. He wasn't a hardcore criminal! He was an idiotic plant whisperer! *The* idiotic plant whisperer, thank you very much, and right now, he just might crap his pants from sheer panic.

"I don't belong here!" he hollered, tugging frantically against his restraints, only to find that the harder he pulled, the tighter his bonds became.

He screamed. He was not about to become some psycho killer's cellmate. The military should have killed him when they had the chance.

"Yo! Vomit boy! Pull it together!"

Vomit boy? Was someone talking to *him*?

Devon froze. He obviously wasn't alone. Leaning forward, he was able to survey his surroundings a bit more easily. It looked as if he were in the cargo hold of some kind of aircraft, judging by the way the walls sloped concavely around either side of the room. He counted five other kids in the room. Two guys sat across from him—one skinny and bald, the other with long, greasy blond hair. A Latino kid sat two seats down on Devon's left, and a pale blonde chick with trippy dark circles beneath her eyes sat just to his right. There was also a brooding musclehead in a black leather jacket sitting next to the door. The guy looked like he could bench-press a tank.

All of them sat chained like rabid dogs to their fortified recliners from hell, which could only mean that they too were guests of the US government…and in a serious shitload of trouble.

Five pairs of starburst eyes gazed coolly back at him.

Devon had seen those judgmental glares before at the North Central Psi Facility—usually right before some jackass slammed him into a locker.

Inwardly, he groaned.

Note to self—no more freaking out in public.

"That's better," said the skinny bald kid sitting across from him. He had unusual piercings on the sides of his face around his eyes and he was dressed in a dirty, stretched-out T-shirt and shredded jeans. "That conniption fit of yours polluted our airspace. You reek, vomit boy! Like, *bad!* And it's not like we can just get up and move, ya know."

"Leave him alone, Alison," growled the big guy next to the door. His starburst eyes were rimmed with kohl eyeliner, giving him a dangerous, don't-mess-with-me Goth vibe. He sat facing everyone, looking buff and badassed enough to break them both in half if he wasn't constrained.

"The name's *Nevada*," the bald kid said, turning to scowl at the big guy. "Don't make me say it twice."

Hey, wait a sec…the bald kid's a girl?

Devon's eyes instantly locked onto her chest, but the circus tent of a T-shirt she wore gave absolutely nothing away.

Dang it! Now he was picturing her naked!

"Well, the feds called you Alison," the big guy said, gazing at her with an alien intensity. "It wasn't like I could read your mind."

"Not like any of us can right now. Even if you *were* a telepath." The greasy blond guy was talking. "These wrist shackles? They're called disruptors. None of us will be able to access our abilities."

"No shit," smirked Alison—Nevada—whatever-her-name-was. When she noticed Devon staring at her chest, she seductively licked her lips. "See something you like, vomit boy?"

Devon's eyes widened. For a bald chick, she sure could come on strong.

And in a weird way, that was kinda hot.

He noticed her more feminine features now—her thick, pouty lips, her small, delicate ears, and her long, artistic fingers.

And then there was that blue tattoo inked all around her head in what appeared to be something akin to Celtic runes.

It matched her vibrant starburst eyes. And it pulsated with energy as if it had a life all its own.

"I—I like your tat," Devon said.

Nevada sat back in her seat and gave him a wide, provocative smile. And in that moment, she was eminently beautiful. "Why, thank you," she said. "My late husband gave it to me as a wedding gift."

Devon gaped at her in astonishment. She couldn't be much older than him—eighteen at the most. "You're married?"

"Was." Her beautiful smile faded. "He's dead."

"Oh. Sorry."

"Don't be sorry. It wasn't your fault." Nevada turned the side of her head toward Devon so that he could take in the full effect of her tattoo, with its intricate patterns created entirely from psionic energy deposited just below the surface of the skin. "He did beautiful work, didn't he?"

"Oh, yes. It's incredible—I've never seen a psionic tattoo up close before. It's really amazing."

She nodded, the attitude gone from her voice. "Even though he's dead, I'll have a part of him with me forever."

"I didn't think psi-tats lasted but a few weeks," the big guy said from over by the door.

"Unless you're a *baseline*, of course," added the greasy blond with a bit of a sneer. "And then, well, you're dead."

He was right. Psi-tattoos were completely harmless for psions, but for baseline humans they were a death sentence. Not that Devon had ever even met a psi-tat talent, but he resented the fact that dangerous abilities like that had made it impossible for him to live with his family anymore.

"Yeah, well, who even cares about the stupid baselines, anyway?" said Nevada. She turned to the big guy by the door. "And for your information, I'm gonna have my psi-tat inked over before it fades. Capisce?"

"That might be kind of hard to do where we're going," the big guy replied. He didn't look angry when he spoke, more like resigned—like he had already accepted his long walk to the gallows.

"Where *we're* going?" Nevada growled. "You might be going down without a fight, but I'm not."

"*Shhhh!* They're listening!" The pale blonde to Devon's right was speaking. She had a thick foreign accent, and Devon was suddenly curious as to where she was from. "They'll hold anything you say against you. Make you regret your boasting."

"I'm not boasting," Nevada replied with a shrug. "And I don't care who's listening."

"Well, you should." The blonde girl was looking paler by the moment, and Devon thought that she might faint dead away.

"Alya," the greasy blond guy hissed from his chair across from hers. *"Enough!"*

"Alya?" Devon asked, turning to her. "Is that your name?"

"Yes," she whispered, half-closing her eyes. She nodded toward the guy with the greasy hair. "Alek—he's my twin."

"Twins? No way…" Devon glanced over at Alek and then back again to Alya. Other than the fact that they were both blond and a bit pasty-looking, they sure didn't resemble each other very much. Alya's face was soft, with delicate characteristics that one might find in a Renaissance portrait, while her brother had the oversized but well-proportioned features of a sitcom star. Unlike his sister, who possessed an ethereal quality more akin to an angel, Alek was good-looking in that average, I-don't-have-acne kind of way, and he didn't have that freaky accent, either.

"So, where are you from?" Devon asked, admiring the graceful curve of Alya's profile. He had never chatted up a girl as pretty as Alya, but he wasn't about to let the opportunity pass him by.

"It's no business of yours," Alek growled.

"Romania." Alya gave Devon a little smile, and he noticed how wearily she was leaning against the headrest. "At least, that is where we were born."

"Alya! Hush!" Alek hissed from across the aisle, but Devon ignored him. He was more concerned with how white Alya had turned.

"Uh, are you okay?" Devon asked. He wished that he could move his arm and feel for a pulse or something. That girl looked seriously weak.

Alya's sweet smile stayed on her lips while she managed a nod, but then her eyes closed as if the effort had been simply too much for her. "There is nothing to be done," she said softly. "It is merely a condition of my power."

"She's a healer," said Alek. He was glaring outright at Devon now, his eyes brimming with malice. "She draws people's diseases into her own body when she restores them to health. She needs to rest. So leave her the hell alone!"

"Language, Alek," Alya said with her eyes closed. "There is no need to be rude."

"Alya, I—"

She held up a finger, and Alek fell silent.

"You see," she said, her eyes opening ever so slightly as she turned to Devon. "There is always time for manners. Don't you agree?"

"Yes—yes, I do," Devon replied softly. Alya was as fragile as a glass butterfly, and he feared that the sight of his vomit-coated face might shatter her.

Once more, she conjured a sweet smile. "That's good," she said, her voice drifting away as her eyes closed. "Manners are ever so important."

"Indeed," said the musclehead from beside the door. "Too bad our hosts don't seem to agree with you, Alya. I think we could all use some food and water. Maybe even a bathroom break before we lift off again."

"Hey! Yo! Yo! I gotta pee!" Nevada cried, addressing a camera that hung above the Latino kid's chair. "You gonna do something about that?"

Devon glanced over and saw the Latino kid cower in his seat as Nevada started yelling. It sounded as if the little guy was praying…in Spanish.

"Uh, Nevada?" said Devon.

"What is it, vomit boy?"

Devon nodded toward the Latino kid. "I think you're scaring him."

Nevada glanced over at the boy. The kid's hands were folded before him in prayer, eyes squeezed shut, head lowered. "Aw, shit," she sighed, rolling her eyes. "Hey, kid! KID!"

Trembling, the Latino kid looked up.

"Honestly, kid, I wasn't yelling at you. There's a camera above your—"

The boy shook his head and went back to praying in Spanish.

"Aw, for the love of Pete! Get over yourself, you little shit-sucking twit!" Nevada was yelling again.

"I don't think he speaks English," said Devon. He knew he was taking a big chance pissing Nevada off, but he really didn't want the kid sitting two seats down from him to crap his pants, either.

"Seriously?" Nevada asked. Her gold-and-sapphire piercings sparkled in the light. "I thought everybody spoke English these days. Look at the Russian freaks."

"We're not Russian," Alek snarled.

"Whatever," Nevada said, with a dramatic eyeroll. "It's not like I wanted to scare the Mexican kid, I thought he was, you know, just shy or something."

A red light began to rotate above the door, and an alarm sounded.

Devon's first impulse was to put his hands over his ears, but that was impossible at the moment. Instead, he found himself cringing at the horrible noise with his eyes glued to the doorway. He just prayed that whoever was about to come through that door wasn't coming for him. Not yet, anyway. He *so* wasn't ready to face the feds.

And orange definitely wasn't his color.

The heavy metal door slid to the side, and two burly federal agents wearing dark suits with long, skinny ties dragged an unconscious Asian chick into the room. The girl's long black hair fell dramatically around her pretty face, but she hung limply between them, lifeless. Devon wondered if she might be dead.

The alarm stopped, but the red light continued to rotate as the two men slammed her into the chair next to Nevada and quickly went to work chaining her in. While one guard closed the shackle on her right wrist, the other bent over to secure the wide bar across her hips. As soon as he reached across her, the girl's knee came straight up, popping the guy right in the nose. *Hard!*

The man cried out as a torrent of blood poured onto the girl's lap. The other fed glanced up from his work in time to receive a head-butt between the eyes.

Before either man could recover, the girl continued her attack in a blur of motion as she handed out a martial arts butt-whooping all over their federal asses. She struck the guard she had just head-butted with a series of quick chops to his throat, while at the same time wrapping her legs around the guy with the bloody nose to flip him onto the floor. She moved insanely fast. Only her right wrist remained cuffed to the chair. As the fed beside her held his throat, gasping for air, she searched him with dexterous fingers and produced a set of chip keys, which she quickly narrowed down to one.

"Dang," Devon said, eyes wide as he watched from his front-row seat. "Who *are* you?"

The girl didn't even look up when she dropped the chip key into the lock on her shackled wrist. "Bai Lee Chen," she said. The shackle popped open, and in the next instant, she knocked out the fed next to her.

As the man crumpled to the floor, Bai Lee looked over at Devon. And winked.

"See ya around, killer," she said with a bright grin. And then she was out the door.

Whoa…now, *that* was hot.

Bai Lee would definitely be making an appearance in Devon's dreams tonight. Though hopefully, she'd be completely naked and armed with a can of whipped cream.

Gunfire startled Devon from his thoughts. His eyes slid to the door, where he saw the big guy straining to get a view of what was going on outside their room.

Oh, no! Not Bai Lee! Devon hoped that they hadn't caught her so quickly.

But they had.

This time, a team of armed guards dragged Bai Lee to her seat and held her down by beating her with riot sticks around her head and shoulders. Devon cringed with each blow as the girl sat helpless to defend herself. But she didn't cry out. She took the blows in silence, until the guards were satisfied that their prisoner had been secured.

Fear rose up from his guts like an arrow-shot to his brain. "They're going to kill me." Devon was only half-aware that he had spoken aloud.

The guards carted off the unconscious federal agents and left behind Bai Lee's bloody and broken body. No longer did she look hot and kick-ass.

She needed help.

They all needed help.

But Devon was helpless.

"No," came the soft reply.

Devon turned to find Alya staring at him. She reached out her hand; to his surprise, the chain around her wrist was loose enough to allow her to touch his arm.

"They won't kill you," she said with that sweet smile of hers, and Devon noticed tears in her eyes. "You're no threat to them."

"You're right—I'm a loser," he said, staring hard at the bar that held him firmly in his seat. He looked up when he felt Alya gently caress his arm with a fingertip.

"No, not a loser," she said. "A good person." Their starburst gazes met. "You care more than most."

"It's a curse."

"Why? Because you find love a weak virtue?"

Devon chuckled. "Nah…I'm just a sucker for punishment."

Alya's smile waned and Devon heard her sigh as she withdrew her finger and lay back in her chair. "I wish I could heal you," she said.

Devon glanced down at his arm, locked firmly to his seat, and immediately missed her touch.

"Yeah, me too," Devon softly replied, but Alya's eyes were already closed as she rested in her chair. He didn't think that she had heard him. He hoped that she was sleeping.

Glancing across the aisle, Devon caught Alek glaring outright at him; he quickly averted his gaze. The last thing he needed was to get his ass kicked by her twin for talking to her. It was just like back at North Central. Geez! When was he ever going to get a break?

"Hey! Psssst. Vomit boy!"

Devon looked over at Nevada. She gestured with her head toward the seat next to her.

"Is she dead or alive? I don't wanna be chained next to a stinking corpse, ya know? I got rights."

Devon leaned forward and took a careful look at Bai Lee. Her face was a swollen bloody mess with an oozing gash across her right temple. Her nose looked broken, and her lip was bleeding, too.

"Uh…" Devon said as his eyes wandered her small frame in search of a sign that she was still breathing.

And that's when he saw it.

"Oh, yeah, she's alive."

Bai Lee was giving him the finger.

Chapter Three

"YOU guys are such wimps," Bai Lee chided. "You should have jumped those idiot feds when you had the chance!" Her eyes were open, and she was grinning at them with blood-coated teeth. She looked up at the camera above the Latino kid's head. "They're probably in the command center right now with a pair of tweezers and a hand lens trying to locate the whereabouts of their pricks!"

"Watch your language," said the musclehead by the door with a scowl. He didn't look the least impressed with Bai Lee. "We may be prisoners, but we don't have to behave like animals. Besides,"—he nodded toward Alya—"we have a lady present."

Bai Lee glanced down the row with a look of disgust. "Who? ...*Her*? I don't see no lady—she's practically a corpse!"

"Says the blood-splattered Chinese *be-otch* who couldn't even manage a proper escape," Nevada replied with a smirk. "Enjoy your ass-whooping much?"

Bai Lee flashed her a deadly smile—one that had Devon seriously concerned for Nevada's safety. "Oh, yeah, and I'm ready for seconds."

Nevada leaned forward as far as her restraints would allow so that she was towering over Bai Lee, nose to nose. Their eyes locked, and the tension in the room rocketed into the stratosphere. Someone was about to get her face chewed off—and by no means was that a good thing.

"Bring it, bitch!" Nevada growled.

"NO!"

The word came out more as a roar of rage than an actual command. And every pair of starburst eyes in the room was suddenly trained on Devon.

Great... Why'd he have to go and play the hero?

"What is it, vomit boy?" Nevada cooed with a deadly glare that slid from Devon back to Bai Lee. "You afraid there won't be anything left of your new girlfriend after I finish ripping her face off?"

"My name's Devon McWilliams, not vomit boy," he corrected her. "And it's not about that. I was just—"

"What?" demanded Bai Lee, her eyes cold with fury, "You don't like girl-on-girl action?"

"Actually, I do enjoy a little girl-on-girl action as much as any red-blooded American male. However—" He was about to blurt out some lame-sounding *something* when he felt Alya's reassuring touch on his arm.

"Now is not the time to fight amongst ourselves." She had finished his thought and Devon could hear the exhaustion in her voice. "We must unite if we are to survive."

"Unite," Bai Lee spat. "Yeah, right." She narrowed her eyes at Alya, as if she were lower than the dirt on a sidewinder's belly. "Bite me."

"Excuse me?" Devon cried in outrage. He threw his weight forward, straining against his bonds. "How dare you speak to her that way? You don't know what she's been through! *What we've all been through!*" He felt Alya's gentle squeeze for him to stop, but the pain and panic of the last three days continued to spew from his lips. "You might be some bad-ass ninja Barbie where you come from—but here? In this room? On this one-way flight to hell? We're pretty much all equally screwed! Together! *Sideways!"*

The entire room was silent.

No one moved.

Devon's heart thumped so rapidly that he thought that it just might explode from his chest and take flight. Too bad he wouldn't be able to soar out of the room after it and disappear.

Bai Lee slowly shook her head. "Sideways, huh?" Her icy glare softened, and she looked like she might actually laugh outright in his face.

Geez! How stupid had he sounded?

"Yes, sideways!" Devon spurted. "You'll be screwed in whatever way you *won't* like it. That's what the feds are gonna do to you."

Bai Lee shrugged. "Doubful. When it comes to being screwed, I'm usually up for anything."

Devon groaned and fell back against his seat. He couldn't talk to that madwoman! She was seriously depraved! *And* she could probably kick his scrawny little chicken ass with her left eyebrow alone.

And that's when he realized that Alya's hand was no longer resting on his arm.

Devon looked over at her and found Alya slightly turned away from him, her cheeks wet with tears. Oh, man, had he made her cry?

"Alya? Are you okay?" he asked softly.

"Fine," she replied, but Devon could hear her choking on a sob.

"You're not fine, Alya." Devon tried to reach over and touch her, but the shackles held him firmly in place. Damn it! Why weren't the feds helping her? It was beyond obvious that she was dying.

Like I told you, the feds won't help because they're cowards. They want us all to die.

What the hell?!

That voice was Bai Lee's!

And it was *inside* his head!

Devon's head snapped toward her. Bai Lee was a telepath! She had no right to be rummaging around inside his head without his permission! "How in the heck are you able to—"

Watch what you say! The feds are listening!

Bai Lee offered Devon a little smirk from across the aisle as he struggled to change what he was going to say, mid-sentence.

"—uh, uh, uh…kick ass like you do?"

Yeah, well, that was stupid, but what the heck else was he supposed to say? She could come at him with the speed of thought. If he'd been able to access his own powers, he'd at least have had some kind of mental barrier to protect himself with, lame as it was. Most psions could defend their thoughts from telepaths, even if telepathy wasn't their specialty. But take away a psion's power and he was as helpless as any baseline.

Actually, everyone in this room was now at Bai Lee's mercy. And if Devon was going to get any answers, then he was going to have to be a heck of a lot more delicate in his approach. Defenseless, it was hard to hide much of anything from a telepath.

Bai Lee was looking at Devon with a smartass grin on her face. "You want a lesson in ass-kicking?" She glanced up at the camera positioned over the Latino kid's chair. "Maybe the feds would like to come back in here and allow me to give you another demonstration. I know I'd love it."

"We probably all would, but I'm pretty sure that's not going to happen. The feds aren't *that* stupid," Devon said. He wasn't about to take his eyes off Bai Lee, not until he knew what she was up to and how the heck she was able to access her psionic ability while restrained. "So, tell me, then, Miss Chen, what brings you aboard our little flight to Club Fed?"

Bai Lee's grin widened. "Oooh, you like to jump right in, don't you?"

Actually, Devon mostly *stepped* into things—like dog crap.

Or fell off of them—like *towering buttes*. So, "jumping in," like he was about to do, was an altogether new experience.

"I like to get to know someone I've just met," Devon said. He was spewing so much bullshit that it was hard for him to think straight. Bai Lee was a telepath. Why did she have access to her powers when no one else did? "Besides, I'm sure it's a long flight to Washington, DC, from wherever we are—"

"We're in Artesia, New Mexico," Bai Lee said, interrupting him.

"Great," Devon shot back a killer smile, which he didn't feel in the least. "Then there's plenty of time."

Bai Lee's eyes narrowed as she scrutinized him, and Devon could tell that she was trying to figure out what kind of game he was playing. He held his breath and waited. Talking was about the only thing he was good at—well, that and *listening.* His powers being as lame as they were, Devon often had to talk his way out of another swirlie in the boys' locker room. He'd take conversation over a physical altercation any day.

"Okay, fine," Bai Lee said. "I'm open to discussion. So, what are you offering me?"

"Offering you?"

"Yeah, you know…a little wager." Bai Lee was grinning now. And that wasn't a good thing.

"Oh, I don't think—"

"What kind of wager?" Nevada asked.

"The best kind," Bai Lee said with a vicious smile that chilled Devon to his core.

Your freedom.

Bai Lee's voice came through loud and clear inside Devon's head. And judging by the shocked looks on the faces around him, she had distinctly broadcast herself into everyone's minds at once.

"How'd you—" Nevada began, but a look from Bai Lee instantly shut her up.

Even the Latino kid had stopped praying. He sat in his chair, eyes wide open, gaping at her.

Oh, crap! The big, fat, freaking cat was out of the bag.

"Let's hear her out," said the musclehead by the door. "I'm not much of a gambler, but the way things stand I don't believe any of us has much to lose."

"I'm with him," said Alek. "I'm always open to new experiences, especially when there's a little wager involved."

"Me, too," Nevada said. "Count me in."

The Latino kid sputtered something in rapid-fire Spanish at Bai Lee, and she nodded in agreement. Apparently, Ninja Girl was bilingual too.

"Okay, Miguel here's onboard," said Bai Lee. She then turned her attention down the aisle to look at Alya. "What about you, princess?"

"I am *not* a princess," came Alya's soft reply. "However, I would very much like to entertain your little wager."

"Excellent." Bai Lee grinned. "I'm not sure when the feds plan for us to take off, but if we're all in agreement, we should get started."

"Hey, wait a minute," Devon said with as much indignation as he could muster. "Did I miss something? I only agreed to a conversation, not some crazy wager where you'll be insisting on God knows what kind of satanic ritual as compensation."

"Oh, Devon, you've got it all wrong," said Bai Lee with a sweet grin that contrasted starkly with the blood smeared across her face. It made her look confident, sexy…and more than a little scary. "Don't you know? You're the inspiration for this little fête…and I just love to party."

A fête? In this place? *Oh, come on now!*

Where was a patch of grass to step on when he needed it?

Bai Lee sat up straighter in her seat, all the while retaining her pleasant demeanor. "Devon wants us to get to know one another. So let's get to it." She pointed across the aisle to the Latino kid. "His name is Miguel Antonio Martinez Ruiz."

Upon hearing his name, Miguel started speaking rapidly in Spanish. Bai Lee nodded as he spoke and translated.

"Miguel says he's fourteen. From Guatemala. And that he's an untrained telepath."

Miguel continued to jabber on and on, until Bai Lee held up her hand and said, "Look, kid, enough already."

"Why?" asked Devon. "What'd he say?"

Bai Lee rolled her eyes. "A bunch of dumb shit about how nice it is to finally be able to speak to someone in Spanish, yadda, yadda."

Devon turned to Miguel and waved his right hand as best he could, which wasn't much. "Hey, Miguel. Nice to meet you."

Miguel smiled back in return, probably just happy to be referred to by name.

Next, Bai Lee turned her attention to the big guy beside the door. "So, what's your story, tall, dark, and brooding?"

"Vahn de Montague. That's Vahn, with an H. I'm seventeen…psi-blade."

Oh, no wonder the guy was so beefed up. Psi-blades were considered the true warriors of the psionic disciplines. They could generate powerful force-field projections from their hands that appeared like colorful swords or blades. A psi-blade's projection reflected the color of his or her aura. Many could create shields or armor as well. Like healers, tech-heads, and seers, psi-blades were highly prized by powerful people worldwide; as a consequence, they often didn't mix with the general population of psions at the facilities. Mostly, they were carted off to secret government installations to be used in matters of "national security."

Devon strained to get a better look at Vahn. Outside of his bottled dye job and smudged eyeliner, Devon could make out the hard edges of his jawline and the ragged combat scar that ran down the side of his face only to disappear into the collar of his T-shirt. His hands, too, were zigzagged with thin, pale scars that appeared whenever he balled them into beefy fists.

"Oooh, I just love me some psi-blade," purred Nevada. "How kick-ass…and manly."

Vahn grunted. "It's not so manly when you can't protect the one you love."

Bai Lee's grin stretched wider. "Oh, I *do* detect a story there."

"It's not for your ears," Vahn growled.

Bai Lee shook out her long, dark hair. "But it's why you're here, isn't it?"

When Vahn looked away, Devon knew that Bai Lee had hit upon a painful truth that the psi-blade wished to remain his and his alone.

So much for secrets when there was a telepath around.

And Devon was suddenly very worried about where this little wager of hers was going to take them.

"So, what about you, Nevada?" asked Bai Lee. "What's your specialty?"

"My *what*?" Nevada turned to face Bai Lee. "You gotta speak up. I'm a bit deaf in that ear."

"Your psionic discipline," Bai Lee clarified. "What is it?"

"Windwalker," Nevada replied with a shrug. "Hence the hairstyle, or lack of one. Though I can't say that I wasn't pleased with the reaction I got from my mother when she saw it."

"So, you fly?" Devon asked before he could stop himself. Windwalkers could manipulate air molecules in fantastic ways. "What's it like?"

"Way overrated," Nevada said with a sigh. "Humans just aren't meant to fly. First off, it's freezing up there in the atmosphere. And the higher you go, the more difficult it is to breathe because of the lack of oxygen. Landing *always* sucks. And long hair will whip your face raw when you're being propelled by high winds."

"Oh," Devon said, surprised by her answer. "I had no idea."

Nevada smiled then, and Devon thought that he had never seen a more beautiful woman. "But I have to say, when I wear an insulated flight suit and I'm gliding across the earth, just me and my element? I'm one. I fit. I'm not just some freak anymore." She paused, a faraway look in her eyes. "I belong, you know?"

Actually, Devon had no clue as to what truly belonging felt like; instead, he said, "Yeah…sure."

"Oh, bravo," groused Alek. "How disgustingly sweet."

"What's your problem?" Devon shot back, suddenly defensive.

Alek turned to Nevada. "You never once mentioned to the poor boy that you are in fact the daughter of a very powerful US Senator…*Alison*."

"Don't call me that," she said, the color draining from her cheeks.

"I heard your father turned you over to the government in exchange for his Senate seat," Alek continued spitefully. "Is that true?"

"Alek!" Alya cried; her voice, even in its outrage, barely carried above a whisper. "Leave her alone!"

"Why?" he retorted indignantly. "She's a spoiled-rotten celebrity! Everything she does—her marriages, her psi facility escape attempts, her psionic tattoos—it's all because she wants to make headlines! She craves fame and doesn't give a crap about what it's doing to her own kind!"

Devon gaped at Nevada in surprise. "You've been married more than once?"

Nevada shrugged. "A few times."

"Uh, you stupid Americans," Alek said in disgust. His Romanian accent was more pronounced the angrier he got.

"Don't you understand that you're playing right into the hands of the worldwide media? You're just giving them an excuse to eradicate us!"

"Alek," said Alya, "This is not the time or the place for one of your sermons."

"Oh, but it is, dear sister," Alek said, shaking his head. "God made us the way we are for a reason. We have a purpose. A destiny to fulfill. And I'm pretty sure it doesn't include serving mankind."

"Talk like that will only get us killed that much quicker," said Vahn, glowering from his seat by the door. "Just because you feel mightily connected to your truth doesn't mean that you should spread it like gospel."

"So, comrade, you are not a believer?"

"I didn't say that." Vahn balled his large, scarred hands into fists. "What did you say your discipline was again?"

Alek smiled. "I didn't."

"Well, maybe you should." The intensity of Vahn's gaze could have melted steel.

"I'm a popper," Alek replied with a slight wave of his hand.

"A what?" Devon asked.

"I teleport." Alek leaned back in his chair.

"That's so cool," said Devon. "So, I guess you've seen a lot of the world."

Alek shrugged. "Not really. Mostly, I moved large weaponry for the Russian military."

"But I thought you said you were Romanian."

Alek chuckled. "Oh, yes, Alya and I *are* Romanian. The blood of Romanian kings flows through our veins."

"Alek, no…don't," pleaded Alya.

"And why not, dear sister?" Alek asked. "Does the truth so frighten you?"

"No, not the truth."

"What, then?"

Alya didn't answer. Instead, her head lolled to the side as she turned to Devon. Her cheeks wet with tears, the only thing she could offer him was a weak smile. Devon feared that she just might fade away right before his eyes.

"Alya?" said Alek. "Alya?!"

Devon pulled against his restraints. "Something's really wrong. Can't somebody help her? Alya needs help! Now!"

The lights dimmed, and the red light began to rotate over the doorway. An instant later, the entire room shook with a deafening roar.

"What's going on?" Devon cried.

"We're taking off," Bai Lee shouted above the din. "Hold on!"

"But what about—" Devon was thrown back into his seat as the aircraft lurched straight up into the sky. There was no doubt about it now. He was on a military transport, the kind reserved for secret missions and the invasion of other countries. He was on a one-way trip into the heart of darkness. And the thing that saddened him the most was the knowledge that he would never be allowed to see his family again.

His mom, the worrier, the one who knew just how to cheer Devon up on a bad day with a slice of her famous lemon pie.

His dad, the bravest man he'd ever had the honor of knowing, the small-town doc who'd quietly refused to give his son away—even when it meant his family's livelihood.

And his eight-year-old sister, Linny, the bratty, comic-book-stealing troublemaker who loved nothing more than to mess with Devon's stuff—which usually resulted in mondo breakage. *His* stuff, not hers. Linny's ear-piercing scream could shatter concrete, but that was nothing compared to her uncanny ability to break wind *loudly* in close quarters and blame it on *him.* He would absolutely die whenever she would let one rip in an elevator with a hot girl beside them.

It was totally humiliating…as if he wasn't enough of a freak show already.

Oh, how he missed them!

Amidst the chaos and clamor, as the large aircraft lumbered into the air Devon was pulled from his thoughts when Alya reached for him in the red-tinged darkness.

He looked over at her then and was relieved to see her smiling wearily back at him.

He returned her smile and felt his heart soar when she took his hand.

Together, they held on for dear life.

Chapter Four

HIS ears ringing with the unearthly roar of the thrusters, Devon endured what felt like an eternity of bone-jarring, teeth-rattling shaking. In short, being hog-tied at the base of an erupting volcano would probably have been a slightly more pleasant experience. Devon just hoped that Alya was surviving this, because he sure as heck couldn't turn his head to check. The g-forces had him pinned to his seat like a lab rat on a dissection table.

With a great *swoosh* followed by a deafening *pop*, the mighty thrusters cut off and the much quieter drone of the propulsion engines took over. The monstrous beast of an aircraft had reached cruising altitude, and the crushing weight of the g-forces subsided.

"Alya?" he said, opening his eyes, and then just as quickly, he squeezed them shut.

What the hell?!

The room around him had become a sea of dazzling white light.

Was he dead?

Flapping his way over the cuckoo's nest?

Dehydrated?

It's me, stupid!

Bai Lee's voice was once again inside his head.

I've linked our minds. Just open your damn eyes already!

Oh, great…more telepathic bullcrap. Devon took a deep breath and slowly opened his eyes.

As his eyes adjusted to the brightness of the room, the six other people around him came into focus. Miguel was kneeling on the ground about five feet away, his head bowed in prayer over his clasped hands. Devon just hoped the guy had enough sense to know that this wasn't heaven—that they were rattling around inside Bai Lee's head like a set of oblong croquet balls. He wondered when the gigantic mallet would appear and smack the hell out of all of them.

Glancing just to his left, he caught sight of the blond Romanian twins sitting together on a stone bench a few feet away, and his heart sank like a torpedoed destroyer. When had Alya released his hand? And why was she sitting so damn close to her brother like that?

"Alya?" Her name came out of Devon's throat in a desperate rasp. "It looks like she's busy," said Bai Lee, stepping up to him. She was dressed in what could only be described as a trio of delicate yellow robes that gave her an exotic warrior-princess vibe, and Devon had to work hard to keep his jaw from flopping open in awe. Without blood caking her face, she was a total babe—dangerous, lovely, most definitely in charge…

And way the hell out of Devon's league.

"But—but Alya was just sitting right next to me," Devon said. He sounded whiny and juvenile, but he didn't care. He was still in a bit of a daze over the whole mind-meld experience, and Bai Lee's hotness sure wasn't helping him focus any.

"And she still is," Bai Lee explained. "None of us have left our seats."

"Because we're all in your head."

"You got it, Sherlock," she said with a crooked smile. "I didn't want to freak the hell out of you, so I picked something basic."

"Basic?" echoed Devon. Bai Lee's "basic" landscape was more like nineteenth-century retro limbo. "You mean we could be sitting in a tropical paradise if you wanted us to?"

"Sure." Bai Lee held out her hands and the long silk sleeves of her gown draped sexily to the ground. As she moved her arms, the world around them instantly changed to a lush jungle setting with an enormous waterfall roaring down the side of a sheer cliff face. A towering weeping willow with a lush canopy of descending branches stood sentry beside the waterfall's pool. Birds called from the trees. Devon felt a gentle breeze caress his skin.

"Wow," he marveled. "You're good."

Bai Lee crossed her arms. "Just so you know, I can change all of this with a thought…so don't piss me off. Okay?"

"Sure." Devon grinned at the sensation of grass beneath his feet. And the grass wasn't screaming. "You know, this is pretty awesome, Bai Lee."

She flashed him a tiny, girlish smile. "Thanks."

"So, what's the plan, then?" asked Vahn as he rose from the boulder he had been sitting on. Devon did a double-take—Vahn had a head full of golden curls. His blond locks softened the harsh angles of his face, making him appear younger and much better-looking. The smudged black eyeliner was gone too, and with it the badass Gothic-punk look. Vahn now resembled a bronzed Roman god or an underwear model fresh off a Times Square billboard. It made him more approachable. And much less scary.

"Uh, what happened to your hair, dude?" Devon couldn't help it. It was a question begging to be asked.

Vahn gave him a curious look before reaching up and tentatively touching his flaxen locks. "Oh… I, uh…"

"He's a natural blond," Bai Lee explained. "This is how he sees himself." She extended her arm and pointed behind them. "Take Nevada, for example. She's no longer bald. And surprise…she's a brunette."

"The best ones always are, honey, and don't you forget it," Nevada said as she walked over to them from where she had been standing before the glorious willow.

Devon gasped when he laid eyes on Nevada. Her short hair was styled in a pixie cut that framed her face and enhanced her starburst eyes. The contrast of her dark bangs and her splintered blue eyes was at once startling *and* beautiful. The face piercings were gone as well, which softened her features and made her look even younger than her eighteen years. She was a natural beauty, once pared down and relieved of her hardware. And Devon now understood why she had had so many husbands in her short, flamboyant life.

She was simply…gorgeous.

"What are you gaping at?" Nevada asked with a frown.

"N-nothing," Devon managed with concerted effort. He had to remain focused. This wasn't the time or the place to be flirting with a couple of way hot girls who were completely unattainable—except maybe in his dreams. He sure wouldn't mind Nevada and Bai Lee making an appearance in the world championship of naked mud-wrestling— Oh, no, he was doing it again.

Devon shook his head in an attempt to clear his thoughts. "I'm just, uh…tired, is all."

Nevada turned to Bai Lee. "He's acting funny. Have you done something to him?"

"Not me," she replied, her eyebrows twisting themselves into a genuine look of concern. "Devon. Come here," she instructed.

"There's nothing wrong with me, I'm fine," he said, standing his ground.

Bai Lee raised an eyebrow. "Now, Devon…I won't ask nicely twice."

Remembering what she had done to the two unlucky feds back in the aircraft carrier, Devon thought it might be prudent to do what she said. "Okay, fine," he mumbled as he stepped over to her.

Bai Lee took Devon's face gently in her hands and gave him a quick once-over. "Huh," she said.

"You see? I told you I was—"

Bai Lee punched Devon hard in the arm.

"Ow!" he cried, retreating a few paces. His bicep throbbed. Dang, that girl could hit! "That hurt!"

Bai Lee gave Nevada a satisfactory nod. "See? He's fine."

"I am *so* not fine," Devon said massaging his arm. And that's when it registered that his left arm was no longer broken.

"Oh, wow...wait a sec," Devon held his left arm before his face and opened and closed his hand a few times. "There's no pain! Holy cow! You fixed it!"

"No, I didn't," Bai Lee corrected. "You weren't listening to me. None of this is real. I have merely linked our minds and provided you with a semblance of reality so you won't freak out on me."

"This is so cool," Devon said with a grin. He'd been living with such intense pain for so many days that he had entirely forgotten what it felt like to be whole and healthy again. "Is this all part of your escape plan?"

Bai Lee scoffed. "Hardly."

"Then what is?" Vahn asked, looming over them. The guy had to be six-four, maybe even taller. "It's time you told us how you're able to access your psionic ability when none of us can."

"I'm about to get to that," said Bai Lee, "but first, I need one last piece of information." She turned to Devon. "What's *your* psionic ability?"

"Who? M-me?"

"Yes, you," Bai Lee replied with a smirk.

"Why don't you just dig around in his brain and pull the information out for yourself?" Nevada sneered.

"Because she can't," said Vahn. "Linking our minds is requiring all of her concentration. In fact, she has possibly altered reality for our federal friends as well, so that they won't notice how suddenly quiet we've become in the cargo hold." He focused his gaze on Bai Lee. "Am I right?"

"I never pegged you for an Einstein," Bai Lee said, returning his piercing gaze with one of her own. "But yeah, it would be easier for all of us if Devon just told us what the hell the government is hauling his bad ass in for."

All eyes turned to Devon.

Oh, crap.

"Oh, yeah…right," Devon said, as he felt his stomach drop straight to the floor. Of course, he had no intention of sharing his true and laughable talent with any of his fellow prisoners. He felt certain that Bai Lee wouldn't hesitate to leave him behind if she thought, even for an instant, that he was too lame to help her break out of here. After all, that was what his peers had thought of him back at North Central. If it hadn't been for his roommate, Colton, he definitely would have been left to rot inside that psi facility. No, Devon had to keep cool if he wished to survive. It would take every ounce of chutzpah he had to appear confident and collected with what he was about to do next—

Which was to lie his ass off.

"I'm a psi-cannon," Devon said with a little shrug as if it weren't any big deal.

"A psi-cannon?" echoed Nevada. Her perfectly arched brows were knitted in a look of confusion. "That's funny. I just thought—well, you just seemed more—uh, I don't know…*elemental* to me." She shook her head, looking disappointed. "I thought for sure you were an earthmover, or perhaps a waterwielder, but I would never in a million years have pegged you for an egotistical, backstabbing, piece-of-trash psi-cannon. I'm usually a much better judge of character than that."

Devon hadn't anticipated that kind of reaction—and from Nevada, of all people. His confidence in his plan began to waver.

"Yeah, well, uh, you know…uh, sorry to disappoint you," Devon muttered. Colton had been a psi-cannon, and Devon had never once thought his roommate to be egotistical, or a backstabber—let alone a piece of trash. Colton was the coolest guy Devon had ever known. What was so wrong with shooting bursts of energy from one's hands? Wasn't that, like, the greatest thing ever?

Bai Lee scrutinized Devon with that steely gaze of hers. If she suspected him of lying, which she probably did, Devon just hoped that she wouldn't do anything too horrible, like melt his brain or call him out in front of everyone. For the first time in a long, long time, "Plant Boy" wasn't in the picture. He wasn't being ridiculed for something he couldn't control, and best of all, the grass beneath his feet wasn't shrieking.

"Well, I must disagree with Nevada on one point... I don't think psi-cannons are backstabbers," said Bai Lee with an unreadable expression.

"Oh, yeah?" Nevada crossed her arms and stood taller, ready to argue. "And why's that?"

A hint of a smile appeared on Bai Lee's lips as she looked pointedly at Devon. "Because in the eyes of the government, I too am a psi-cannon."

Oh, shit! If it took one to know one, then Devon was definitely screwed.

"Wait a minute," said Vahn shaking his head. "You're a telepath, we all know that, so how can you be a psi-cannon, too?"

Bai Lee tapped her temple. "Because I'm both. And the disruptors can only cancel out one psionic discipline at a time. I'm a para-psion."

"They're real?" asked a voice from behind Bai Lee, as Miguel stepped into the circle. He was short for a fourteen-year-old, but his wide brown eyes held all of the sadness and misery of an eighty-year-old man. "I thought they were a myth, like the chupacabra."

"Oh, no," said Nevada. "Para-psions are real. Except you wouldn't know it because the government pulls them out of the psi facilities as soon as they're discovered, and then they're never heard from again."

Miguel looked at Nevada as if she had just sprouted wings. "You—you can understand me?"

"Yeah, well…duh," she replied with a dramatic eyeroll.

"You can *all* understand me?" he asked the group, his eyes alight with excitement.

"They can understand you, Miguel," Bai Lee said with a sigh. "That's why I linked our minds in the first place. So that we can all get to know each other a little better."

"And why would you want to do that?" asked Alek with a sneer. Devon wasn't sure when he and Alya had joined the group, but they were standing less than four feet away from him. Alya was still so weak that she leaned heavily against her brother, her eyes closed, and Devon wished that he was the one Alya leaned on for support, instead of her cocky twin.

"Because I am still proposing a wager," Bai Lee said, crossing her arms.

"Which is?" Vahn asked with an anxious intensity in his eyes.

"I'm going to need some help breaking out of here. So, you show me a glimpse into your lives, like maybe some spectacular event that led to your being here, and I'll tell you if you're worth my while to take you with me."

"What?" Devon cried. "That's your big wager? That's what all of this has been about?"

Bai Lee met Devon's gaze and held it. "Actually, it was *your* idea. And I *could* just go it alone and leave you all to rot in your government-appointed cells."

"Hey, I don't mind sharing," said Alek, "if it will get me and my sister the hell out of here." He stepped forward, pulling Alya with him. "I suppose you're going to replay our memories for everyone to see—so go ahead. The sooner we get this over with, the sooner we're free."

"You want my crappy memories? Then fine, they're all yours," said Nevada. "No skin off my backside."

"Count me in," said Vahn.

"Me too," said Miguel.

Bai Lee turned to Devon. "You see? They're all on board for a memory replay. So, what are you so worried about?"

Devon worked hard not to visibly squirm beneath her steely gaze. "Well, okay—fine. Suppose we tell you our tales? What then? How the hell do we even know you *can* get us out of here? It didn't go so great for you the last time."

"She's got access to her abilities," said Vahn. "Her telepathy will give us the edge we need to escape."

Devon glanced over at Vahn. "But how can you be so sure it will work?"

"I can't. No one can," he replied with a shrug. "But what other choice do we have?"

"There *is* no other choice," Nevada interjected. "Except perhaps to go ahead and *let* the feds interrogate us, torture us, and dump our carcasses in a landfill once they've had their fun."

Nevada was correct, of course. There really was no other choice. However, there remained plenty of room for negotiation with Bai Lee.

"It's not that I don't want to escape, or that I think Bai Lee's a second-rate telepath," Devon said, shaking his head in exasperation. "It's the wager that bothers me."

Bai Lee's glare turned murderous. "So, you're saying you don't want to participate?"

"I'm asking you for assurance that you can get *all* of us out of here, not just one or two of us. If we *all* tell you our stories, and we *all* wow you with our—I don't know—our pathetic little lives, then we can *all* go with you. We don't leave anyone behind."

"You want me to put my neck on the line for all of you?"

"Yes. Yes, I do," Devon said with a conviction that had his heart pounding in his chest like a bass drum. Speaking up felt good. He felt alive. He was tired of being left behind and shoved aside because he gave a damn. It was time that he stood up for himself—for everyone here—knowing full well that no one else in this mental paradise would have returned the favor. Screw 'em! He wanted to see his family. And he knew that he would never be able to look his father in the eyes again if he didn't stand up for what was right. "Because if you can free one or two of us, you can free us all."

"You sound so sure of yourself."

"That's because I am." His heart was banging against his ribcage, threatening to burst through. Acting cool was seriously strenuous, like chewing nails in an effort to spit bullets.

Bai Lee looked skeptical. "I can see that."

"So…all or nothing?" Devon ventured. He had no idea what the hell he was doing.

Bai Lee paused, her eyes locking onto his. "What if I hate every one of you?"

"You won't," he assured her, steeling his gaze.

"And you know this because…"

Devon glanced over at Alya. She was watching him. Her lips turned up in a tiny, hopeful smile. And he knew instantly that what he was doing, he was doing in large part for her; in the state she was in, he knew that she would surely be left behind. Just like he would have been left behind back at North Central without Colton's intervention.

"Because I give a damn," Devon said. "It's a curse, I know. But this is the way I choose to live."

Bai Lee raised her delicately arched eyebrows in surprise at Devon's response. For the first time, Devon saw her cool, controlled façade slip aside to reveal a mixture of hope and fear. They were all trapped within the same sinking vessel.

In order to survive, they would have to find a way to work together.

"There are spies," Bai Lee said softly. "Even among our own kind. It's not safe to blindly trust."

Devon reached out and took Bai Lee's hand. He held it gently between his own and gave her his best encouraging smile. "My father used to say that he'd never judge another unless he'd walked a long, hard mile in that person's shoes. And I like to think that's sound advice. Especially when it comes to our own kind. I mean, haven't the baselines judged us and found us all guilty of, well, just about everything you can imagine?"

"Hell, yeah," Nevada cried. "I'm called a bank robber every time I use the ATM, a jaywalker when I cross the street, and a slut whenever I'm photographed with a member of the opposite sex, regardless if I'm related to 'em or not." She tried in vain to look the victim, but it was futile. She barked out a laugh. "Okay, I'm a slut. So shoot me."

"Like the paparazzi?" Alek quipped with a grin. "In high-definition?"

"You better believe it," Nevada replied playfully. "I don't expect anything less than the best from the tabloids."

"Then it's agreed," said Bai Lee, pulling her hand free from Devon's grasp. "You will each allow me to replay your memories, so that we can see firsthand what makes you tick. If I'm satisfied with the whole stupid lot of you, we make a break for it...*together*." Bai Lee's sharp gaze was leveled at the entire group. "That acceptable?"

"Hell, yeah!" Nevada shouted, high-fiving Miguel. "Bring on storytime!"

Devon looked around at the six people standing before him. They were beaming with excitement and—dare he even think it?—*hope*. Yet despite the inclusive spirit that permeated the air, Devon could feel fear gnawing at his guts.

He knew that everything was bound to change once Plant Boy was revealed.

He was, after all, loser incarnate.

"Devon?" said Alya, with a hopeful smile. "You're with us…right?"

He returned her smile and stepped closer to her. "Yeah, I'm with you." Devon reached out to take her hand, but Alek yanked her out of reach.

"Hands off my sister," he hissed.

Devon could take a hint. But he didn't have to like it. He settled for standing next to Alya. Despite the fact that this was all an illusion, he could feel her body heat and smell the sweet scent of her hair. He was as close to her as he could be without touching, and that was probably for the best, because no matter how long he put it off, sooner or later, they would all come to know what a lame-ass excuse of a psion he was.

Alya included.

He just hoped that somehow he could find a way to convince them not to leave him behind.

Chapter Five

"ALL right, kiddies," Bai Lee said, with a clap of her hands. "Let's get to it. Who's going first?"

No one said a word, and Devon could see in his peripheral vision that he was by no means the only one to stare hard at the ground and wish himself invisible. Heck, it was just like being back in Mr. Wrenforth's speech class at North Central all over again—that terrible sensation of dread that sat in his belly like a hundred pounds of quick-drying cement, because he knew that, no matter how well prepared he was, Mr. Wrenforth would be sure to make him look like a complete idiot in front of his peers.

There was no way he was going to willingly subject himself to ridicule now. Especially if he could avoid it.

Devon chanced a glance over at Bai Lee, and saw that she was glaring at all of them with disapproval. "Oh, come on," she chided. "I'll make you draw straws if I have to."

That hundred pounds of cement dropped down Devon's legs and into his toes. He had horrible luck. If he was forced to draw straws, he knew for certain that he'd pull the shortest one. Then he'd have no chance whatsoever of getting around his wimpy psionic ability. Devon was a weak link, and a liar besides. They'd be certain to leave him behind.

There was a shuffling of feet behind Devon as Vahn de Montague stepped forward. "I'll go first," he said. "There's no use waiting; we'll only be that much closer to DC. And once I'm there, I'm pretty much a dead man."

"You can't be sure of that," Nevada said.

"Yes, I can." Vahn ran his hand through his thick hair, frowning. "I killed two men."

"Oh." Nevada said, and Devon could see the sadness in her eyes. If Vahn had killed two baselines, then he was indeed a dead man. He probably wouldn't even get a trial.

"It wasn't by choice," Vahn said as if in explanation. "Things just got…crazy." He looked down at his scarred fists and stared hard at his knuckles. "Let's get this over with. What do I have to do?"

Bai Lee took Vahn by the crook of the elbow and led him toward the gigantic weeping willow that overlooked the pool at the base of the waterfall. As they approached the great canopy provided by the willow's lithe, descending branches, the earth at the base of the tree began to tremble and a tiny shoot appeared.

"Whoa," Devon said, intrigued. It was the first time that he hadn't been responsible for a tree's sudden sprouting. But, then again, this wasn't a *real* tree. A real willow would have spoken to him or graced him with a song, but Bai Lee couldn't have known that. Not many people did. Outside of his family, Devon spoke very little about his psionic ability—not that anybody cared. Not many people gave a crap about a plant's opinion.

Devon trailed after Bai Lee and Vahn, all the while marveling at the shoot's rapidly expanding form. It appeared to have a will of its own as it twisted and stretched into a long, low bench that resembled something akin to a wooden psychiatrist's couch.

Stepping beneath the willow's canopy, Devon heard Bai Lee instruct Vahn to lie down. "Try to relax," she said, assisting him onto the wooden lounge.

Vahn grunted in reply and laid his head back against the expanding headrest, where leaves had sprouted from thin, decorative branches to create a soft pallet.

"Gently, now," Alya instructed Bai Lee while clinging to her brother's side.

Vahn gave the healer a tiny grin that ignited a bitter flame deep inside Devon's chest. Was the psi-blade hitting on her?

"Believe it or not," Vahn said, "it's more comfortable than it looks."

Alya tried her best to return his smile, but the effort appeared to be too much for her. Instead, she reached out her hand toward Vahn, only to have her brother pull her back.

"What are you doing?" Alek asked, holding her upright with both arms.

"I must get closer," she said softly. "He mustn't be alone."

"Alya, don't do this." Alek was doing his best to appear stern and in control, but Devon could hear the panic in his voice. "You're too weak."

"Please—" she begged.

"Allow me," Devon said, wrapping his arm around Alya's shoulders. "You both must be exhausted."

The look he got from Alek was murderous, but Devon knew better than to stand around and get himself punched in the face. Alya shifted her weight toward Devon as he gently led her away from her twin. With Alya resting comfortably against him, he guided her toward Vahn. "Why don't I take you closer?" he said softly to Alya. "You can hold Vahn's hand if you'd like."

"No!" Alek cried. "She must sit and rest! She's mentally and physically exhausted from her last healing session with that guy Vladimir—"

"Viktor," Alya corrected. "His name is Viktor."

"Well, *Viktor* and his disease have exhausted you. You're too weak to stand through Vahn's replay, mental projection or not. If you pass out, chances are you'll break your connection with Bai Lee and expose us all to the feds!" He stood only inches away, shadowing them like an angry wolf whose dinner had just been stolen.

"Okay, fine," Devon replied with a shrug. He couldn't believe how light Alya felt, nor how lovely she looked despite her illness. "No standing, then, which probably means no hand-holding, either. But I'll set you up as close as I can." He flashed Alya a devious grin. "Can you handle that?"

Alya managed a wan smile in return. "Yes…yes, I can."

Devon's heart soared to see such a lovely smile, but he worked hard to keep his cool. He was Plant Boy, after all, and bound to mess up eventually.

When Devon reached the wooden lounge, he helped Alya sit down on the soft grass so that she could make eye contact with Vahn. When Devon attempted to leave, he was surprised to find that Alya still clung to him.

"Don't go," she said. "Please. Stay with me."

Whoa. A hot chick had never said that to Devon before.

"S-sure," he replied, his heart thumping so hard that he knew everyone around him was bound to hear it.

Alya made a motion for Devon to sit behind her so that she might lie back against him. He had no sooner sat down than there was a flurry of movement to his right. It was Alek, and he was set on overprotective-brother mode. He glared outright at Devon, his hands balled into fists, just waiting for a reason to clean Devon's clock. But Devon had had his share of bullying; he knew better than to mess with a pissed-off sibling. Averting his gaze, Devon ignored Alek. At times like this, denial was a means of survival.

"This seat taken?" Nevada asked as she plopped herself down on Devon's left.

"No, not at all," he replied, a bit dumbfounded. Devon wasn't used to being the center of attention—especially when it came to hot girls. Though he could definitely get used to it.

"Good." Nevada turned and signaled to Miguel. "Get your butt over here, Miggy-boy. It's no fun way back in the cheap seats."

Devon turned and watched Miguel cautiously sit down cross-legged beside Nevada. The way the kid kept watching Nevada out of the corner of his eye, Devon got the sense that Miguel was a bit dubious of her intentions.

"You idiots ready?" Bai Lee asked from her perch on the edge of Vahn's wooden lounge.

Devon frowned. "Don't call us idiots."

"Then don't make me wait forever like a group of gawking five-year-olds," Bai Lee huffed. "I've got to concentrate—so give me a minute." She closed her eyes and sat very still, becoming all Zen-like.

Nevada made a sound in her throat. Devon glanced over in time to catch her flipping Bai Lee off with both hands while mouthing the word *bitch* as if she were screaming it.

It wasn't the most mature response, but it sure made Devon feel better. It truly sucked being ordered around all the time.

Bai Lee didn't appear to notice Nevada's obscene gestures, as she sat still as a yogi lost in meditation. When next she moved, it was to take Vahn's hand.

"Vahn," she said. "When you're ready, simply close your eyes and open your mind. I'll do the rest." The tone of Bai Lee's voice was lower, and her words were thick and smoky. The calm her voice held was both reassuring and relaxing, and Devon felt his fear evaporating with his every exhale.

"She's hypnotizing us," Devon whispered, and Alya gave him the slightest of nods.

Vahn kept his gaze locked on Bai Lee while he settled his bulk into the contours of the exotic chair, which continued to weave and move around his body. The way the tree held him reminded Devon of a mother cradling an infant.

Bai Lee released Vahn's hand and sat up straighter, the sleeves of her robes gathering on the ground in tranquil pools of silk. "Before we begin," she said to Vahn, "is there anything you'd like to tell us first?"

Vahn blinked at her for several seconds, perhaps a bit stunned by her softly spoken question. He turned his head slightly to address Devon and Alya and the rest of their motley group sitting in silence before him.

"I'm a soldier, just so you know."

"Yeah, we kind of guessed that," said Devon with a grin, and he was surprised when Vahn smiled in return and nodded, acknowledging the humor behind his obvious statement.

"Then I guess you've also noticed that I'm not the subtle type," he said.

"And you sure as hell don't talk much, either," interjected Nevada with a salacious grin. "You're the strong, silent, *sexy* type if you ask me. I'd rock your world any damn day of the week!"

Vahn frowned and turned away from them. Lying flat on his back, he focused his gaze on the tree branches overhead, his jaw muscles twitching with turbulent emotion. He was through talking.

"Nevada," Bai Lee growled. "Not cool."

"What?" The windwalker shrugged. "I didn't mean anything by it. What I meant to say was— Oh, come on! He's *gorgeous*. All you have to do is look at him."

"Shut up, *Alison*!" Bai Lee was glaring at her full bore. "This is Vahn's time to speak."

Nevada grumbled something under her breath, but she kept her gaze glued to the ground, while Vahn remained staring into the stratosphere.

Great. Now two people had been shamed into silence.

Alya shifted her weight in Devon's arms and extended a delicate hand toward Vahn. "Please continue, Vahn. How long have you been in training?"

Keeping his gaze locked skyward, Vahn answered. "Since I was three. Up in Alaska—I was being trained for the government's Psionic Special Forces." Vahn paused, his hands curled into fists.

"What happened?" Alya gently prodded. "Did they hurt you?"

Vahn shook his head. "No. Not me… Emily. They took Emily away. And I knew that I had to find her."

"Emily. She was your girlfriend?" Alya's voice quivered.

Vahn turned his head toward her and nodded. "We grew up in the facility together." A sad smile turned up the corners of his mouth. "I loved her from the very first moment I laid eyes on her…and my superiors knew it, too." Vahn paused and licked his lips, his gaze hardening. "Emily was a low-powered clairvoyant until they started pumping her full of chemicals to enhance her ability. Her visions became so vivid, so *real,* that she had no idea if she was awake or asleep. All I could do was hold her for as long as they would let me while she sobbed uncontrollably in my arms.

"And then one day, she was gone. Her room was cleared out. Not a trace that she had ever been there."

"Where did they take her?" Alya's voice was hardly more than a whisper as she wrapped Devon's arms tighter around her. Her eyes were half-closed from sheer exhaustion.

"I don't know," Vahn replied, his frown lines deepening. "That's why I'm here. I escaped so that I could make contact with the Psionic Underground. They're the only ones who can help me find her.

"And I will find her, or die trying…God help me."

Vahn lay quietly for a moment, a faraway look in his eyes, and Devon wondered if the psi-blade was thinking about Emily. Clairvoyants, also known as seers, were prized psi-talents for their ability to accurately predict the future. Devon's abilities paled in comparison to someone like Emily. Yet it was the fact that his psi-talent was so lame that had made it possible for him to live almost fourteen years with his family in Springfield, Illinois before he was removed. Had he been a seer like Emily or a healer like Alya, the government would have forced his parents to give him up when he was a toddler. It saddened him to think of all the psi-talents out there who had grown up without knowing their families.

Bai Lee shifted her weight on the bench beside Vahn and her silk robes rustled, snapping the psi-blade from his thoughts. He blinked his eyes a few times before finding a comfortable position for his head on the pallet of soft leaves.

"Let's do this," Vahn said, and then closed his eyes.

Before Devon could draw his next breath, the world around him folded in on itself like some insane origami exercise, before bursting into hyperdrive. It was as if a million pinpricks of light spun all at once. He felt himself pulled forward at the speed of thought. There was no time to scream. There was only a sensation akin to rocketing down a drainpipe at warp speed.

A moment later, Devon McWilliams ceased to exist.

Vahn de Montague's Story

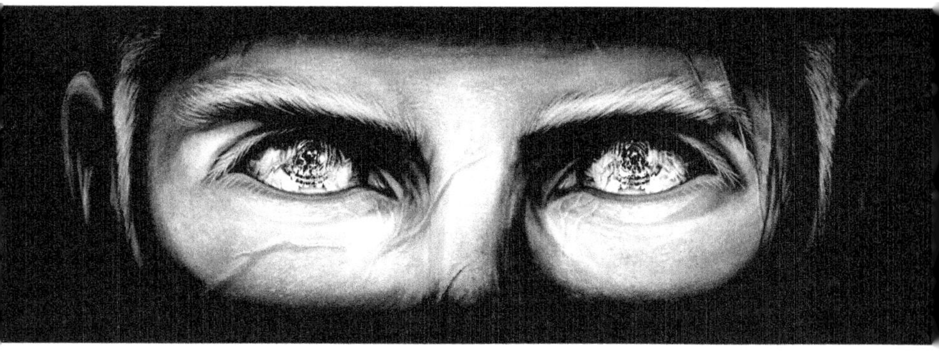

Chapter Six

THE buzzing from the overhead lights fills the tunnel as I make my way to the arena for the final round of the Psi Games. My shoulder aches, but I ignore it. The pain's there to remind me that my last bout in the pits could have gone a whole hell of a lot better. It had taken everything I had to keep my last opponent at bay; as a consequence, I'd been on the defensive throughout most of the battle. Twenty minutes into the round, I'd spied an opening and landed a blow to my opponent's diaphragm. I followed it up with a shield sweep that slammed him hard to the ground.

Match, de Montague.

I shake my head in an effort to remain focused. I've made it to the finals. The first part of my plan is complete—only the team competition in the arena remains. My escape hinges on a Tiger Squad victory. Anything less, and I will lose Emily forever.

"Concentrate," I say aloud as I suck in air through my tight-lipped grimace. The Alaskan Psi Facility director, Major General Allen, is well-known for changing the rules of the Psi Games as they're being played. Surprise attacks are his specialty. I must remain focused and present at all times.

I pause when I hear a raucous cheer from the stadium echo through the tunnel. The sound races through me, touching me deep inside. The pit of my stomach drops, and instantly I know—

Something isn't right.

Surely my Tiger Squad has emerged victorious from the early-round matchups—but if they have, why haven't they waited for me to join them before stepping into the arena?

The pitch of the crowd rises even higher from the stadium above, and my insides grow cold with dread. I am certain now—

Something has gone horribly wrong.

This is no time for failure—especially during the last game of the season. Everything hinges on a victory!

I break into a run, but as the arena entrance comes into view and the roar of the crowd becomes deafening, I realize that there is no sign of my teammates.

"No…" I can't be the only victor.

Sticking close to the shadows of the arena entrance, I can see the expectant faces of the baselines as they cheer ecstatically over some new Lion Squad arrival. The spectators have it easy, viewing the games from their luxury boxes and VIP sections, with their gourmet food and endless supply of microbrewed beer.

The Alaskan Psi Facility's final-round stadium, known as the Imperium Arena, was built in the tradition of the ancient Roman Coliseum. The wealthy and powerful enjoy themselves as they watch the latest in psionic gaming warfare. From the comfort of their high-tech chairs, they can place bets as the games progress or request a special audience with a psi-blade of their choice—at an exorbitant fee, of course.

I sink deeper into the shadows as a hovercam zips past. The little round machines are as pleasant as overgrown gnats in the arena. They're programmed to get the latest full-blown, in-your-face action for the government's secure internet broadcast to its powerful allies around the world. I'm supposed to feel honored, but the idea disgusts me. It's not their lives on the line. It's mine.

"Vahn? Where are…" Diana says, trotting up behind me. She is my second in command, a fiery redhead whose skintight battle suit leaves nothing to the imagination when it comes to her curvy figure. And that's on purpose. A cunning warrior, she uses all of her assets on the battlefield to keep her opponents distracted. *Especially* her cleavage.

The hesitation in her speech tells me all I need to know as she quietly settles into the shadows beside me. "We're it?"

"Looks like it," I say with a nod, though I keep my eyes locked on the arena. I am relieved that she has made it this far too. Diana is our unit's best swordsman and she's fearless on the battlefield. If there were anyone I would hope to have my back, it would be her.

Another cheer from the crowd reverberates around us, shaking the dust from the pipes overhead.

"What are the Lions doing out there?" she asks quietly.

"I don't know. But whatever it is, it's going to be hell for us."

I can hear Diana stirring nervously behind me. "Surely Jason will be here… Maybe we could wait a little bit longer before stepping into the arena? You know, just give him some more time—"

"Time?" I say with a growl. It sounds threatening, but Diana has no idea how much this victory means to me, or what losing will cost me. "Time is not a luxury we have right now. If your boyfriend can't fight his way out of the early-round melees, he has no business being out there with us!"

"*Boyfriend?!* Jason is *not* my boyfriend!" Diana is pissed; I can hear it in her voice. But she's too much of a professional to reveal any more. She hesitates, retreating further into the shadows, and I realize what a complete ass I have just been.

I lower my head, pressing my thumb and forefinger against the bridge of my nose, and release a long, pent-up sigh. "Look, Diana, I didn't mean—"

"Forget it," she says. "We've got heads to bash." She pauses, then adds, "Two against what? Eight? Think we can overcome those odds?"

"Surrendering isn't an option." I glance at Diana, and for the first time notice the angry bruise above her eye and the blood oozing down the side of her face. "You get that in the last round?"

A ghost of a smile plays across her lips. "You should see the other guy."

I force myself not to grin. Diana and I have been friends since she arrived at the facility ten years ago. When a situation gets tense, she becomes harder to read, and right now I'm not certain if she's joking or completely serious.

Movement high up along the arena's far wall catches my attention. The refs are taking their positions on the observation platforms. I turn back to Diana and retrieve a couple of butterfly bandages from my forearm pocket. "We haven't much time," I say as I rip them open. "You notice anything different about your opponent last round?"

"Other than the fact that he almost took my head off?"

"And that surprised you?" I say, but I realize my mistake the instant I look in her eyes.

She's angry. With her hands on her hips, she frowns at me. If I were any closer, she would probably slap me across the face. "No one ever catches me off-guard. And you know it."

"Yes, I do," I say, meeting her gaze. "That's why I'm concerned. I'd never even seen my last opponent before today. He called himself Skullcrusher, of all things. Was hell to bring down, too."

"Skullcrusher…huh." Diana winces as I squeeze the skin around her laceration and seal it closed with one of the small bandages. "Mine called himself Carnage. What's up with that?"

"No clue." I quickly secure the other bandage, then tuck the wrappers into a thigh pocket on my battle suit. "But they weren't trained in our facility. So that could only mean one thing—"

"The rules have changed," Diana says, following my thought.

I nod solemnly. "We need a plan."

"I've got your back," she says, clear-eyed and excited by the prospect of the overwhelming odds. There is very little on the battlefield that frightens Diana.

"Count us in, too," says a voice from behind me.

I turn to find Michael Via slowly making his way toward us. A descendant of the famous Apache outlaw Geronimo, Michael is the youngest psi-blade in our unit at fourteen and a half, but he's quick and crafty in combat, and he follows orders well. Despite the fact that Michael looks like hell and is bleeding from a cut across his cheek, he is half-carrying, half-supporting another kid whose soil-coated hair and face make him hard to recognize.

"Jason!" Diana gasps, racing to help Michael with his burden. "What happened?" she demands.

"Don't rightly know," Michael says. "I found him unconscious on the tunnel floor."

I step up beside Jason and lift him into my arms. He's covered with dirt, as if he's just crawled out of his own grave. I have never seen anything like this at the Psi Games. And that worries me. What the hell are we about to face in the arena?

"Careful," Diana says, hovering beside me, and I can hear the concern in her voice.

I lay him down against the wall as gently as I can, then reach into the med-pouch at my waist and rip open a moist towelette. I start with Jason's nose and mouth. His breathing is labored; I fear that he might have breathed some debris into his lungs.

"We need to run a vitals scan," Diana says, rummaging through Jason's med-pouch. "But where the hell's his card?"

"Check his breast pocket," Michael suggests, kneeling beside her.

Diana rips into his battle suit and withdraws the thin white card with Jason's photo on it. "Got it!" She turns to me then, her eyes pleading for me to intercede. "Please," she begs, and it is as if a hot blade has pierced my heart.

Only the squad commander can authorize a vitals scan… but in order to do so, we will lose precious time. What's left of my Tiger Squad must step into that arena before the final-round cannon sounds. The referees have already taken their positions. We may have ten minutes—*tops*—before the final round commences. If I am not on that arena floor in time, I won't have another chance to escape for a very long time.

And Emily's trail is already growing cold.

Diana grabs my hand and presses Jason's medical card into my palm. She doesn't have to say a thing, because her eyes convey the depth of her emotion. And for an instant, I see Emily's starburst eyes and her sad yet endearing smile. How could I deny her plea, when I am risking my own life for a woman I can no longer hold in my arms?

"Unzip his battle suit. It might help him breathe," I say, and insert Jason's card into my med-scanner.

As quickly as I can, I activate the oblong machine and let it go. It hovers over Jason's body, projecting a bevy of colorful hard-light beams that scan Jason from head to toe. In a matter of seconds, it homes in on Jason's ribcage and the beams give way to a detailed, three-dimensional, hard-light image of Jason's left lung. It doesn't look good.

"Right tension pneumothorax," the med-scanner says in its dry, computerized voice. "Rib fractures detected—four, five, six. Heart compressed. Stroke volume down to thirty percent. Medical intervention recommended. Manual code 389."

"What's that mean?" Michael asks, tilting his head in confusion.

"It means three broken ribs and a tear in his lung that has forced air into the cavity between the lung and the chest wall. Right now, there's too much pressure on his heart and trachea," I reply as nonchalantly as I can. I don't mention that there's a chance his heart might stop. I'm not in the mood to stir up any more drama where Diana is concerned. I need her to be clearheaded in the arena, not stroking out over her boyfriend's injury.

"Ah, geez," Michael says. "That's gotta hurt. Even if we release the pressure, he'll be useless in the arena."

In an instant, Diana is in his face. "Shut the hell up, Mike! You don't know shit! There are worse things than a little chest pressure and a few broken ribs!"

"Not by much," I say, in an effort to take the heat off of Michael.

Diana whirls on me. Jason's body is the only thing keeping me out of striking range. "What're you saying? You're not going to revive him?"

"He can't fight in this condition. We've got to call in the medical team."

"And what? Take a forfeit?"

The idea of a forfeit makes me grimace. It's the last thing in the world I want to do. "What choice do we have?"

Diana is outright glaring at me, and for a long moment, she holds my gaze. Then she slowly shakes her head. "No. No way. I'm not going to let you do this. Jason would want to fight. Release the pressure. Get the air out of there."

"Diana, we don't have time—"

"Do it."

"He'll be useless in the arena—"

"Do it!"

"No."

"DO IT!!" She screams, her eyes wild with anger.

I stand my ground and glare at her in return. If I didn't need her so desperately right now, I'd have her on KP duty for a month for insubordination. I'm about to inform her of this, when I hear Jason say—

"Yes...do...it..."

I turn to find Jason looking up at me, his face contorted in agony.

"Jason!" Diana cries in relief. "What the hell happened to you?"

His face is a mask of pain, but Jason manages to utter two words. "...earth...mover..."

Michael looks stunned. "What the hell are elemental psions doing in *our* games?"

"Kicking our ass," Diana replies dryly. She turns to me, meeting my gaze. "It looks like we're going to need all the help we can get out there."

I know she's right, damn it. Two teams of forty are whittled down to ten finalists in the final arena battle. Any team advantage depends on the number of one-on-one matches won in the earlier rounds. Four of us in here means six of *them* out there. If I turn Jason over to the medics, that would mean the Lions would be allowed to pick someone who had lost in the earlier rounds and add that person to their team. This being yet another example of the major general's twisted little rules. In his opinion, a psi-blade too injured to fight after a preliminary round is no victor at all. I sure as hell think that four against six is much better odds than three against seven. Even if Jason can't fight, if he can walk into the arena with us, then that would at least prevent the Lion Squad from adding Jason's last opponent, an elemental psion, to their final-round roster.

"Override code 389. De Montague, Vahn. 5-6-4-4-4-8-5-9," I say, addressing the med-scanner, which hovers patiently over Jason's chest.

The med-scanner chirps, then says, "Override accepted. Needle thoracostomy commencing."

I grip Jason's right shoulder and place half my body across his because I know what's coming next. When I see Michael and Diana hesitate, I frown and say, "Hold him down. This won't be pretty."

They spring into action. Michael throws his weight on top of Jason's legs, while Diana takes hold of Jason's left arm, putting all her weight behind it.

The med-scanner lowers a three-inch 16 gauge needle from its underside compartment as it hovers over Jason's chest near his left clavicle. Everyone's eyes go wide.

"You gotta be flippin' kiddin—" Michael starts to say, but at that moment, the med-scanner drops down and inserts the needle into the second rib space in the mid-clavicular line.

Jason violently struggles as the pain shoots through him, and I lean my weight into him to keep him from smashing the med-scanner.

"Don't struggle, baby," Diana coos close to his ear. "It's almost over."

The med-scanner chirps again, and I close my eyes before the burst of air hits me in the face as the scanner extracts the air from Jason's chest cavity.

"Aaaaahhhhh," Jason sighs, both from pain and relief. "I—I...can...breathe!"

"Nanobots released," the med-scanner says.

"Nanobots?" Michael asks dubiously.

"They're the latest advancement in battlefield medicine. The med scanner has programmed them to close the tear in his lung from the inside to prevent any further leakage," I reply, watching the med-scanner pull itself free. Its needle drips with a bit of blood as it retracts back into the scanner's lower compartment.

"What about his ribs?" Diana asks. "Will the nanobots repair those, too?"

"In time," I say quietly. "But just so you know, he's going to be in agony out there in the arena."

"Needle thoracostomy complete," the med-scanner says, as I reach for it to remove Jason's medical card.

"How you feeling?" I ask Jason.

He coughs deeply and grimaces in pain. "Like…shit," he replies. "But at least…I can…breathe now."

I tuck the scanner back into my belt and hand Jason his vitals card. "You think you can stand?"

Jason grunts in reply.

Diana and I each take an arm and hoist him to his feet. We're cutting our entrance close and we all know it. There's no more time for thinking—we have to move.

Michael leads the way to the arena's entrance. He pulls his battlesuit hood over his head and powers up just as he arrives at the entrance to the arena. His armor takes shape around him—transparent plate mail that radiates a vibrant sapphire color with a roaring tiger, our squad's insignia, depicted on the breastplate and his shield. As a tribute to his heritage, Michael manipulates his psi-energy armor to include dangling feathers on the sides of his helmet. Because no bladed projections are allowed in these games, he creates a quarterstaff complete with feather embellishments as he waits for us to catch up.

"Get out there, Corporal!" I shout at him. "What the hell are you waiting for?"

He turns back to me then, his eyes wide with surprise, but he knows better than to question a direct order. With one last glance, he strides forward, his game face on—an Apache warrior ready for combat.

The crowd goes absolutely wild when Michael emerges into the arena. The pipes above my head rattle, and more dust rains down on us as Diana and I drag Jason to the arena's entrance.

"You sure you're up to this?" I ask Jason.

He grunts in reply, and I level my gaze at Diana. "Whatever you do out there, don't allow another hit to his chest. Have him kneel in forfeit as soon as the cannon sounds. You got that?"

"Yes, sir," she says, but her gaze shifts just slightly, and I know that her pride may not allow Jason to forfeit so easily.

I turn back to Jason. "I don't want any kind of heroics from you out there today. Your injury's too great."

Jason stops walking long enough to look me straight in the eyes. Standing as tall as he can, he says, "I know about your plans."

I freeze as soon as Jason's words hit me.

"You confiscated a key to the old back gate," Jason continues. "You're planning to run right after you take the victor's walk."

Dread fills my insides faster than quicksand, because if Jason knows about my plans, then there is no telling who else knows. But before I can get any words out, Jason leans forward, his breathing ragged, determined to say something more.

"You *have* to win today, Vahn—for Emily's sake. And I want you to know that I will have your back…as long as I can stand. So, with all due respect, *sir*…I will not forfeit. This day…or any day."

I can only gape at him as I work to still my thoughts. Though relieved to hear that he won't turn me in, I still can't get over one major fact. "How the hell did you—"

"It's not what you think," Diana interjects. "No one else knows. Jason saw the gate key in your gear bag yesterday. That's all. The Administration has no idea what you're planning."

But the dread in my guts tells me otherwise. The lack of final-round victors from Tiger Squad, the inclusion of elemental psions, facing opponents we have never seen before—and I thought I had been so clever in stealing a forgotten key.

The major general is toying with me. Odds are that my Network contacts have already been arrested.

Emily is already lost to me.

Diana reaches over and grips my arm. "It's not over yet. We can do this. I know we can."

I try to nod, but I'm overwhelmed with fear. If the major general is on to me, then he will see that Emily is punished as well. And if that were to happen, I don't know how I could ever look at myself in the mirror again.

But what choice do I have? There's no going back. I have three troops to protect. Anything less than my complete and best effort in the arena will be noted by the major general and his Administration.

"You're right," I say to Diana, despite my reservations. "Let's do this." I hope I sound more positive than I feel, because I'm only going through the motions now—a dead man walking.

"Power up," I say as I pull up my hood and form my armor. All of us have been trained to conjure plate mail armor, and mine radiates a crimson glow. My bladed projection of choice is a longsword. I've always favored its reach and weight. But since we are not allowed to use bladed projections in today's games, I round out the edges of my weapon while still maintaining its weight and shape. My sword resembles something a novice would use in training, but I don't mind. I'm allowed to wield it on the condition that I do not stab with it. Of course, the officials have been known to overlook a jab or two if it's an exciting fight.

Standing at the threshold, I glance at Diana. She's powered up in her electric violet armor, with a three-dimensional tiger roaring on her shield. She conjures a three-dimensional Medusa head complete with writhing snakes for her breastplate. This is something she has always done, and I think the image suits her perfectly. In her hand she projects a blunted broadsword. Her game face set, she's ready for action.

Jason, on the other hand, is having trouble projecting his armor. Sweat beads his brow and his mouth is set in a painful grimace as he concentrates on bringing into focus his vermilion plate mail. After he finally sets the roaring tiger across his breastplate and shield, he barely has the wherewithal to conjure his war hammer.

"We've got to move," I say. "Can you do this?"

"Let's go," he replies through clenched teeth. He pulls away from me and strides toward the arena.

"Right behind you," Diana says, following closely, but not too closely, after Jason. The last thing she wants to do is tip off our opponents to Jason's condition.

As I stride into the arena behind Diana, I add a touch of flame to my crimson armor, igniting it for show. The roar of the crowd slams into me with the force of a speeding locomotive. It reverberates within me, the pure energy of it, and deafens me to the point of pain. I promptly adjust the force-field helmet covering my ears to temper the sound.

Looking up into the stands, I raise my sword over my head and give a long, loud battle cry. This only whips the crowd into an even greater frenzy, but I have an ulterior motive. Focusing the hovercams on me lessens the threat of a skyscreen holographic projection of Jason looking pale, exhausted, and weak.

Michael joins me in the battle cry, and we both gaze up at the arena's thirty-foot onyx walls, smooth as glass and hard as steel. Hovercams the size of large golf balls swirl around us. I fight the instinct to swat them away by tilting my head back and focusing instead on the stands before me, where the faces of baselines peer down from every conceivable angle—and they're all hungry for blood. It would be easy for a novice to get distracted by the wall of sound, which is amplified by the colossal stadium and directed at the participants on the arena floor. But that's all part of the Psi Games, and Michael and I know how to play it up for full effect.

The crowd loves us, but what I really want is for that stupid cannon to fire! Crowd preening is definitely not my style, and I am fully aware that somewhere in the upper echelons of this stadium, peering down from a luxury box on high, sits the major general. He'll guess what I'm up to if this lasts much longer, and change the rules on me in some terrible way.

BOOM! BOOM! BOOM! The cannon fire finally resounds overhead, and not a moment too soon.

Diana and Jason join me and Michael as the officials break free from the stadium walls and hover above the arena floor on their floating platforms. Each referee wears black battle armor and a helmet with the dark visor pulled down for protection. They're all baseline adults, most of them career military, so they know better than to take any chances when officiating the Psi Games.

"Squad leaders to the center of the field," announces a voice over the arena sound system.

"That's my cue," I mumble as I depower my longsword and stride forward, weaponless, looking to the world like a competent and able leader. In truth, I feel on the verge of panic. I'm afraid I'll crack if I think too deeply about Emily and what the major general might do to her if indeed my escape plans have been compromised.

I clench my hands into tight fists in an effort to focus on the battle ahead, but no matter how many cleansing breaths I take, I am unable to shake the dread that fills me. These are not the games I have come to expect...but I hate myself regardless. Because, in truth, I should have known better—nothing escapes the major general.

Not even me.

I glance to my left as an official swoops down and matches my gait with his hover-platform beside me. I can feel him staring hard at me through his visor.

When I turn to look at him, he extends two gloved fingers and points to his eyes hidden behind his helmet's dark faceshield. Then he points the fingers back at me. I get the message loud and clear—he's going to be watching me.

I grit my teeth, angry that I'm being challenged by an official, and flare the crimson in my armor. I will not be intimidated.

I have no idea how my retort has been received, because I turn away from him and busy myself waving at the spectators on the opposite side of the stadium. A moment later, he glides past, but the anger that I feel does not ebb when he leaves. I'm disgusted with myself for not realizing that my "brilliant" escape plan may have put the girl I love in jeopardy.

I may never see Emily again…and I'm not sure I want to live without her.

"Focus," I growl to myself. I can't go there right now.

With my next step, my boot sinks several inches into the loose, rich dirt that covers the arena floor, and I hesitate. Studying the ground before me, it's obvious why so much earth has been trucked in. *Earthmovers.*

And they mean to use their skills in combat.

Damn it!

A cheer rises up from the crowd as the Lions' captain approaches. But something's off. Captain Kastich's armor is reflecting an ominous ebony flame, and he carries a menacing-looking mace projection in his right hand, its round head held aloft in the grip of three dragon talons. Oh, no…it's not Kastich at all, but Arthur Eichler.

He is the last person in the world I want to see today. Arthur was transferred out of the Alaskan Psi Facility over two years ago for insubordination. Growing up, he had been my rival at every turn—even when it came to Emily's affections.

I loathed the creep.

Swallowing my surprise, I continue trudging through the soft dirt. Two officials await us in the center of the arena. It is time for the reading of the rules, and there is no telling what surprises await.

Arthur grins at me in that smug way of his, and I find myself gritting my teeth. "Good to see you, old friend."

"Artie," I reply with a nod, and I'm satisfied to see the grin vanish from his lips.

"Your Tiger Squad hasn't fared so well today. Looks like you've gotten slow and lazy in my absence. Hardly Alpha Squad material."

"Really? And how would you know about Alpha Squad material? You were headed for a detention camp in Washington, DC, last time I saw you."

He laughs at me then, in that condescending, piercing bray of his. "Is that where you think they sent me? Oh, that's precious."

I stand there, glaring at him, refusing to dignify this jerk with a reaction. Right now, it's all I can do *not* to slug him.

"Major General Allen didn't send me to a detention camp, you idiot. I was traded to a private government-funded military academy. It's called The Stillwell Agency for Psionic Integration and Development, but that's just its bullshit title. People in the know refer to it simply as "The Agency," because there's only one like it in the world. They're building us a new facility off the Carolina coast. Nice of 'em, huh?"

"Yeah, real nice." I am so through talking to this bag of shit that I glance over at the officials hovering just five feet away on their platforms. They've made no attempt to break up our little tête-à-tête, and I can hear the crowd growing restless in the stands.

I am about to question the official to my left when I catch sight of a gilded hover-platform floating toward us from the luxury boxes above. Whoever's coming can only be bringing more bad news for me and my squad.

"Oh, and Vahn," Arthur calls to me, in that irritating singsong way of his.

"What?" I snarl, ripping my eyes from the descending administrator's platform.

That smug grin of his turns sinister. "*Emily* sends her regards."

My blood runs cold as ice flows through my veins. My heart drums in my chest, and the world around me drops away. I am stunned beyond words and can only gape at my opponent.

Arthur brays like a donkey, satisfied with my reaction. "You should see your face! Oh, if only I controlled a hovercam right now!"

His laughter alone is enough to pull me from my stupor. My hands curl into fists as I attempt to channel my rage. I'm satisfied only when I hear the buzzing of my force-field gauntlets grinding against each other.

"Attention!" the officials cry in unison, and I instinctively turn toward the descending platform and snap to attention.

"At ease, captains," commands a voice I'd know anywhere. And once again, I find myself caught off-guard by the change in protocol. Palpable dread fills me as the major general strides to the front of his platform.

I allow my training to take over. I stoically regard him in his military dress blues and gleaming black shoes. The sheer weight of the ribbons on his chest would topple most men, but it's his piercing gaze that holds me now, and in a strange way, it is the presence of the major general himself that gives me the strength to stand my ground. Though I despise the man before me, I deeply respect him as well. He may be a sadistic son of a bitch in his battle training methods, but he has always been fair and impartial when it came to governing the Alaskan Psi Facility.

Until he sent Emily away.

The hovercams swarm the major general, and his image instantly appears fifty meters high in midair, projected by the arena's gigantic floating hologram projector. Called the ImperiumTron, there is no other optical device like it in the world. The crowd roars with excitement at the sight of the major general, who politely smiles and raises his hands. He waits for the spectators to quiet down before he begins.

"Ladies and gentlemen, noble dignitaries and world leaders," the major general says, his voice booming over the arena's sound system. "Today, you have witnessed three rounds of intense one-on-one combat. These psionic warriors are unmatched in their training and combat readiness. From eighty well-honed troops, we are down to our top ten combatants, each of them vying for the honor of top cadet." He pauses, his eyes falling on me and Arthur.

"Captain de Montague. Captain Eichler. I am very pleased to see you both standing here before me." The major general turns away from us, addressing the crowd. "These two young men have trained hard over the last fourteen years, and both of them deserve to wear the victor's crown in these games.

"However, this round is a team event. And it is up to what remains of Captain de Montague's squad of psi-blades to defeat Captain Eichler's combined psionic battle squad on loan to us from The Stillwell Agency for Psionic Integration and Development."

An enthusiastic cheer rises up from the crowd, though for the life of me, I'm not sure why. It is then that I feel the earth tremble, and a moment later, a pillar of dirt rises from the ground beneath Arthur's feet. But instead of falling, Arthur stands tall and throws his arms out wide as if embracing the crowd's favor. He rises more than five feet above my head before the pillar of dirt recedes and gently lowers him back to the arena floor.

How the hell is my squad supposed to defeat *that*?

Arthur flashes me one of his grins, and all I want to do is punch him in the face.

"Yes, an earthmover has made it to the final round," says the major general, addressing the crowd. "We are entering a new age of warfare, where psionic disciplines of all kinds will train under one commander in order to better utilize our talent on the battlefield. This is the future, my friends. Embrace it or be conquered. Let the final round commence!"

The crowd cheers, and I can see people jumping to their feet and wildly applauding. The sound is insane and it rolls over me in waves as the baselines begin chanting, "Let's go! Let's go! Let's go!"

I notice movement above me and look over in time to see the major general deftly leap over the side of his hover-platform. His spit-polished shoes sink six inches into the dirt, but he doesn't appear to notice as he salutes Arthur and then shakes his hand. The major general's beaming smile makes me want to pummel something as he shares some encouraging words with my opponent. There hasn't been any mention of what happened to Adam Kostich, my friend and the Lion Squad's previous captain. Just like Emily, he too has apparently vanished.

I wonder if that will be my fate as well one day.

"Vahn, my boy," says the major general as he approaches me, wearing a disarming smile.

"Sir!" I cry. I jump to attention with a perfect salute.

The major general remains smiling as he returns my salute, then reaches out to shake my hand. Several hovercams buzz about my head as I take his hand, broadcasting my face high above us in midair and God knows where else around the world.

"Good luck, soldier," he says. He remains smiling as he pulls me closer into a firmer handshake. He leans forward then, and speaks quickly and directly into my right ear so as not to be overheard. "The earthmover's one sadistic bitch, but she's green. Her last opponent managed to level the playing field using Jackson's bubble."

My mind is in overdrive as I take in his every word. It's obvious that he's giving me critical information. But two questions loom in my mind. Why would the major general break rank to give me this information? And, more importantly, can this information be trusted?

The major general's face reveals nothing as he releases my hand, and it takes all of my discipline to stay calm while he strides back to his hover-platform. The stadium crowd continues to chant, "Let's go! Let's go!" And that's when I realize that I really don't matter in the least to the people in the audience. To them, I'm just an amusement in a dirt-covered ring, stuck smack dab in the middle of a crazed, bloodthirsty circus.

"You know the rules," shouts the official to my left from his hover-platform. "Blunt weapons only. No stabbing. A five-second takedown means you're out. Let's fight honorably out there!"

"Sir! Yes, sir!" I shout in unison with Arthur.

"Shake hands," the ref orders, and I extend my hand to Arthur.

As we clasp hands, Arthur squeezes with all his might. I return the sentiment in kind.

"Emily's mine now," Arthur says.

"Bullshit," I growl in response.

He holds up his left hand then, to reveal a tiny gold cross dangling from a cheap silver chain. I recognize it instantly as Emily's.

"Where'd you—"

That smug grin returns as he closes his hand over the necklace. "Emily gave it to me…for luck."

I don't believe him. Like me, Emily doesn't believe in luck. Hard work, sweat and guts…those are the things we put our faith in. But it's apparent that he has her necklace, and suddenly I'm very motivated in seeing this battle through to a victory. Escape or not, I'm going to beat the truth out of Arthur Eichler.

I squeeze his hand even harder before releasing the handshake, and am rewarded when I see him wince.

Turning on my heel, I stride back to my squad, but he calls out after me. "We're going to crush you, golden boy! Tonight, you're going down!"

The noise of the crowd swallows up the sound of Artie's hollow promises.

Chapter Seven

AS I return to my squad's end of the arena, I find Michael standing at the point where the loose dirt begins, waiting for me. Though he appears collected and coolly alert, I can tell he's anxious to speak with me.

"Artie Eichler is Lion Squad's leader?" he asks in disbelief as soon as I am within earshot. "The guy's a jerk! He used to pick on me all the time when he was at the facility! I can't stand him!"

"Join the club," I reply, and Michael falls in step with me as we walk toward Diana and Jason.

"So, where the hell is Captain Kostich?"

"I wish I knew," I say, and I can hear the resignation in my voice. "Right now, there's not a whole hell of a lot that's making sense in these games."

Michael frowns. "I know what you mean."

We walk several meters in silence before Michael turns to me and asks, "So…do you have any idea how many earthmovers we might be up against?"

"One. And she's a bitch." I flash him a grin. "But don't think that makes her any less of a threat." Apparently, I have decided to trust the major general's information.

Michael laughs, shaking his head. "Oh, no, sir, I won't… Four-legged or two, an earth-movin' bitch isn't something I want to mess with."

"What's going on?" Diana asks, shouting over the din of the crowd as she jogs over to us. I can see Jason standing a few meters behind her, serreptitiously leaning on a force-field projection. To the unattentive spectator, Jason looks as if he is standing of his own accord—relaxed, perhaps, but not holding himself up on a force field that extends several feet into the ground. Suddenly, I have a plan…one that just might give us half a chance out there.

"Jason," I say, indicating his force field. "How deep were you able to penetrate the arena floor?"

"I'm extended eight feet down…but there's probably more room than that. Why? What's going on?"

"We've got an earthmover to contend with," I say, addressing the three of them in a private huddle. "The major general tipped me off to a couple of her particulars."

"Wait a minute… You're talking about *our* major general, right? Major General *Allen*?" Diana asks, her expression a mixture of disbelief and concern.

I nod. "He hinted that the girl might be unskilled in battle, and then he mentioned something else…Jackson's bubble."

"Jackson's bubble?" Jason asks. "Should I know what that is?"

"Oh, wait!" Michael interjects, his eyes lighting up with excitement. "I was there when that happened! Back when I was with Beta Squad—Jackson Medincoff, that was the kid's name! We were on a training exercise in the mountains when he fell down an ice fissure and tumbled headlong into an underground river. He survived by projecting a spherical force field around himself. He stayed dry and fully oxygenated until he could find a place on the riverbank to land."

"I think we should consider the properties of an arena full of loose dirt the same as if we were dealing with a major body of water," I say with a nod.

"So, reshape our armor using curved lines instead of straight," says Diana. "No surface area for the dirt to pile onto."

"And therefore no way for it to smother us," Jason adds with a scowl. "Wish I would've thought of that."

"Think outside the box, people," I say while forming a four-inch force field bubble in my hand. I hold it up and then make it grow larger and larger. "By expanding the force fields around us, we'll force her to use more and more dirt to cover the surface area."

"Just watch out for the one-two punch," Jason interjects. "They can make the dirt form giant fists to hit you with, or grab you and drag you under. They can also form columns that explode right out of the ground beneath your feet. Step on one of those and you're airborne."

"Damn…" Michael says. "One earthmover can do all that?"

"All that and more, probably," I say. "Just be ready for anything. And improvise!" I look directly at Michael. "You're the quickest one here. I want you constantly moving downfield toward the earthmover. Keep the pressure on her and your guard up. I want her as distracted as possible."

"You got it," Michael says with a nod.

I address Diana next. "I want you to hold your ground here until after the first wave of attack. Artie's not stupid. He's going to send his two best swordsmen at you at the same time."

"Let them come," she growls. "I'm more than ready."

"Excellent attitude. Exactly what I wanted to hear." I turn to Jason next, and I'm more than a little concerned by how pale he looks. "I'm not going to ask you to forfeit—"

"Good. Because I think we've already covered that," Jason says, narrowing his eyes at me.

"—but I am going to ask you for a favor."

"A favor?" asks Jason.

I nod. "I need you to use your reserves to set a trap." I grin then, because I simply can't help but imagine the surprise on Artie's face when he sees what I have planned for his precious psi-blades.

Jason returns my grin. "You're talking about stunning bunnies, aren't you?"

"I most certainly am."

Jason shakes his head. "We'll need a carrot."

"We have our carrot."

Jason looks at me in surprise. "Who?"

I point at Diana. "Her."

"Me?" Diana says, hands on hips. "I am *no* carrot."

"No, you're not," I agree. "But you're the one they'll be gunning for the moment the trumpet blares. So, be ready… Jason and I will take care of the rest."

Diana's frown deepens. "This better be one hell of a bunny stunner, gentlemen, or I'm kicking both of your asses when this is over."

Michael snickers, and Diana throws him a murderous look. "You want your ass kicked, too?"

The youngest of us instantly straightens up, swallowing his laughter. "Oh, no, no…no ma'am. Not me. I was just… Uh, I think I'll go take my position on the field."

"Good idea," I say after him. The noise from the crowd has died down in anticipation of the starting trumpet. It won't be long now. "Let's take our positions."

Diana stands stoically where she is and powers up her blunted broadsword, while Jason and I start walking in opposite directions. I power up my projected weapon as I cross the arena and come to a stop approximately ten meters away on Diana's left. With a glance down the line, I see that Jason stands in position ten meters to Diana's right, powered up and ready.

Michael powers up his quarterstaff from a position seven meters to my left, well out of range of our bunny-stunner. He knows what we're up to, because he was part of our squad during last summer's extreme wilderness survival camp, when Jason and I came up with our unique method for stunning prey. It was either that or go hungry for five days.

Needless to say, we all had our fill of roasted rabbit that week.

I glance up at the hovering ImperiumTron the moment it buzzes, signaling the start of the one-minute countdown.

As the crowd begins to stir, I turn my concentration inward. What I'm about to do takes timing and precision. Baselines have never even seen this kind of thing before, and in that respect I am a bit worried. No telling how many hours of debriefing I'll be in for once my superiors see this.

Relaxing into myself, I release my power flow from the bottom of my feet. I work a cord of power as far as I can go, which is about twelve feet into the hard-packed dirt; then, like a hungry earthworm, I extend my energy in Jason's direction. While I work, I also keep my armor and sword powered up without appearing distressed. It takes every bit of strength I have.

The ImperiumTron's projected clock hits the thirty-second mark, and the crowd screams with delight. Voices from the stands rise in chorus as they count down to the starting trumpet.

I'm straining now to reach Jason under twelve feet of earth and over sixty feet of space.

"Ten…nine…eight…seven…" The crowd is on its feet.

Where the hell is Jason's energy thread?

"Six… five…"

My energy thread is extended as far as I can possibly reach.

"Four…three…"

Where the hell is Jason?!

"Two…"

I stretch myself out another foot—

"One!" The trumpet blares over the sound system and the ground ominously rumbles.

And that's when I notice the five-foot swells of earth rising from the ground like a damn ocean of soil.

"Jason!" I yell at the top of my lungs. I somehow manage to send my energy thread out another two feet—

The crowd roars with excitement as the swells roll closer. It's then that I notice the three psi-blades riding the rolling earth on force-field surfboards…and they're moments from contact!

"Oh, you gotta be kidding me!" I cry, and put everything I have into my energy thread.

Somewhere deep inside the earth, I make contact with Jason's energy thread and the power surge is immediate.

"NOW!" I scream.

As one, Jason and I extend our force field straight up from the ground. Higher and higher! My armor winks out as I pour everything into raising our grand force field.

The swells of earth loom high overhead at the exact moment that Jason and I break through the ground. In an instant, our wall rises thirty feet into the air, with traces of crimson and vermilion sparking within our combined effort.

I will myself not to turn away as the giant waves of soil smash into our wall. I see a flash of blue, then green, then yellow before I realize that I am looking at three psi-blades hurtling at full speed into our wall. I hear their voices cry out in alarm above the din of the crashing waves, followed by three sharp thuds as the psi-blades smash into our force field and tumble headlong into the raging brown earth below.

For several long minutes, the onslaught continues. Over and over the waves come, with the force of a hurricane.

And there is no sign of the three psi-blades from the first attack.

From behind the force field, I can look out over the arena. Four officials point at something within the turbulent sea of soil. Two officials hold up white flags, and it's apparent that two of Artie's psi-blades will be benched from further play.

In other words, they're out.

A horn blares from the ImperiumTron high overhead, and images of the two exiting psi-blades are projected midair. Since I've never even seen these kids before, their faces mean nothing to me. I scan the arena for the third psi-blade and find him bobbing around in the calming dark waves in a jade-tinged sphere, looking angry and pissed off. I also notice how much he has to struggle to remain standing in his force-field bubble. That's some swiftly moving dirt out there.

It only takes a few minutes for the officials to pluck the two retiring psi-blades from the turbulent battlefield, and the "game on" horn sounds overhead.

In the blink of an eye, the earthmover changes tactics. The waves drop back into the earth, and the dirt begins to roll backwards as if being sucked up by a giant vacuum cleaner. I watch in horror as a giant fist rises out of the ground and begins to grow at a rapid rate. The larger it grows, the less dirt remains to fill the arena. I can already feel the soil rushing around me as the monstrous fist takes shape before my eyes.

"Diana!" I scream, looking back at her. But she already sees what's coming her way. Her feet slipping over rolling soil, she scrambles to redirect her force-field armor to keep from falling. I want to laugh out loud when I see her generate a snowboard and boots and ride the cascading soil like a ski run.

My relief is short-lived, however. I turn in time to see the goliath soil fist slam into our wall. The impact tosses me backwards, but because I'm connected to the wall, I rebound and crash face-first into my own force field. *Hard!*

"Shit!" I cry, thankful that I had managed to maintain my helmet projection. I'm just about to catch my breath when the giant fist smashes against the wall again.

This time, I outright scream my rage at the top of my lungs as I lash about helplessly. And that's when I feel the tension in my power flow with Jason wink out.

"Jason!" I cry, knowing he has fallen…but there is nothing I can do for him. He's in the care of the officials now.

As our force field vanishes, I am fully aware that my squad and I are headed for a world of hurt. The crowd is going absolutely nuts as the giant fist rears back for a third blow. It's a grotesque and slow-moving thing, and it's going to pound me into the ground in about two seconds.

I'm just about to power up into Jackson's bubble when I'm plucked from the ground by Diana, zooming by on her snowboard—or should I call it an earth-skimmer?

"Miss me?" she asks.

"Definitely," I reply as I power up a new set of armor, complete with my own earth-skimmer.

"Where'd you get the idea for the footwear?" I ask.

Diana grins and points across the arena. "Michael."

Sure enough, I catch a flash of Michael tearing around the base of the growing fist on an earth-skimmer. He's deft and confident over the rippling dark waves as he raises his quarterstaff and rips it through the fist's thumb.

The entire soil digit crashes to the ground, and I smile.

Chancing a glance behind me, I am relieved to see an official and a med tech loading Jason onto a hover-platform. He may be out for the rest of these games, but his supreme effort on my behalf will never be forgotten. If I have even the slightest chance of seeing Emily again, it is only because of loyal friends like Jason.

As the hover-platform carrying Jason speeds off toward the arena exit, the ImperialTron buzzes overhead and Jason's image appears midair. Since no one has been buried beneath a ton of dirt this time, play doesn't stop. Diana and I race across the retreating soil, keeping well to the right of the looming fist as it draws in massive amounts of dirt to replace its missing digit. Out of the corner of my eye, I catch a flash of the Lion's jade-armored psi-bade riding a projected surfboard as he comes ripping around the towering soil fist on a collision course with my second-in-command.

"Diana!" I cry in warning, but it's too late. The psi-blade swings his blunted flail at her.

She ducks low on her earth skimmer, narrowly missing the blow, but she's off-balance and tumbles head over heels into the deep, turbulent soil.

"No!" I shout in fury. I change direction and race after the jade-armored Lion. I catch a flash of his armor as he rounds the base of the growing fist ahead of me. Putting my weight into it, I close the distance between us and lean into the turn as the soil moves of its own accord beneath my skimmer, which picks up my speed. I whip myself around the base and am stunned to find an indigo-tinged knight barreling straight at me.

There's no time to change course, so I swallow my surprise and lean further into my turn around the base of the rising fist. I can hear the bits of dirt and rock grinding as the soil draws together. I am less than a foot away from the growing column of dirt, but that may be to my advantage.

The indigo psi-blade stands almost a foot taller than me, and the angry grimace he bears leads me to believe that he is all about taking my head off with one sweep of his projected war hammer. My suspicions are confirmed when I see his left arm twitch, and I do my best not to tip my hand as I hurl myself even faster at him.

My opponent's grimace deepens as I close in, and I allow him to think that he has me. When I see him rear back to swing, I don't even raise my shield. Instead, I hold my position as long as I can while speeding over the swiftly moving soil, the giant fist at my back—

The whites of my opponent's eyes go wide as he swings at my head with all of his might.

At that moment, I plant my sword deep into the growing column of soil behind me. I crouch low and lean as far away from my opponent as possible. Using my sword for balance, I am able to stay low while still in control of my earth-skimmer, well out of my opponent's reach.

Just as I predicted, the undisciplined energy behind my opponent's blow hurls him off-balance, smack into the base of the still-forming soil fist. I can hear him screaming in rage as he collides headlong with the massive column of dirt.

I don't wait around. I withdraw my sword and use my momentum to sail free. As I speed across the arena, I can hear the audience roar. Glancing up at the ImperiumTron, I smile just a tiny bit when I see the monstrous fist crash hard to the ground in one massive deluge of dirt.

The crowd's thunderous applause practically blows me over as the ImperiumTron's buzzer sounds—not once, but twice! Not only does my opponent's image appear midair, but the jade psi-blade's image does as well. Diana must have dispatched her opponent at the same time. That's two more Lions out of play. Perhaps we do have a chance for a victory.

All four officials wave their white flags, indicating a pause in play as they proceed to search for the indigo psi-blade beneath the ton of dirt that has just fallen on top of him. I can feel the moving earth slow as it swirls around my calves. Scanning the battlefield, I catch sight of the jade psi-blade arguing with one of the hovering officials, but I don't see Diana anywhere…

Three hovercams fly directly in front of my face, buzzing and chirping incessantly.

"Give 'em a smile, chief," says Michael as he sweeps his earth-skimmer to a stop next to me. He points skyward. "You're large and in charge."

"Yeah, I see that," I reply with a fleeting glance at the instant replay of my opponent tumbling headlong into the earthmover's soil monstrosity. "How're you holding up?"

"Covered in dirt, but otherwise fine," he says with that bright grin of his.

"Where's Diana?" I ask.

Michael points behind us, across the arena. "She was right behind me… Oh, there she is."

And sure enough, I see Diana, powered down and slogging through the dirt toward us. Since the earth has stopped moving, there's now no way to move quickly over the soft, deep soil.

I glance over at the officials and note that they're still searching for the indigo psi-blade.

"Let's walk," I say to Michael as I power down. "We haven't got much time before play resumes."

Michael powers down and stays close as we make our way through the soft dirt toward Diana.

"Did you get a good look at her?" I ask.

"Who?" Michael replies, with a confused look on his face.

"The earthmover."

"Oh, yeah, her… I caught a glimpse of her standing beside Artie just on the other side of that hellacious mound of dirt they're digging in. She's a tiny thing—hair up in pigtails, with these big pink pom-poms dangling down both sides of her head. Even in a battle suit, she looks like she's about eight—but I'm sure that's what they want us to think." Michael turns to me, looking grim. "But I have to tell you, Captain…you know I don't enjoy hitting girls. Especially tiny girls who remind me of my sister. But if I *do* get the chance today, I'm not going to have any trouble smacking that little chickadee upside the head with my quarterstaff."

I work hard not to grin, but it isn't easy. Even on a field of battle, Michael can make me crack a smile, just by being Michael. "Duly noted, Corporal," I say with a nod. "It looks like we're going to have our work cut out for us."

"More like dumped on our heads," says Diana. She's covered in dirt, well beyond pissed off, and ready to punch someone in the face. "I have never been so filthy in my entire life! I can hardly move in this muck, let alone fight in it!"

"What happened after that psi-blade knocked you into the dirt?" I ask, ignoring her grousing.

"He didn't knock me into the dirt—I *fell*," she growls at me, her eyes narrowing to slits.

"Right," I reply in an effort to keep Diana focused, "so what happened next?"

"The dirt was unusually deep there, so I bubbled up, crouched down and waited. The next time the idiot surfed by, I ambushed him and pulled him into the dirt with me." She shrugs and rolls her eyes. "It wasn't even a challenge after that. The guy almost looked relieved when I took him out."

"Good to hear," I say with a nod as a hovercam buzzes around my ear. I turn and address the little plastic machine as it studies me with its one large, unblinking lens. "Do you mind?"

With a whirl and a beep, the hovercam floats away, and I turn my attention back to what remains of my squad.

"They're bound to change tactics once play resumes." I look pointedly at Diana. "I want you gunning for Artie as soon as the horn blares."

"With pleasure," she says, flashing me a crooked grin.

"Good." I turn to Michael. "I need you to keep that earthmover busy at all costs. If you can get in for a smackdown, go for it, but it's all going to depend on what the earthmover decides to throw at us."

"Or slam us with," Michael adds.

"Just keep moving." I point to Diana. "That goes for you, too. Let's make that earthmover work for her victory."

A low roar builds from the crowd, and I glance over Diana's shoulder in time to see the officials pull the indigo psi-blade from the towering mound of dirt. The guy waves weakly to the spectators in the stands as he's loaded onto a med-sled.

"I guess we know whose side they're on," quips Michael with a shake of his head. "Dang, that's loud."

Diana scowls. "Let's just get this over with. I need a shower."

"Good idea," I say. "Spread out. And be ready for anything."

Michael and Diana trudge through the soft soil and take up positions ten meters apart. I decide to stay to the left of the two of them while Michael closes in on the massive mound of dirt.

The moment the med-sled glides into an exit tunnel, the starting horn sounds, and I instantly feel the loose earth take on a life of its own. I have barely finished powering up when—

KACHOOM!

A giant spout of dirt flies sky-high like some sort of ancient sea monster's tentacle. The shower of dirt that pours on me is full of dangerous rocks and debris. There is no way I can warn Michael and Diana; it's all about survival now.

KACHOOM! VERR-OOSH!

It's like running through a minefield, as the earth explodes all around us. To make matters worse, that stupid hovercam has returned. It knocks into my helmet as I zigzag toward the arena's far wall.

"Get away from me!" I shout at the hovercam, and then the ground explodes beneath my feet—KACHOOM!

I am soaring through the air, head over heels, arms flailing. The black arena wall comes at me way too fast. I have a nanosecond to strengthen the shielding around my head before I crash face-first into the cold, hard steel. *Damn*, that hurt!

I drop another five meters before I hit the soil-covered arena floor. My ears ringing, my vision swimming, my entire body aching, I work overtime to pull myself together from the crumpled heap I have become.

I have only five seconds to stand up, or I may never see Emily again.

Somehow, I manage to roll onto my hands and knees, mindful that an official is hovering over me, keeping a close eye on his stopwatch. I squeeze my eyes closed and take a deep, cleansing breath, willing the vertigo to cease. The next time I open my eyes, I find that my bearings have returned and that I am able to sit back on my knees. I inhale deeply again, and the pain in my shoulder lessons.

"Resume play, soldier," the official calls, and he speeds away on his hovering platform.

Despite the fact that I have been cleared to resume the battle, despair fills me. I have absolutely no idea how to prevent my squad from being slaughtered out here. I never expected that I would have to battle an elemental psion during the Psi Games, and I feel helpless in my lack of adequate battle strategies. How does one even go about defeating an opponent that one cannot get close to?

It is then that I notice the cracked and useless hovercam lying on the ground between my knees…and I'm struck with inspiration.

Projectiles have never been allowed in the Psi Games… but then again, neither has an earthmover.

Scooping up the broken orb, I stagger to my feet and take in the battlefield before me.

I must have flown more than ten meters in that blast, because I can see Artie and the earthmover now. They are standing close to the far arena wall, up on a wide mound of dirt, four meters off the ground so that they have a clear view of the action. Artie stands smugly beside the tiny earthmover, so confident in his victory that he hasn't bothered to extend his shields to protect the unarmored girl from attack.

I stick close to the wall for as long as I can while I make my way toward them. Thankfully, the explosions of earth have caused clouds of dust to drift over the battlefield, and this provides me a bit of cover as I approach.

The earthmover squints in concentration while she focuses on a moving target somewhere in the arena before her.

KACHOOM!

A monstrous explosion of dirt shoots high into the air, and I can only watch helplessly as a purple-tinged figure flies across the battlefield.

Oh, no! It's Diana!

Anger rolls through me, and I find the strength to push free from the wall. I have to end this now. I cannot allow this slaughter to continue!

The ImperiumTron's buzzer sounds, but I don't have to look up to know whose image has been projected midair. In an instant, I have formed my new weapon and loaded the projectile. It's then that I notice Michael out of the corner of my eye as he bounds across the arena and directly into the earthmover's line of sight.

The earthmover's pink pom-poms bounce around her cherubic face as she locks her gaze on Michael.

I want to shout to him in warning, but it is too late—

KACHOOM! VERR-OOSH!

Michael is thrown mercilessly into the air.

My anger carries me forward as I sprint across the soft dirt toward my quarry. Whirling my sling overhead, I let loose a battle cry at the top of my lungs. I race through the explosion's billowing cloud of soil and am rewarded with the earthmover's startled expression when she turns to me. I release the projectile.

The broken hovercam rockets from my force-field sling like a missile. The girl has absolutely no time to react before it strikes her square in the middle of her forehead.

She drops unconscious to the ground like a sack of wet concrete.

It is then that I realize my mistake. In my anger-driven haste to take down the earthmover, I hadn't considered one thing.

Artie.

With a primal scream, Artie leaps off of the dirt platform, wildly swinging his mace at my head. I manage to duck the blow, but I'm off-balance and I lose my footing in the soft earth. Collapsing onto one knee, I am unable to power up my shield in time, and Artie's mace cold-cocks me across the left side of my jaw. My force-field helmet protects my face from the weapon, but not from the power behind the blow.

"Nighty-night, de Montague," Artie sneers as I am sent reeling from the blow.

Time slows as I fall to the ground. I have lost, and that little insight has sent my mind into overdrive. Artie's eyes shine with malice, his lips curled into a savage grin as he watches me tumble to my doom. He is a beastly victor, but judging by the crowd's approving roar, the spectators could care less. It is spectacle they crave…that, and my blood all over the arena floor.

Consciousness fading, my last thought is of Emily. It's her smile I see—that sad, sweet, heartbreaking smile that tears me to shreds inside.

Because I have failed her.

I have failed *us*.

Chapter Eight

I awaken on a med-sled hovering a few feet over the exact spot where I fell. A medical tech stares down at me as he examines the side of my face.

"How you feeling, sport?" he asks, with an absurdly cheerful smile across his face.

"I'm fine," I lie. In truth, the side of my face painfully throbs where Artie whacked me, and it feels like a hot poker has skewered my left shoulder. But none of that matters now. I have failed to win the Psi Games. By this time next year, Emily will have disappeared for good. I have lost my one and only chance to find her.

"How is the rest of my squad doing?" I ask in an effort to focus on my present surroundings.

"They're fine. They've already been sent back to the facility."

I nod, glad to hear that Michael and Diana didn't suffer any major injuries during that last explosive encounter with the earthmover. I'll be joining both of them and Jason soon, no doubt. The Administration wastes no time returning defeated psi-blades back to the facility for a headcount and lockdown.

The crowd cheers wildly, and I glance out into the arena to see what's going on.

It's Artie. He's riding a six-foot column of dirt around the arena like some kind of ancient pagan god. He holds his arms wide as if embracing the crowd, lapping up the adoration with the pomp of Caesar.

I look around for the earthmover and find her sitting on a med-sled not more than five feet away. Her drooping pink pom-poms are damp with what appears to be blood. A white field dressing has been wrapped around her head with a tiny red stain evident where I had beaned her with the hovercam. She looks fragile now, and very childlike. She's probably close to Michael in age, but her small size makes that difficult to assume.

She's looking away from me, out at the arena where she guides Artie's dais around the battlefield, so I'm not able to clearly see her face. But I do see the extreme paleness of her skin and the effort she is putting into her psionic discipline… and I have to admit that I am concerned for her well-being.

I turn back to the med tech. "Is she all right?"

The man glances over his shoulder. "Oh, yeah, she'll be fine. Mild concussion is all."

Turning my attention back to the arena, I see that Artie is making his way over to us atop his pillar of earth. His gaze locks with mine as he approaches. When he is within earshot, he points his mace at me and flashes me that smug grin of his.

"Told you I'd crush you, Goldilocks," he shouts down at me from atop his pedestal. "Ha! I bet it sucks to be you right now."

I don't reply. Instead, I turn to the med tech, who is retrieving a disruptor band from his pack for my short journey home.

"I'm sure you've already heard," Artie calls down at me. "But they're planning to close the Alaskan Psi Facility. They're going to incorporate all of you into a private elite military program!"

I look up at him the moment his words register. Why the hell would they close the facility? It's the only home I've ever known.

Artie's grin turns sinister as he scowls down at me. "Looks like your golden-boy days are over, Vahn." His lips twist into a sneer and his glare hardens until I can feel the full measure of his hatred. "I can promise you that I'll fill *Emily* in on every last little detail of your downfall."

I have no idea if what he is telling me is true, but if it is, I've lost not only the Psi Games, but my soulmate as well.

"Is it true?" I ask the med tech. "Are they closing us down?"

When the med tech doesn't answer right away, I have my answer. "Yeah," the med tech says while fiddling with a disruptor band. "We all got our pink slips about a month ago." He throws me a quick glance. "Sorry, kid."

Artie laughs from his dirt perch above us, playing it up once more for his adoring fans. His idiotic braying rakes my nerves raw. All I want to do is return to my bunk at the dorm. I am beyond ready for these games to be over.

"Hey, Sylvia!" Artie calls from above. "Sylvia!"

The earthmover turns to him, looking paler than before. And I notice that the spot of blood on her bandage has grown in size.

"Raise me higher!" Artie shouts at her.

The girl's eyes widen, and for a moment I think she is going to swoon.

"You hear me?" Artie cries. "Raise me higher!"

"But—but—" the girl stammers, her starburst eyes full of fear.

"That's an order!" Artie shouts. "Higher, you pygmy bitch!"

The earthmover looks troubled, and I notice that her hands are trembling. It's obvious that she doesn't want to do this, but it's nearly impossible for a soldier to disregard a direct order from a superior. I watch helplessly as she squeezes her eyes shut and channels her remaining strength into controlling her psionic ability.

I try to move toward her, but a hovering official descends and blocks my way. "Sit back down, soldier," the official says, his voice muffled by his helmet's visor.

"Yes, sir," I reply as I ease back down. "But I think Sylvia may need help."

The med tech hands the disruptor band to the official. "I'll go take a look at her," he says, and leaps across to the earthmover's sled.

The crowd roars in delight as Artie takes his second victory lap around the arena, but this time his pillar of dirt has risen over thirty feet. Artie smacks hands with the spectators, all the while braying in triumph.

"Can you stand?" the official asks me.

"Yes, sir."

"Good. I need you to step onto my platform." The official holds up the disruptor band, and I understand what he wants me to do. It's against the rules to transport a psi-talent outside of the facility without a fully activated disruptor band.

"Yes, sir," I say as I start to rise. It's then that the pain in my shoulder burns a hole right through me. I hesitate, my breath caught in my throat. And suddenly, I'm not so sure I can get to my feet.

"Medic!" the official calls, and the med tech leaps back across to my side.

"Where does it hurt?" the medic asks, as he takes out his portable med-scanner.

"Left shoulder," I manage to say through clenched teeth.

The med tech runs the scanner over my shoulder. "You've separated your shoulder. Unfortunately, I'm fresh out of nanobots, so it looks like a visit to the infirmary for you, soldier. In the meantime, I'll give you something for the pain."

He searches through his pouch and produces an injectible cartridge. Placing the tube on the front of my shoulder, he presses down firmly. I feel a sting, then hear the *hiss* of the cartridge discharging the painkiller. The relief is instant, and I can breathe freely once again.

"That's much better," I say to the med tech. "I can—"

All of a sudden, I feel a bone-numbing rumble. Judging from the collective gasp of the stadium crowd, they can feel it too. Normally, I would say that this is what it must feel like to encounter a massive earthquake, but I am hovering on a med-sled five feet above the ground.

I take in the horrified expressions of the spectators. Following their gazes, I turn to the arena in time to see the massive pillar of dirt collapse beneath Artie. He is instantly pulled under by the dirt's momentum and disappears from sight. The earth rolls over him as it loses its form, its sheer mass spreading out across the arena like a great beast lolling to its death.

I should be happy that my rival has been toppled from his pedestal, but I'm not. There have been too many injuries and too many surprises at these Psi Games. I can only hope that Artie was able to somehow save himself from suffocating beneath that massive mound of dirt, but I doubt that he had the time.

"Sylvia." The earthmover's name escapes my lips before I have full command of my senses. My eyes dart over to the med tech, but he's no longer beside me. He's hovering over the prone earthmover, performing CPR.

"Breathe!" he cries as he continues his efforts, pumping both hands over her sternum, willing her heart to beat of its own accord.

"I've called in backup," the official tells the med tech. "They'll be here momentarily."

The medic doesn't respond; he's fighting to keep Sylvia alive, but she's not responding. And then it occurs to me that I can help.

"I'm authorized to use a med-scanner," I say to the official hovering on his platform between our two med-sleds. "It might have some nanobots left. Perhaps I could—"

"No," the official says, cutting me off. "You're needed elsewhere. Now get on my platform. The medic can handle the girl."

I gape at the official for a moment too long, and he snaps at me again.

"Get your ass on this platform *now*, soldier!"

I jump to my feet and step onto the hovering platform. The official gestures for me to sit behind him in the jumpseat while he stands to pilot the craft. As I sit down, I glance over at the med tech who's working hard to revive Sylvia, and my insides wither with despair. The earthmover is deathly pale, her lips as blue as her starburst eyes; the bandage on her temple is saturated with blood.

I know my actions in the arena are responsible for that girl's condition, and I shudder at the thought that she might die. The Psi Games are not meant to be a killing field. Sure, accidents have happened in the past, but never like this. Why were things allowed to go so far this time?

"Hold on," the official says to me before maneuvering his platform between the med-sleds and out into the arena.

As we speed away, another med-sled arrives with two more medics, and a part of me brightens a bit with hope. No matter how horrible it was for me and my squad out there tonight, I didn't want anyone to die…not Sylvia, not even Artie.

The platform I'm riding on slows down midway across the arena, and I look over the siderail to see what's going on. Below me, there are more than a dozen administrator platforms gathered around the humongous pile of dirt, and about thirty facility guards digging through the earth in hopes of finding Artie alive.

"They should call in another earthmover," I say, more to myself than to the official.

"An earthmover has been called," the official replies. "But the facility is over twenty minutes away."

"Do you think that maybe I could offer my services?" I ask the official tentatively. "I could perhaps burrow an energy thread through the mound and locate him—"

"That won't be necessary," the official says. "You need to get out of here."

I'm about to press him once again about helping Artie when I realize that I am not wearing a disruptor band. I stare hard at my wrist, and then spot the disruptor band lying on the floor next to the official's spit-polished dress shoes.

Psi-Game officials wear boots, not dress shoes.

And those dress shoes are definitely military issue.

"S-s-sir?" I say the word softly, my mind a whirlwind of disbelief, my heart drumming with fear. "What are you doing? Where are you taking me?"

From where I'm sitting, I can see his shoulders visibly relax, like he's relieved that I have figured out who he is. "I'm getting you the hell out of here."

"You mean back to the facility."

"No, son," he says, turning to me. He presses a button on the side of his helmet and his faceshield retracts. "There's no going back to the facility for you."

"I don't understand, sir, I—"

Major General Allen holds up a gloved finger. "You've always been my best and brightest, Vahn. And I'll be damned if I'm going to just hand you over to a no-account private corporation so they can turn you into a mindless mercenary for hire. Where's the honor in that?"

"A private corporation, sir?" I am struggling to keep up with the deluge of information that the major general is throwing at me.

He nods. "The Stillwell Agency for Psionic Integration and Development, aka The Agency."

"That's where Emily is," I say without thinking.

"No, son, Emily isn't at The Agency."

"Then where is she?"

The major general sighs. "I don't know. It was the federal authorities who took her, and they were tight-lipped during the whole affair."

"The feds," I feel my heart sink to the floor. "But Arthur had Emily's necklace, he said he'd spoken with her, he said—"

"*Artie* has no honor. He's a liar and an egotistical, smart-mouth punk. If he had a necklace of Emily's, then I have no idea who gave it to him. I had nothing to do with it."

"But what about what you said at the beginning of the games? All that 'new age of warfare—embrace it or be conquered' stuff?"

"I may be a son of a bitch when it comes to tactical training, son, but I want you to know that I had absolutely no part in the planning of these games. None. I've been held prisoner since last year in my own facility by my very own administration." He pauses then, the hover-platform once again picking up speed and heading toward the arena exit. "Now…you got that back gate key card I left for you?"

I can't help but grin like an idiot. "Yes, sir."

Major General Allen returns my grin with one of his own. "Very good, Captain. Very good."

Chapter Nine

MAJOR General Allen guides the hover-platform out of the arena, through a transport tunnel, and into a vast arched dome that serves as the central staging area. As my eyes adjust to the dim lighting, I realize that it's a hive of activity. Hundreds of psi facility guards wearing full riot armor swarm into the staging area from the monorail station thirty meters above. Almost all of them carry retractable shovels in addition to their guns and neuro-stunners. They are all on a mission to rescue Artie.

A large hover-barge crowded with over fifty guards pulls away from its docking moors just ahead of us.

"Get down," the major general orders, and I crouch low behind the railing.

Looking up at the ceiling, I notice the monorail station high above us. From what I've been able to figure out over the years, the monorail has only two destinations. The first is the five-star Imperium Arena Hotel; the second—and the only route that I've ever taken—goes directly to the psi facility. The exact place I would be headed to right now if it wasn't for the major general.

It's still a bit hard for me to wrap my mind around that fact that the major general was held prisoner by his own administration. That kind of betrayal must have cut deep for a man of honor like himself. Yet he never let on to any of us. Was that to keep us safe from the powers that be?

More importantly, I wonder if my absence will make things harder on my squad. I can't imagine any of my troops willingly serving as mercenaries alongside Agency psions named Skullcrusher and Carnage.

"There's a helmet in that duffle bag beneath the jumpseat," the major general says, eyes locked on the airspace ahead. "Put it on."

Reaching beneath the seat, I remove a black psi-facility-issue duffel bag. I unzip it, pull out the riot helmet, and shove it onto my head. Before I lower my faceshield, I see that the bag is packed with a complete set of riot gear, along with two extra sets of boots. The major general has indeed come prepared for our escape.

With my face now hidden from view, I find that I can relax a little in the knowledge that I will be harder to spot from above. I can hear the hundreds of booted feet stomping across the unloading platform of the monorail as the psi facility guards race down to the arena floor.

"Do you think they'll find Artie in time?" I ask.

But the major general doesn't reply. He continues staring straight ahead.

I'm about to chastise myself for asking such a stupid question when I hear him say, "Hold on."

Gripping the rail tightly, I brace my feet against the base of the jumpseat just as the hover-platform makes a sudden dip and veers right. I watch the monorail's giant concrete columns rise up around me like a haunting alien forest, while the tracks above me get farther and farther away. The hover-platform sways as it dives into the bowels of the arena. Everything appears jumbo size above me and much, much darker. I retract my faceshield so that I can see more clearly the strange structures that have been built down here.

Red blinking lights attached to the monorail's massive concrete supports are our only guide as the major general whips us about the maze of support columns and a gracefully arching glass-and-steel structure, which looms like a giant silver spider. It's too dark for me to make out just what that building houses, but it gives me a chill just the same.

"Uh, sir?" I say. "That building…what's in there?"

It's almost pitch-black out here, but the glow from the control panel enables me to see him lower his head in resignation. "Dissection rooms."

"*What?*" I have never heard of such a thing…and all at once, I'm very frightened. "Emily's not—"

"No, no, no… Emily's *useful*; she's in no danger of that."

"Then who is?" I ask, trying hard not to sound like a scared child. "Why would anyone build dissection rooms beneath the Imperium Arena?"

The major general takes a deep breath and slows the hover-platform before answering. "They've been pressuring me for years to make the Psi Games a fight to the death. The strong versus the weak. But it was just an excuse." He pauses to retract his faceshield. "The truth is, the government's not going to rest until they find out what makes you kids tick."

"It was that vaccine they gave our mothers during the Ebola-X pandemic—that's what did this to us."

"Is it?" the major general quietly asks. "Or is that just what the government wants you to think?"

I hesitate, his words shattering things that I thought I knew for certain. "What are you saying, sir?"

"I'm saying that not one scientist in all the world has yet been able to replicate the psionic syndrome in a lab. Haven't you ever wondered why there haven't been any youngsters born with starburst eyes in the last twelve years?"

"Then how *did* we happen?"

The major general chuckles. "I think you happened by the grace of God, son. And you have as much right to this earth as any of us." He levels his gaze at me. "We're monsters for what we've done to our own children…and I hope that, one day, you can find it in your heart to forgive people like me."

I have no idea how to reply, because I've seen the major general as the warden—and my own personal oppressor—for so long that to hear him ask for forgiveness is almost as absurd as him asking me to sprout wings and fly. Has he ever truly been my oppressor? Or was that the only way in which he knew how to protect me—all of us—from the whims of a cruel and unjust world?

"There's nothing to forgive," I say. "Baselines have a right to be scared of us."

"But not a right to cage you, *use* you, and then allow a horde of scientists to pore over your remains," the major general says in disgust. "And it's only going to get worse as all of you get older. The governments of the world are panicking. They want to cull the number of psions."

"Cull? You mean kill."

"Yes, son," he says, looking grave. "They mean to lower your numbers to a more manageable headcount. And they plan to keep alive only those who they feel they can control."

"So, none of us are safe."

The major general lowers his eyes. "I'm sorry, son."

I stagger under the weight of his words and find myself gripping the railing for support. My mind reels from the sheer magnitude of the information, and what it means for me, my classmates…Emily. And suddenly, I have to know—

"Is Emily safe?"

The major general nods. "For now. With her newfound power boost, I'm sure the feds will keep her alive. Indefinitely, perhaps."

"Good," I say. "Then I have a little time to find her."

"Yes…perhaps a little."

I look at the major general then and really see him for the first time. Not as my commanding officer, but as a fellow human being. And as perhaps the greatest ally I never knew I had.

"Thank you, sir."

He looks surprised by my words. "Whatever for, Captain?"

"Well," I say, hoping that my sincerity will carry my meaning well beyond my simple vocabulary, "for protecting us for all these years. I'm sure it couldn't have been easy."

He flashes me a grin before returning to the control panel. "Well, for whatever it's worth, you're welcome. Now let's get the heck out of here." He takes the projected guidance controls in both hands and we speed off into the darkness.

This time, I ease myself into the jumpseat, mindful of my injured shoulder, and buckle in. With my helmet on down here, I don't expect anyone would be able to identify me from a distance. The hover-platform dips and rocks as it glides around support structures and giant sewage pipes. I spot a red light in the distance that appears to grow in size as we approach.

"I know it's dark," the major general says, "but do you think you can get into that guard's uniform? It's in the bag."

"You want me in the armor, too?"

"You bet. Oh, and Vahn?"

"Sir?"

"Don't forget the boots."

I grin. "Yes, sir!"

I don't bother taking off my battle suit, because the high-tech fiber is extremely thin, skin-tight, and supple. It offers extra protection, and it could prove useful in case we run into trouble and I need to power up. Unlike regular clothing, my bladed projections won't tear my battle suit to shreds. So, retaining my dignity during a fight will be one less thing I'll have to worry about. After I remove my boots and unstrap my utility belt, I manage to pull on the guard's uniform, taking care not to jostle my injured shoulder too much. The pants and shirt are a bit loose, but it's nothing that anyone will notice under the layer of riot armor.

By the time I finish latching the last shin guard to my boot, I resemble any other psi facility guard in the area—

except for the starburst eyes, of course. Thank goodness for the helmet's polarized faceshield.

The last thing in the bag is a neuro-stunner, and I hesitate before picking it up. Neuro-stunners resemble long billy clubs and transmit a neon blue glow when activated. The weapons act very much like disruptor bands in that, upon contact, they instantly neutralize a psion's power. Unlike the more humane disruptor bands, any psion a guard feels the need to zap gets whacked with fifty thousand volts of electricity.

I shudder at the memory of my first and only encounter with a neuro-stunner. I was ten and desperately trying to break up a fight between Jason and this really huge kid whose name I can no longer recall. The guards rushed the room without regard to the situation at hand and I was zapped in the neck with such fury that I was laid up in a medical suite for two days with second-degree burns and minor nerve damage.

A neuro-stunner was a weapon that I definitely didn't want to mess with.

"You're going to have to take that, too," says the major general over his shoulder. "Neuro-stunners are standard issue down here."

"Why? Are there wild psions on the loose?" I ask, only half-joking.

"No," he replies, shaking his head. "Large rats."

"Oh." With that little gem of information, I decide to holster the neuro-stunner without further thought.

The flickering light in the distance has grown considerably, and I can feel the heat radiating from what I can only assume is a boiler room. The massive arena must consume a lot of fuel to keep its VIPs extra cozy as they watch the midwinter Psi Games. From the massive size of the building that looms before us, I'm confident that this boiler room also heats the surrounding ten smaller domes that host the early rounds of the games.

Noticing how bright it has gotten from the glow of the flames heating the boilers, I lower my faceshield and belt myself back into the jumpseat. I can see people in coveralls moving along metal ladders and catwalks on either side of the arched docking bay before the concrete-and-steel building.

Without a word to me, the major general guides the hover-platform into a docking stall and waits for the magnetic clamps to attach before signaling me to hand him his boots. He pulls them on without a word, then motions for me to follow him as he steps onto the concrete dock and walks to a ladder at the far end of the station.

I try not to gawk at the bright orange glow that flickers twenty meters above our heads as I match pace with my commanding officer. I am thankful for the riot-gear gloves the moment I touch the first rung of the ladder; it's hot. The gloves keep my hands protected, but just barely. With my injured shoulder, I climb the ladder awkwardly at first. It's hot and exhausting work, but my grip is strong; by using my legs and favoring my good arm, I fall into a rhythm as I ascend. The warmth I feel is uncomfortable at best, and I must constantly remind myself not to brush any other part of me against the metal rungs.

I join the major general on the catwalk at the top of the ladder. He gives me a nod and we cross into a huge room where a row of large industrial furnaces burn brightly behind thick metal doors. I am awed by the sheer size of this place. Dozens of men wearing blue coveralls and yellow safety helmets move effortlessly along the ladders and catwalks that crisscross the room in a dizzying display. Gigantic pipes extend every which way throughout the room, disappearing into the walls, floor and ceiling at irregular intervals. I barely have time to glance around as the major general confidently strides across the catwalk ten meters above the boiler room floor.

It's clear to me now that, on my own, I would never have been able to find the back gate, let alone make it there alive. *What the hell had I been thinking?*

The heat is oppressive, and I am relieved when we step into a dimly lit hallway. The major general takes a left, and I follow suit. He picks up his pace, leading me through a maze of hallways, catwalks, and stairs. Smaller pipes and ventilation shafts snake their way out of the boiler room above our heads. The hiss of steam and gurgle of water are constant.

The major general signals for me to hold up, and I immediately lean back against the wall to wait. Instead of gripping my neuro-stunner, I ready my psionic ability by conjuring up a power thread until I can feel it tingling just beneath my skin.

I hear the footfalls and voices of two psi facility guards as they approach. My heart drums harder in anticipation of an encounter. Though it's been one long, hellacious day for me in the arena, the combination of my military training and the ample amount of adrenaline coursing through my body has left me more than up for the challenge.

While my heart thumps, the guards walk past us, oblivious to our position only a few feet away. We remain where we are for a half a minute longer before the major general motions that we're moving out.

I lose count of all the quick turns we take as the major general navigates the maze of corridors and back stairways. After ten minutes of brisk walking, we come to a catwalk that crosses high above what looks to have been an old cargo bay, and he signals me to hold up.

He points across the catwalk to a rusty loading bay door. We've made it. That has to be the back gate! I'm about to say something when I hear the soft scuff of a footfall behind me.

"You fellas lost?" says a man.

I turn to find the two guards from earlier standing behind us. The guard who spoke has his faceshield up and I can see he sports a mustache, but what worries me most is his holstered gun. The second guard keeps his faceshield down, but his right hand doesn't stray from the butt of the service revolver at his hip.

I'm not thrilled to see that both of them have guns. That first shot rarely gives me enough time to power up an effective shield. I draw on my power thread until my skin tingles, ready to throw up a protective shield big enough for both of us.

"We're not lost," the major general says. "We know exactly where we are. You may carry on."

The fellow with the mustache chuckles unpleasantly as he uses his thumb to pop open the safety snap on his piece. "You must not be from around here, because down here, when people address me, they tend to call me *sir*."

"Sir," replies the major general stepping up beside me. "That's interesting. Now, why would anyone call a homicidal piece of trash like yourself *sir*?"

The man's eyes narrow to murderous slits. "No one calls me a piece of trash!"

The man draws his gun, but I'm ready for him. I raise as powerful a shield as I can muster, just in time for the first shot to ring out.

"They're ex-military. Watch yourself," the major general tells me as I deflect yet another bullet.

"Damn it, Junior! He's a psi-blade!" cries the mustached guard to his partner. And that's when I see the second guard reach between his shoulderblades and unsheathe a neuro-stunner.

The mustached guard shoots two more rounds at me while his partner charges me with his neuro-stunner. I can't allow him to hit my force field with that weapon, so I conjure a longsword and charge the guy shooting at me.

My change of tactics throws off the mustached fellow just enough to cause his aim to go wide. I swing. The flat of my projected blade catches him hard across the face and sends him crashing to the ground. His gun goes flying over the side of the catwalk, but there is no time to rejoice. I turn back around to find the major general locked in hand-to-hand combat with Junior, the second guard, who has retracted his faceshield and revealed his ugly, hateful mug. The major general holds his own until Junior tags him with a vicious uppercut with the neuro-stunner, which sends his helmet flying off his head.

I close in, but Junior's too fast. He grabs the major general and puts him in a choke hold. Junior now has the upper hand, and he knows it. He crushes the end of his revolver to the major general's temple. "Well, if it isn't Major General Allen come for a visit," he snarls through a jumble of crooked teeth.

"Let him go," I growl.

"No can do, little man. When the Administration hears what this one's been up to—stealing government property, transporting underage goodies like yourself—well, let's just say that I'd probably be doing your friend here a favor if I just up and blew his brains out right now."

"You wouldn't dare," I say, narrowing my eyes.

Junior flashes me a sadistic grin. "You'd better power down, sonny, if you want your sugar daddy here to live."

The idea that my relationship with the major general is somehow perverted makes my blood boil. I want to rip Junior's face off. But the reality is, I'm powerless to act at the moment. I'm going to have to be patient and wait for an opportunity to present itself. Very slowly, I rein in my power, all the while holding Junior's gaze. "Don't do it!" shouts the major general, but Junior silences him by tightening his hold around his neck.

When the last bit of my armor vanishes from sight, the mustached guard grabs me roughly from behind. "Gotcha!"

he snarls in my ear, his face so close to mine that I can smell his putrid breath. Despite the pain resonating from my shoulder, the moment I hear the hum of his activated neuro-stunner, I throw everything I have into conjuring the largest, sharpest weapon possible from between my shoulder blades.

I feel it form instantly and expand it with a thought. I waste no time launching the blade with all of my mental might through the guard's riot armor, straight through his chest and out the other side. It all happens so fast that Junior's not even aware of his partner's demise until the moment I dismiss the force-field blade and the body drops to the floor behind me.

"What the hell—" Junior starts to say, and that's when the major general twists into him and punches him viciously in the guts.

I power up into my full armor and join in the attack. There is no going back for me now. I have already killed one baseline today; two won't make my sentencing any less severe.

Rushing in, I manage to land a gauntleted uppercut with my good arm; it rips the helmet off Junior's head and sends him reeling backwards and straight through the catwalk's flimsy chain railing. I watch impassively as the man falls. He hits the cement floor with a sickening wet *crack*. Moments later, blood begins to pool beneath his head.

"I'm as good as dead now, aren't I?" I hear myself say as I power down. I'm unable to rip my gaze from the sight below me.

"Aren't we all?" the major general replies. He clasps me on the shoulder and gently guides me away from the edge.

Before I know it, we're both walking toward the back gate. My thoughts jumble as I struggle to understand what I have just done. I was never trained to kill, only protect and defend. How has all that incessant instruction come to this?

I am now a killer. Some might even say…a murderer.

"May I have the key, son?" the major general asks me.

I blink several times before the question registers. "Oh, yeah—yes, sir." Unstrapping my left gauntlet, I push up my sleeve. I retrieve the key from a small forearm pocket in my battle suit. It's a flat plastic card with the interface sequence prongs evident on the back. I hand it to the major general.

Without a word, he takes it from me and inserts it into a control panel in the wall. A moment later, the old cargo bay doors slowly slide open. Arctic air blasts through the opening, and the chill rouses me from my troubled thoughts. I glance over at the major general and find that he is studying me. "You okay?" he asks.

I nod. "Yes, sir." There's no need to mention the dull ache in my shoulder, nor my arm's limited movement. That's pain I've trained my entire life to manage. It's the deep ache I feel inside my chest that I'm less confident about, but I'm the one with blood on my hands. It's up to me to deal with the repercussions, not the major general.

He points toward the open doorway. "Your helmet is equipped with a headlamp. Activate it once you're outside. You're going to jog due south for half a mile until you come to a pond. There'll be a boat waiting for you there. The captain's name is Josiah Johnson. He'll have a warm coat for you and necessities for your journey."

"B-but, sir," I interrupt. "Aren't you coming?"

My heart sinks when I see him shake his head. "I can't, son. I have to go back for the others."

"You mean you're going back to free the rest of my squad?"

"Soon, but not yet. You'll be the only one who escapes tonight." He holds my gaze, and it is then that I see the truth of his intentions.

"You're not leaving, are you?"

"Not by this exit. I have work yet to do." He glances around the storage bay, and then points to something behind my left shoulder. "Look up there."

My eyes travel to where he is pointing, and I understand immediately what he has planned when I see the string of plastic explosives barely visible along a ceiling support beam. "Oh, sir…you're going to blow up the Imperium."

"For the last year, I've been planting explosives around the stadium. One hour after you head out that door, the whole place goes up in flames."

I want to argue with him, to beg him to come with me, but I can't find the words…mostly because I realize that this is the only way to ensure that those dissection rooms are never used.

"You remember the name of your contact in Vancouver?" he asks.

I nod in reply, because I fear that my voice will fail me if I try to speak. And right now, I don't want to appear weak before the major general.

"Good," he says with a confident smile. "Now, get out of here. Go find that pretty little gal of yours."

"Yes, sir," I manage to say. "I will, sir."

"John."

"What?"

"My name. It's John. John Allen." He extends his hand to me. I hesitate a moment before I take his hand, because I'm so used to saluting him. As we shake hands, he says, "Good luck out there, son."

"Thank you, si—John."

Releasing his hand, I walk to the door. But before I go, I turn back to the man who has risked everything to free me. A man I have killed for. A man I would have gladly died defending.

"I promise I'll find her," I say. "After everything…I will find her."

He gives me a reassuring smile. “I know.”

I give my liberator one last nod, and then I race into the arctic night. The headlamp in my helmet clicks on, and my training takes over. My body finds its rhythm as I run across the snow-covered ground.

These are my first steps as a free man.

Emily, I’m coming for you.

Chapter Ten

In a dizzying, vomit-inducing whirlwind of motion, Devon McWilliams was suddenly himself once more. As he blinked his eyes and felt the grass that wasn't truly grass beneath his derriere, the extreme letdown of no longer inhabiting the memories of a noble, ass-kicking, modern-day paladin-in-training came crashing over him in waves. It left him feeling deflated and…ordinary. Much like leaping off a skyscraper and, mid-jump, realizing that he was no longer Superman.

Damn, that was a long, hard way to fall!

The only good thing about coming back to his own lame senses was the lovely Alya snuggled against him, her head resting on his chest. He could feel her every breath through his sweater. His arms were still wrapped around her, but he didn't dare move. Sitting here with Alya made Bai Lee's mental paradise complete. He had no intention of messing this up—not right away, anyway. In the back of his mind, however, he knew that he would have to tell the truth about himself when his turn came.

Until then, he would simply enjoy his time holding Alya.

"Oh, man, Vahn. That was, like…awesome!" Nevada cried. She sat beside Devon, shaking her head in disbelief. "You are so kick-ass! And I just want to say that you look a hell of a lot hotter as a blond. Black is *sooo* not your color."

"Somehow, my dear, I think you missed the point," said Alek in that condescending tone of his. "Major General Allen made it quite clear that the government is making preparations to eradicate us from the face of the planet. Doesn't that alarm you just a little bit?"

"As opposed to what?" Nevada asked with a scowl. "Drugging us out of our minds? Messing with our DNA? Turning some of us into psionic vampires so we'll cannibalize our own kind?" She looked pointedly at Alek. "What fairy tale have you been living in? Life *already* sucks for us."

"Wow…the American princess speaks," Alek said mockingly. "I guess being killed in a death match on live TV as entertainment for the baseline masses is something you'd be partial to?"

Nevada's glare turned ice-cold as she met Alek's heated gaze. "It's better than slowly being poisoned to death as some lab experiment."

The tension was once again rocketing toward the stratosphere. Before he fully realized what he was doing, words were tumbling from Devon's mouth. "You know, I remember reading something online about an explosion in Alaska this past January, but I don't think I heard that it was a stadium." Devon looked over at Vahn, who was slowly getting over the effects of Bai Lee's memory replay. "Do you know anything about that, Vahn?"

As Vahn struggled to get his bearings, Devon was pleased to see that Nevada was no longer looking in Alek's direction. The tension had subsided. All eyes were turned to the wooden lounge, awaiting the official word from the noble psi-blade himself.

"The press referred to it as a chemical plant explosion," Vahn said groggily. "Then they buried it."

"Did Major General Allen get out of there in time?" Alya asked, and Devon was thrilled to hear her voice. He wanted to squeeze her—*something!*—to show her how much he cared, but he didn't want to appear like he was coming on too strong, so he held back.

Vahn lay silently before them, gazing upwards. He looked reluctant to answer Alya's question. Then again, perhaps he had not heard her.

"Vahn?" Alya asked.

"I don't know, Alya," he said softly. "No one could tell me anything for sure about the major general. Not even my Network contacts."

"How about what Alek just said… Is that true?" Miguel asked. "Does the American government really have plans to kill us?"

Vahn struggled to sit up, and the tree's branches tenderly unfurled from around his body. "Unfortunately, yes, Miguel. My contacts in Vancouver pretty much confirmed everything. It's like the major general said. Smaller numbers are easier to control."

Miguel nervously ran his fingers through his hair. "When my family told the Guatemalan general that I was dead, he had his army destroy my village. When they still wouldn't tell him my whereabouts, he murdered my mother in cold blood." He shook his head as if trying to clear the memory from his mind. "I thought I was leaving all that behind when I came here."

Gripping an overhead tree branch, Vahn managed to sit up and plant his feet firmly on the ground. "Well, I don't know what to tell you, Miguel," he said wearily. "The grass just isn't any greener on this side of the Rio Grande."

"But what about life, liberty, and pursuit of happiness?" Miguel asked in earnest. "Your Constitution protects you, does it not?"

"Not." Nevada chimed in. "Because ten years ago, *my father* pushed through an emergency law that deemed all psions a domestic threat. Like all baselines, he believes that we have to remain locked away in order to assure life, liberty, and pursuit of happiness for the ordinary citizens of the United States of America." Nevada dramatically rolled her eyes. "My old man is such an ass."

"Oh, but he's a powerful ass," Alek smirked. "Senator Wingate is running for President. Isn't that right, Alison?"

"Up yours, Alek," Nevada sneered. "You have no idea what hell that man has put me through."

"Then why don't you enlighten us?" Alek's grin reminded Devon of a hungry jackal. "Bai Lee's couch is now vacant."

Nevada glared outright at him but didn't say anything more. She hesitated a moment before slowly getting to her knees and then turned to Miguel. "I'm really sorry about your mother," she said, and Devon could hear the sincerity in her voice.

"Thank you," Miguel whispered. He flashed her a shy, grateful smile.

Rising to her feet, Nevada looked over at Bai Lee. "I guess I might as well be your next victim." She pointed at Vahn, a playful smile on her lips. "Though I have to say, good-lookin', you're going to be one tough act to follow."

"Oh, I don't know about that," Vahn replied, as he rose from the wooden lounge. "I'm sure your story is going to be just as harrowing."

"Yeah, right," Nevada flashed him a salacious grin. "You're just saying that because you can't wait to inhabit this body." She laughed when she saw Vahn blush. "Wow! For a guy who bashes heads in for a living, you sure are a prude."

"He's not a prude," Bai Lee corrected. "He's a gentleman. Now quit messing with him. You're starting to piss me off."

Nevada rolled her eyes. "Says the woman wearing the yellow pajamas."

Devon wanted to chuckle at Nevada's joke, but he didn't dare when Bai Lee's piercing gaze swept over him. No sense getting into the middle of a catfight when he had a lovely lady of his own to take care of.

"So, where do you want me?" Nevada asked Bai Lee as she stood beside the wooden lounge.

"Lie down on your back, please. It's a position I'm sure you're all too familiar with."

"Oh, I know lots of positions, girlfriend. You want me to demonstrate?"

Bai Lee shook her head in disgust. "That won't be necessary. As it is, I'm probably going to have to cleanse my aura after linking with your filthy mind."

Nevada threw her head back and barked out a fake laugh. "Hey—good one! I bet that one took all day to cook up! But seriously, if you'd prefer not to touch my 'filthy mind,' I'd be more than happy to sit back down."

Bai Lee looked angry enough to rip Nevada's face off. "Lay the hell down or I'm leaving you behind."

"Oh, yeah?"

"Yeah."

Nevada lunged at Bai Lee, and Vahn caught her around the waist just in time to prevent the windwalker's right fist from connecting with the telepath's chin. "Hey, hey! Calm down, Nevada!" Vahn said, turning her to face him. "I'm sure this is just a misunderstanding."

"I assure you, Vahn," Nevada growled through clenched teeth, "this is no misunderstanding!"

Devon felt Alya shift her weight as she struggled to sit up. Instinctively, he held her tighter to his chest and gently used his weight to push against her back to help her sit upright. "Thank you," she whispered to Devon, her warm breath caressing his cheek. Devon's heart fluttered with excitement when Alya held tight to his arm and would not let go as she turned to the two girls before her.

"Bai Lee. Nevada. Please stop this," said Alya. "We don't have time for such behavior."

"Alya's right," Devon said, chiming in. "We made a deal, and we *all* need to stick to it. Nevada, you know better than anyone here what those baselines in Washington are going to do to us once we land."

Nevada stopped struggling in Vahn's arms and turned to Devon. "But even if we escape—even if we do find a safe place to hide for a little while—they're still going to keep coming after us. They're not going to stop until they kill us all." She slumped against Vahn, and he had to hold on to her tightly to keep her upright against him. "My life's just been one big mistake after another," she said wearily. "I'm no shining knight like Vahn. Maybe I don't deserve to live."

"No, Nevada! You mustn't think like that!" Miguel cried. The fourteen-year-old was standing up, his eyes locked on the woman before him. "Major General Allen said he thought that we are all here by the grace of God. You have no idea how I have longed to hear someone other than Father Gálvez say that." A hopeful smile played across Miguel's lips as he walked toward Nevada. "Ever since I was very little, I only thought of myself as a mistake, a freak of nature…a slip of science. You have no idea how my heart soared to hear Vahn's noble general friend imply that our kind is as much a part of God's plan as the earth and sky."

Standing before Nevada, Miguel took her hand. Vahn released her and stepped back as Nevada turned her gaze to Miguel. The kid from Guatemala had her full attention. "Through Vahn's story, I now realize that we have always been a part of God's kingdom—not man's. Please, Nevada," Miguel pleaded. "Do not give up now. Show us your story."

"I'm not deserving," she said, clinging to Miguel's hand. "You'll hate me after you've seen what I've done."

"I seriously doubt that. Not one of us gathered here today is without sin. We are all flawed, but that is the beautiful challenge of life, is it not?"

"Well, yeah…maybe." Nevada gave him a hint of a smile.

"There is no one on this earth like you, Nevada. We are all special and deserving in God's eyes." As Miguel spoke, Devon was reminded of a minister he'd once met. The Guatemalan's eyes shone bright with a pure and holy light that radiated from his very soul. "You must remember that life is one continuous work in progress, and mistakes are a big part of how we learn to be better people." Miguel brushed aside a tear on Nevada's cheek. "We can all work on being better people, especially toward one another."

Nevada nodded. "Yeah…" She bit her lip then and looked over at him bashfully. "So, like, when did you become a padre, Miguel? You sound just like my family's priest."

Miguel chuckled. "The priesthood has always been my dream. It's just that, well, my condition makes me an outlaw first and foremost."

"Yeah, I know what you mean."

"So, Nevada," said Vahn, "what *is* your story?"

Nevada shrugged, and Devon noted that she was still holding Miguel's hand. "It's not all that interesting, really."

Vahn grunted. "I'm sure *that's* not true."

It was Nevada's turn to blush. "Well, I *was* married and widowed all in the same day, so I guess that's *somewhat* interesting."

"Yes. It definitely is." Miguel nodded to Vahn, and together they led Nevada over to the wooden lounge and helped her sit down.

"And you loved him, this young man you married?" Miguel asked.

Nevada smiled wistfully. "His name was Jake Kohler. And yes, I did love him. He was my third husband, and the best one by far. I mean, he never hit me, or yelled at me, or threatened to kill me, so that made him a real gem. Plus, he usually listened to whatever I had to say and did most everything I asked—even stood up for me on occasion.

"Looking back, I think he'd been trying all along to save me from myself." Nevada looked sadly over at Miguel. "I just wished I could've saved him from my family."

Nevada slumped dejectedly between Vahn and Miguel on the edge of the wooden lounge, and Devon thought she might actually cry. Instead, she rested her head on Vahn's shoulder and looked miserable. "You know," she said softly,

"I've been called a liar, a thief, and a murderer. But I want you all to know that I am not a murderer. I loved every one of the men I married, even the walking disaster that was husband number one. Sure, I used them for the attention I got from the media, but I'm not the one who killed them. Hell, I didn't even know my first two husbands were dead until a week ago. I just thought they had run off. So, like, what the hell did I know?" Nevada lowered her eyes. "Not much, it turns out."

"Oh, Nevada," said Alya. "I'm so sorry."

"Thanks, Alya, I appreciate that. I thought I had it all under control. You know, messed-up little rich girl wants Daddy's attention and all that jazz. But what I never realized was that my antics—my numerous escapes from the psi facilities—only played into my parents' perverse agenda."

She turned to Alek. "It was just what you said back in the cargo hold earlier—I made a mockery of our kind. I allowed the public to see how wild and dangerous we could be. I became the bogeyman that would steal baseline babies in the night and force them to marry me by morning. I guess you could say that I became the poster child for psionic detainment and control. Only, my overblown ego wouldn't let me see that I never had control in the first place…not until it was too late for Jake."

She looked up at Vahn and Miguel. "I think I'm ready."

Miguel held her hand and Vahn helped slide her feet into position as she laid down on the wooden lounge. As soon as Nevada's head hit the leafy pillow, Devon saw the tree writhe and grow around her to comfortably fit the contours of her body.

"I'll be right here when you come back to us," said Miguel, smiling down at her.

Nevada nodded, then addressed Bai Lee, who stood patiently waiting. "For whatever it's worth, I'm sorry about taking a swing at you."

"For whatever it's worth," echoed Bai Lee, her expression unreadable. "The next time you take a swing at me, I'll break your freaking arm."

"Right," Nevada replied. "Point taken. Now, are we going to do this or what?"

Bai Lee sat down on the edge of the wooden lounge. "Whenever you're ready. You know what to do."

Nevada laughed. "Well, then, buckle your seatbelts, boys and girls," she said, flashing everyone a devious grin. "We're going for one hell of a ride!"

Before Devon could protest, she closed her eyes, and the world around him instantly caved in. He tried to squeeze Alya's hand to let her know that he was with her, but reality had already collapsed into a whirlpool of thought and he was helpless to resist.

Nevada's Story

Chapter Eleven

MARITAL bliss is amazing.

Married eight hours and I'm still orbiting Saturn. And that's saying a lot, seeing as I have an incredibly short attention span. You know, I think I just might have gotten it right this time. Jake's been my best husband by far. Besides being totally hot, he's a true gentleman. Not only does he adore me, but he has terrific hygiene and he doesn't try to have sex with me while I'm asleep.

That's a huge plus in my book.

But the best thing about Jake Kohler, besides being an awesome kisser, is that he *gets* me. He doesn't mind me taking the lead, but he hasn't allowed me to walk all over him, either. In other words, he's a laid-back kind of guy with just enough edge to keep him interesting.

This time, I think I found a keeper.

I just wish I could lie here all night in his arms rather than roust my lazy bones out of bed and over to the hotel room vanity. But I can't. Tonight, there's work to be done. Mainly because we can't afford the room we've just booked at this tiny off-Strip hotel. But lucky us, there just happens to be a slam-banging casino just across the parking lot.

Oh, yeah!

I sit down at the vanity to put in my sclera contact lenses and pause when I catch sight of my big bald head. *Damn*, Jake does amazing work! With his psi-power pulsing through the tattoo he gave me, I look like something out of a sci-fi movie. The tat glows a soothing neon blue throughout a maze of Celtic-inspired designs that delicately curl around my shiny dome. The blue matches my starburst eyes, which gives me an otherworldly flair without crossing into freaky-monster-alien territory.

Too bad I can't walk down Las Vegas Boulevard like this tonight. My tat would rival any of the neon along the Strip, but that kind of thing would only get me arrested. The sight of a psionic tat scares the hell out of any rational baseline, and with good reason—they're deadly.

But not just "it kills you" deadly—more like crazy-zombie-nightmare-inducing, lose-your-mind-as-you-burn-out-at-the-whims-of-a-puppet-master deadly.

Oh, yeah…it's *that* bad. But only for the baselines. We psions are immune to the zombie mind burnout. We merely bask in the pretty glow.

Studying myself in the mirror, I decide that I'm going to be really bummin' when my tat starts to fade in a couple of weeks, because I totally rock this look.

"What're you doing over there, Mrs. Kohler?" Jake asks from the bed.

I grin a little at the thought of being *Mrs. Kohler*. "Getting ready to go out," I say as I unscrew the lids of my contact case.

"Out? I thought we'd stay *in* tonight." He lifts his head up and I can see his handsome face framed by a halo of messy brown hair in my mirror. "You know, being newlyweds and all."

"Yeah, well, someone's gotta bring home the bacon." I open my right eye wide with my left hand and gently place the sclera contact lens over my cornea until it drapes softly across my eyeball. From the first blink, it feels comfortable; however, the vision in my right eye is drastically dimmed due to the dark color of the lens's iris. It's the price we psions have to pay in order to mask the intense color of our eyes. "I gotta rake in a couple grand tonight at the roulette tables to pay for our room."

As I set the left contact lens on my finger, I catch Jake looking deflated in the bed behind me. "So, no more boom-boom?" he asks dejectedly.

I glance at him through the mirror. "No more boom-boom, baby…for now."

He gives me that wounded-puppy look and juts out his bottom lip, and suddenly I feel a little guilty. *Damn, he looks delicious when he does that!*

I slide the second lens onto my left eye, blink it into place, and turn to face him. "Now, dahling, you know we're a far cry from champagne wishes and caviar dreams. Our Network contact can't meet with us until next week, so we've got to lie low and play it cool. And while you might think sleeping beneath the stars is romantic and all, the desert's freezing this time of year."

"Can't your mom, like, wire you some money or something?"

At the mention of my mother, my anger explodes inside me like a solar flare, and I shoot him my most evil look. Jake *knows* better than to bring up my family. "Hell to the no, loverboy! And I better not hear you mention her again!"

Jake holds up his hands in surrender. "Whoa, whoa—hey, I just thought she was the nice one, ya know?"

"Well, she's not!" But the fact he even asked the question fires up the primal rage that boils inside me. "Why'd you even mention her in the first place?"

Jake shrugs. "I dunno. Your parents are just so rich, so untouchable… I've seen those gourmet care packages they send you. Heck, you were the only one in the entire West Coast Psi Facility to have a private room! Professionally decorated—with cable, no less!"

I cross my arms, defiant. "Yeah, *so*?"

"*So*?" Jake rises to his knees on the bed. Married only eight hours, and he's already getting frustrated with me. "Well, why *wouldn't* I think that they'd wire you some money on the outside?"

"Because I *escaped*, Jake. *We* escaped. My parents only like me when I'm safely contained in a secure psi facility.

They'd send me all the Starbucks coffee and Godiva chocolate in the world if it would keep me caged up forever." I sit down on the edge of the bed in a huff. "Geezus, Jake! Why do I even waste my breath trying to explain this stuff?" I stare up at the ceiling; I'm too upset to look at him right now.

There are several long moments of icy silence between us, and then I hear the bedsprings grind as Jake shifts his weight. "Look," he says gently, "I've got a mom too, you know. You remember, I told you about her. Her name's Betsy. She fought hard to keep me for as long as she could. But because of what I am—what my power does—the Supreme Court of California ordered her to give me up when I was eight." He lays his hand lightly on my shoulder. Just to show him that I mean business, I shrug it off.

"Well, that's nice and all, Jake, but what does *Betsy* have to do with our current situation?"

"Actually, I was hoping we could visit her."

I whirl on him. "What?!" I'm practically screaming in his face.

"I just thought—"

"You thought?" I scoff with indignation. "I didn't marry you to *think*, Jake! And I definitely don't want you contacting anyone outside of this hotel room until *after* we hook up with the Psionic Underground next week!"

"But she's my mother—"

"I don't care if she's the first female Pope! You cannot contact her!"

Jake's eyes harden as he scowls back at me. "You don't have to shout, Ali. My ears work just fine."

"Then use them, you idiot!" I shout, anger swirling through my veins like a thousand tiny tornadoes. I want to lash out at him, tell him how stupid he's being—but then I see his wounded expression, and I know I've gone too far.

"Fine," he says quietly. "If that's how you feel... I'm out of here." He scoots to the edge of the bed and makes a mad dash for the bathroom.

That's when I draw the air molecules around me together into one incredible burst of air and hurl it at him. The gale blasts him backwards onto the bed.

"Ali!" he shouts at me. "Stop it!"

I redirect the air into a screaming squall that forces him flat against the bed. The wind howls and the bedsheets rip. With a thought, I could shred the flesh from his bones, but that is not my intent here. What I want is for my husband to just shut up and listen to me. Is that too much to ask?

"Ali! Come on! You're hurting me!"

Like a slap in the face, Jake's plea snaps me out of my rage-fueled attack. The intense need to inflict pain on the guy I adore vanishes instantly. Dispersing the wind with a thought, I scramble across the bed to him. "Jake! Oh, Jake! I'm so sorry!"

He looks at me warily, like he has no idea who I am, and it simply breaks my heart. I'm such a mess that even *I* can't stand myself most of the time. "Forgive me, Jake, please," I plead as I lean over him, checking him for any injury that I may have inflicted.

He sits up and scoots away from me. "I'm fine, Ali," he says guardedly. "You don't have to go psycho on me every time we get into an argument." He raises his eyes to meet mine. "I'm not the enemy, you know."

"I know," I say quietly.

"I love you," he says.

I hesitate, gulping on air as I realize what he has just said to me. "Love you, too," I manage to reply, but with my bad left ear, I can barely hear my own confession. And a very dark part of me wonders if there's even a shred of truth to what I have just said. Nevertheless, my words bring a beautiful smile to Jake's face.

He reaches out to me and caresses my cheek. "You know, you never have to say that back."

"I know." His gentle touch melts my resolve, and I hold onto that warm feeling, memorizing its effect on my cold, black heart. Thankfully, I like it. I like him, oh, so much.

Jake's a good guy.

Way too good for me on more levels than I can count, because I'm probably going to put him through complete hell before I tear out his heart and stomp on it in a heavy-duty pair of combat boots.

I can be that much of a psycho bitch.

And I hate myself for it.

"Jake," I say softly. "I'm so tired. I don't want to play their games anymore."

"What are you talking about?" he asks, the concern returning to his eyes. "What games?"

"My parents' games." I scoot closer to him and look him directly in the eyes. I have to make sure that he really hears what I have to say this time. "They *use* me. And the more I try to fight them, the easier it is for them to gain support for their political agendas." I reach over and place my hand on his knee. "I'm escaping for real this time, Jake. There's no way I'm ever going back. I'm through with the facility. I'm through with them. The Network is going to provide you and me with new identities and a safe place to hide for a long, long time."

Jake's look of concern morphs into one of genuine confusion. "How long is long?"

I shake my head. "I don't know… The only way for me to truly escape is to leave Alison Wingate behind. I can't be that spoiled rotten child anymore, Jake. My antics have only made things worse." I pause for a moment, the seriousness of my own words catching me off-guard. I have to take a deep breath before I'm able to continue.

"I have a lot to make amends for."

Jake leans forward and gives me his sweetest smile. "I'm with you, Ali. You know I'd follow you anywhere."

"But what about your mom—Betsy?" I ask, testing the waters.

He shrugs, his smile withering. "I've waited ten years to see her. What's a few more?"

"But she's your mom."

He chuckles airily as he wraps his arms around me in a heartfelt embrace. "Oh, Ali, where's your confidence?" He pulls back and smiles down at me. "I sure wish you could love yourself as much as I love you."

His words sting, but the horrible anger inside me remains dormant. So what if Jake sees through me down to the frightened, pissed-off little girl that I am? That's probably why he tolerates so much of my bullshit.

But I can only offer him a tiny smile in response. It's definitely time for me to change the subject and focus on more pressing matters. "Jake, we really do need to get out of here."

"Sounds like a plan," he says, and plants a quick kiss on my forehead before scooting off the bed. "I'm going to throw on that suit you made me pack and pop in my lenses while you slip into something more…exotic."

"*Grown-up*, you mean," I say with a laugh. "We have to look well over twenty-one out there on the casino floor. Our fake IDs can only do so much."

Jake chuckles as he walks into the bathroom. "I'll do my best, *dear*." He winks at me before vanishing around the corner.

Damn, he's hot! In a perfect world, I wouldn't have to surround myself with so much drama. But I don't live in that kind of world. I was serious when I told Jake about not going back to the facility. I'm done. I have planned my escape down to the last detail. My mother and father are overseas in France, representing the United States at a global energy summit. That was the only way I could feel safe enough to get this nasty little off-Strip hotel room and not be constantly freaking out that my 'rents would find me in, like, ten seconds.

Walking to the closet, I take out the little black cocktail dress that hangs inside. I'm usually not this conservative, but right now, this isn't just about me. Everything I do from here on out concerns Jake, too. And he's just too good a guy to let down.

I step out of my silk nightie and into the dress. Thank God I have great legs, because I absolutely hate putting on pantyhose. I slip on a pair of black heels and head to the vanity. My own reflection startles me, because I'm so used to seeing my starburst eyes, not the deep brown ones with clear white scleras gazing back at me…but it's my glowing bald head that's going to cause us problems if I don't cover it up.

Unzipping my backpack, I find my black wig and put it on. It's a simple wig—shoulder-length, stick-straight hair with long, blunt bangs. I set it in position on my head and quickly brush through it. When I check out my new look in the mirror, I'm surprised to find a complete stranger staring back at me.

It's definitely a baseline face. My gold and sapphire piercings peek through the bangs of the wig at the edges of my eyebrows, but they have lost their luster without the intensity of my starburst eyes. I sure wouldn't stand out in a crowd with a face like this. In fact, I look downright… *ordinary*.

That's when I begin laying on the makeup. Foundation, liquid eyeliner, fake lashes, eye shadow, blush, and ruby-red lips—outlined and colored in to perfection. When next I examine my reflection, I'm no less ordinary, but I sure look a heck of a lot older…and completely baseline. Alison Wingate is gone.

Good riddance.

"I know you married me because you're such a good Catholic girl—no sex before marriage, that kind of thing," Jake says stepping out of the bathroom. "But what do you think? Could you see us together in, oh, ten, maybe twenty years?"

Jake's wearing a black suit and tie that hang perfectly on his six-foot frame. His deep brown eyes bring a warmth to his face that enhances his ruggedly sculpted features. While I may look like a plain Jane, he looks like an A-list movie star complete with tousled hair and devil-may-care smile.

"So? What do you think?"

"I think I'm a damn lucky girl."

Jake beams at me. "You look ravishing, Mrs. Kohler."

I laugh. "You don't look so bad yourself, Mr. Kohler."

He takes my hand and pulls me up to his lips. Such soft, tender lips. I wish we could snuggle all night in bed and explore each other's bodies, but I can't rest easy until I have several grand in hand—just in case my plans head south in a hurry.

Staring up into his eyes, I'm happy to see that my husband can definitely pass for a twenty-something baseline. And a super sexy one at that. "You remember what I told you about the roulette table?"

Jake nods. "Yeah. After the dealer hands me the chips, you want me to bet the minimum and lose. I'm supposed to look upset—"

"But not too upset."

"Right. And then I'm to place a hundred-dollar marker on any number I like, and you'll do all the rest. How'd I do?"

"Perfect. Just don't play it up too much. Once you win, we leave. We're not there to break the bank."

"And then can we get something to eat? Because I'm starving."

"Sounds like a plan," I say with a laugh as I take his arm. I grab my purse, and together we head to the door.

How a woman walks in high heels is usually a dead giveaway as to how old she is. I learned that the hard way when I was married to husband number two nine months ago. Jonathan Darling was the West Coast Facility's anger management counselor. He was a baseline, of course, and a graduate student at Berkeley, in his early twenties. I found him to be completely adorable, if not just a bit nerdy in his obsession with video games. However, it was my complete lack of confidence in heels that led to our discovery at a chic Los Angeles restaurant, when a waitress noticed that I was teetering in my Christian Louboutins more than I was actually walking in them. She asked to see our IDs and then quietly notified the police as we sat sipping champagne in the elegant dining room.

Of course, both of my previous marriages had been tabloid fodder. At first, I had basked in the media attention, proud of the ruckus I had stirred. But all that changed when I learned that my out-of-control antics had allowed my father to pass anti-psion legislation through the Senate that much faster. I'd had to wise up fast, make a serious plan, and practice walking in heels.

And then, of course, I met Jake. At first sight, I just knew that he would make a perfect husband number three. With a little training, of course.

I wrap my arms around my husband as we walk across the parking lot to the casino entrance. Two sets of baseline couples walk along with us, and thankfully, no one pays us any attention. My heart skips a beat out of nervousness when the casino doors open and we step into the smoke-tinged room amidst the cacophony of ringing slot machines, music, and raised voices.

It only takes an instant for the slot machines' high-pitched ring to cause my bad ear to ache, but I resist covering it with my hand. I don't want to draw the slightest attention to myself out here in the open. I know that cameras are positioned everywhere in this massive casino, with its safari-themed wall art rimmed in gold. This particular casino is beginning to show its age, but it's still lavish, even though it teeters on the cusp of gaudy, like most everything in Las Vegas.

I am taken aback by the sheer number of baselines flittering about the casino floor. As I walk with Jake by my side, my inner ear throbbing, I'm suddenly feeling vulnerable and very much out of my element.

"Are you okay?" Jake asks me in my good ear.

"Yeah," I say, though it's a flat-out lie. My heart drums in my chest. I am on the verge of panic. I hadn't counted on an earache—and this one's sending stabbing pain rocketing through my head. How the hell am I supposed to focus?

I stumble on the carpeting, but Jake reaches out and stops me from falling on my face. "Hey, what's going on?"

"I'm fine. It's nothing," I say, when in fact I'm falling to pieces and I know it…but there's no backing out now. It's only a matter of pushing a silly little ball around a stupid spinning wheel—it should be a piece of cake.

Reaching into my purse, I take out two crisp hundred-dollar bills—the last of our stash—and press them into Jake's palm. "Here. You know what to do."

Jake pockets the money and nods. "Let's go."

Spying the roulette table across the room, I take Jake by the hand and zigzag through the casino as fast as I can manage in my three-inch heels. Mercifully, Jake doesn't say a word. I have to get this over with as quickly as possible; otherwise, I might just blow it. I hadn't anticipated the terrible earache, and the longer I'm here the worse it's going to get. Stupid ear! Courtesy of husband number one, the psi-cannon who preferred to settle arguments with his fists.

I slow up as soon as I get within twenty paces of the roulette table, and take a deep breath. I can do this, of that there is no doubt—but how long will I be able to focus with this painful throbbing in my head?

"Jake," I say, leaning close to him. "Forget losing the first round—we just gotta go in there and do it."

"But—"

I squeeze his hand tightly; he has to know how badly I hurt. "It's my ear—it's killing me." Stepping close to him, I gaze directly into his eyes. "One spin. Straight-up bet. All or nothing."

"Right," he says, sincerely. "Whatever you need me to do… Let's just do this and get the hell out of here."

I try to smile, but it comes out more like a wince. There's no silencing the high-pitched ringing in this cavernous room without causing a hurricane, and I've got to keep the drama to a minimum here.

Hand in hand, we walk over to the roulette table, where three couples hover over the betting area. As soon as we approach, the dealer glances over at us.

"Place your bets," the dealer says, nodding to Jake.

Jake flashes him an easygoing smile and places our last two hundred dollars on the cloth-covered betting area. It only takes a few seconds for the man behind the table to count out a set of sky-blue chips and sweep them in front of my husband.

"Place your bets," the dealer calls out to the table, the roulette wheel whirling madly to his left.

Jake gives me one last furtive glance before staring down at the numbers on the betting area. I draw in a deep breath and slowly release it while he studies the numbers on the layout. The ache in my head feels as if someone is stabbing me with a sharp blade. I rely on years of mental discipline to work through the pain as I wait for Jake to make his choice. I just hope I'm able to focus well enough to control the roulette ball.

He places all of his chips on the black number eight, and I inwardly smile. Eight has always been Jake's lucky number. It's even today's date…the date we got married. I just hope that lucky number eight continues to hold out for us tonight.

Jake wraps his arm around my waist and stands close to me as I turn my attention to the spinning roulette wheel. In anticipation of the dealer's call, I reach out to the air molecules around me, to see what I have to work with—*damn it!* A sharp, stabbing pain rips straight through my eardrum and into my gray matter. My knees buckle, but Jake somehow manages to steady me.

"Ali—we should wait."

I glare back at him. "No," I reply through clenched teeth. "I can do this."

But by Jake's expression, I can tell he's doubtful.

And that's when my anger shoots through my veins like a firestorm. Damn it all! I'm going for broke!

"No more bets," the dealer announces, and I'm riveted to that tiny plastic ball.

The dealer releases the trigger and the ball begins to spin counterclockwise to the wheel as it makes its descent. I reach out with my mind and become one with the spinning currents of air that the ball pushes through on its way to the wheel. In an instant, I *am* that air… I can see the board clearly, and it's as if I am holding that little round object in the palm of my hand.

The ball hits the roulette wheel with a jarring bounce that sends it banging from one slot to the next. My job is to keep it bouncing until I am sure to place it exactly in pocket number eight. The first two bounces happen in rapid-fire succession, but it's nowhere near where I need it to land. As the ball hits pocket number seventeen, I hold it above the spinning wheel just a fraction of a second longer, which takes it off-course from its original destination. It's hard work, what I'm doing, but every rapid-fire bounce and suspension goes unnoticed to the naked eye. And it's a good thing, too, or I'd be busted in a second.

Finally, the ball falls smack dab into the number eight pocket, and I instantly raise the air pressure above the ball to keep it firmly planted there. Success! Oh my God, I did it!

I bite my lip to keep from screaming out in excitement, because the roulette wheel is still spinning too fast for anyone else to read… and that's when the pain stabs through my inner ear again with a searing intensity, and I stumble into Jake.

But I'll be damned if I'm going to allow that stupid roulette ball to move from its spot!

"Hey, you okay?" Jake asks as he holds me close to him.

I wince in reply, but my heart soars the minute I hear the dealer announce, "Black number eight! Winner!"

Jake blanches and gapes down at me. "We won! Oh, my God, we won!"

"Yes, sir," confirms the dealer as he places a doll-shaped score marker on the table layout and begins the process of sweeping away the losing chips and paying out the winners.

Jake gives me a tight squeeze and kisses the top of my head. "Oh, my God—we won! We really won!"

"You say that like you somehow doubted me," I mumble in jest, but I'm not sure that it quite came out the way I wanted it to, because of the strange look that Jake gives me.

"Aw, come on, Ali, I never doubted you." He flashes me that beautiful smile. "I was scared to death that *I* was going to be the one to mess this up."

I roll my eyes. "Let's just cash out and get the hell out of here, huh?"

"You got it," he says as he gently releases me. He makes sure that I'm not going to topple over again before he picks up our stacked winnings off of the betting area.

Before Jake goes, he sets a chip in front of the dealer. "That's for you."

"Thank you, sir," the dealer says, acknowledging the generous tip, before turning his attention back to the next lineup of bets. "Place your bets, ladies and gentlemen. Place your bets!"

Jake and I spare no time cashing out our chips. We've raked in almost seven thousand dollars, and I couldn't be more relieved. My ear still hurts like hell, but at least now we can lie low in comfort for the next week and not have to worry about how we're going to pay for everything.

As we make our way to the exit, Jake studies the giant roll of cash in his hand. "Uh, Ali, I don't know if I want to go out to eat with this much cash in my pocket."

I blow through the exit doors, and the painful ringing in my head finally stops. I massage my ear, mindful of the wig I'm wearing, and glance over at my husband. "You want to go back to the room first?"

He nods. "A place like Vegas attracts a lot of pickpockets."

"And other thieves," I add, stepping up to him. "Why don't you give me some of that?"

He grins at me like a fool as he unrolls his wad of cash and hands me half the stack. "What happened to you in there? You think they had some kind of anti-psion device inside?"

I shake my head as I stuff my half of our winnings inside my bra—shoot, I'm flat as a board; might as well use my bra to hold *something*. "I wish I could tell you some exotic tech-head device did that to me in there, but it didn't. I have a little metal pin close to my eardrum that helps me hear low-frequency sounds—voices, mostly. I think the ringing from the slot machines was simply at the wrong frequency for me to handle."

Jake gives me one of those serious looks. "It was your first husband who caused you to lose your hearing, wasn't it?"

I nod, but I don't say anything. I'm still too embarrassed to talk much about it. How could I have been so stupid as to have picked a wife-beater for a husband?

Jake wraps his arms protectively around me and kisses the top of my head. "Well, I'm not about to let anything like that ever happen to you again."

I stare into his deep brown eyes. "I know." That warm fuzzy feeling fills me all the way down to my little black heart. I really, really do have the most perfect—the most *real* feelings for this man. I want to spend the rest of my life looking into his eyes—contact brown or starburst blue.

"I love you," I tell him. "I really, truly, love you."

A soft smile returns to his lips as he rests his forehead against mine. "I know," he replies. All of a sudden, it's as if the entire world around us has disappeared, and this moment in time is the only real moment of my life. For the first time, I feel safe—I feel loved—and I am able to love just as deeply in return.

My facility psychiatrist would have called this an emotional breakthrough.

Not me.

I call it bliss.

His lips are soft and warm and I simply can't get enough of him. I lean into him, my hands exploring his muscular backside, while his arms gently wrap around my waist, pulling me closer to him. I come up for air as he stoops to cover my neck in tiny kisses. "I love you," I gasp, eager to hear myself say it again. And I can't get over how wonderful it sounds.

"Aw, get a room!" shouts a man in disgust as he passes by on his way into the casino.

"Up yours!" I snap, flipping him the bird.

"You know," Jake grins, "the guy may be right. Weren't we headed back there, anyway?"

I eye Jake suspiciously. "I thought you said you were hungry."

"I bet they have room service. Why don't we go find out, now that we can afford it?"

I laugh. "Fine by me, loverboy."

Arm in arm, we head across the parking lot. For the first time in my adult life, my heart is light and I am happy. No, I mean *blissfully* happy. With Jake by my side I feel like I can do anything…even become the kind of person I have always dreamed of becoming.

I am no longer Alison Wingate.

I am Mrs. Alison Kohler.

And I really like the sound of that.

Jake removes the key from his jacket pocket and opens our hotel room door. He steps aside and waves me forward. "After you, Mrs. Kohler."

"Why thank you, Mr. Kohler. Don't mind if I do."

I step into the dark entry and onto the unfamiliar feel of plastic beneath my feet. It's the thick kind of plastic usually reserved for particularly messy home repair work. At first, I think I might have stepped into the wrong hotel room. Then the tiny hairs on the back of my neck stiffen at the same time alarm bells go off inside my head.

"Jake!" I scream, but it's already too late.

I turn as the gunman's weapon goes off. A silencer masks the gun's blast as a bullet rips through the side of Jake's head.

Screaming hysterically, I watch in terror as my husband's lifeless body falls to the ground. "Jake! God, no! JAKE!" I start to go to him, but the gunman steps in front of me, blocking my way. To my horror, I recognize him as my mother's bodyguard, Benjamin Winston.

Instinctively, I unleash a hurricane-force wind that blows Mr. Winston off his feet and sends him crashing headfirst through the mirrored closet door. I'm just about to send a flurry of broken glass into the man's chest when I hear an all-too-familiar voice behind me.

"Oh, now look what you've done to poor Benjamin."

"Poor Benjamin?!" I cry, whirling on my mother's silhouette as she sits in the darkness at the small table next to the window. "You just murdered my husband!" I send out a burst of air that flips on the light switch, revealing the four people before me.

"I suppose you had that obnoxious Elvis impersonator marry you again," my mother says, blinking her eyes as she primly sits, gloved hands folded in her lap. She's wearing an old-lady Chanel suits that she thinks gives her that Jackie Kennedy, I'm-entitled-to-be-the-First-Lady flair. But let me assure you that no outfit in the world could mask the depravity that lingers behind those cold green eyes. "You're outnumbered, dear. You may as well surrender."

I glance at the three men behind her—all Secret Service agents. All with their guns trained on me.

"What the hell are you doing here, *Mother*?" I say, furious with myself that I actually believed that I could escape her. And Jake…my poor, poor Jake!

"Surprised to see me so soon after the wedding, I bet," she says matter-of-factly. "It's amazing what good intel one gets when one has access to a clairvoyant 24-7." She pauses then and narrows her gaze at me. "Now, then, Alison, I think it's time you put a stop to this nonsense."

"Nonsense? You murdered my husband!" I shout at her. And out of the corner of my eye I see the Secret Service men nervously shift their weight. But my mother doesn't bat an eyelash.

"Oh, my dear," she says in that bored, demeaning manner of hers. "Why, I've had both of your previous husbands killed too. Didn't you know?" Her unflappable expression becomes strained. "Stupid girl—did you really think we'd go through all the trouble of seeking an annulment from the archbishop every time you decided to get married?"

As the extent of her depravity sinks in, I can hardly keep from ripping the woman's hair out in rage. But I know I can't go there. Her death by my hand would only make her a martyr. Then there would be no stopping my father from advancing even more of his anti-psion legislation through Congress. "I hate you," I say quietly.

"It's mutual. Now, about that surrender…"

"Go to hell." And I unleash my fury on the three men before me. They haven't a prayer, because I attack them from behind. Before a single one of them can fire a round, I whip the air molecules into a frenzy, instantly creating a turbulent, gale-force vortex that sucks the men off their feet and slams them against the wall behind them.

My mother's eyes open wide with surprise as the last of her bodyguards slides to the floor unconscious, but it only lasts a moment. She turns back to me and narrows those cold eyes, as if truly seeing me for the very first time. "You've gotten more powerful, I see."

"You're just lucky that I'm not a murdering psycho bitch from hell like you!" And that's when I lash out at her. Drawing the very air into taut, powerful streams, I blast her out of her chair and send her reeling into the back wall. She hits with a thud, the contents of her purse spilling across the floor. The unconscious bodies of her bodyguards break her fall. Lucky her.

Seeing my backpack lying open on the floor, I pick it up and sweep all of my makeup and the contact lens case inside. Then I race to Jake's side, even though I know there is nothing I can do for him now.

At the sight of him, I slowly sink to the floor and release a deep, gasping sob. His blood has pooled beneath him, and his eyes gaze vacantly at the ceiling. He's gone. The love of my life is gone.

"Alison?" my mother calls as she staggers to her feet. "Alison? Where on earth do you think you're going?"

"The hell away from you," I growl. I take a moment to close Jake's eyes with my trembling fingertips. Leaning down, I kiss his cold, smooth cheek.

"Goodbye, baby," I whisper in his ear. "I will always love you." My time growing short, I reach into his coat pocket and remove the cash inside. I know he would have wanted me to have it. And right now, I need every penny of it, if I hope to survive out there alone.

"Alison," my mother says, limping on a broken heel. She looks like she wants to wring my neck, but she wisely keeps her distance. Her rage is palpable, but I continue to ignore her because I'm afraid of what I might do to her if I linger much longer. "You know, it'll only be a matter of time before I track you down again."

"Perhaps," I vaguely reply, as I brush aside a rogue curl from my dead husband's face. *God, I'm going to miss him!*

Rising to my feet, I walk to the door.

"Alison Wingate! Get back here!"

Ooh…my mother actually sounds angry with me.

Holding open the door, I call over my shoulder. "Alison Wingate no longer exists. She's as dead to me as you are."

Stepping out into the cool night air, I close the door behind me, satisfied to hear my mother shouting after me. I stuff all of the money from my bra into my backpack, followed by my wig. I have no idea how I am functioning right now, but I'm thankful to have some extra clothing in my pack to layer against those cold nights I'll be spending out in the desert.

The scream of sirens approaching in the distance signal that my time here is officially over. With one last glance back at the hotel room door, behind which my true love lies, I raise my hands to the night sky and take flight.

Chapter Twelve

THIS time, Devon was a bit more prepared to handle the violent mind-flush as he returned to his body after a dizzying, out of control blur of motion. In a burst of light, he was once again sitting on the silent grass beneath the canopy of Bai Lee's glorious willow tree. His arms were wrapped around Alya, her head resting comfortably against his chest.

Except something didn't quite feel right. His emotions were all backed up in his throat, and his chest ached as if his heart had just been ripped out by a pack of raging dingos, trampled over by a rampaging herd of wildebeests, and then returned to his ribcage with the surgical precision of a blindfolded gorilla.

He ached, but it wasn't in a physical way. It was much deeper than that. It felt as if a hole had been blowtorched through his very soul. He rubbed his chest in an attempt to stop the anguish that lingered inside him, then it dawned on him that what he was experiencing was the residual effects of Nevada's heartbreak. She had indeed lost her soulmate… and that was hurt enough to drive anyone mad with despair.

"I—I'm sorry, Nevada."

Devon glanced to his right and saw that it was Alek who had spoken. The Romanian shook his head miserably as he sat curled in a ball with his arms wrapped tightly around his knees. "I just didn't realize…" His voice trailed off, as if it had been simply too much for him to continue to speak.

"It's fine," Nevada slurred from the wooden lounge. "Nothing to do 'bout it now."

"We can pray," Miguel suggested. He was standing at the head of the wooden lounge, just where he had promised Nevada he would be when she awoke.

Nevada blinked up at him in confusion. "For the dead, Padre?"

Miguel grinned down her. "No. For you, my dear."

Nevada offered him a wan smile. "You know, I think I'd like that."

Bai Lee was unusually solemn as she sat at the foot of the wooden lounge. Her gaze was cast downward, her lips pursed, and Devon wondered what she was thinking about. Apparently, Nevada's replay had had a bit more of an effect on their psyches than any of them could have anticipated—Bai Lee included.

Vahn joined Miguel at the wooden lounge, and together they helped Nevada sit up as she slowly gained her bearings. The mood beneath the willow had become somber, and Devon knew that he would not be able to look at Nevada in quite the same way again. She had grown in his eyes. Like Vahn, she was a warrior, taking on an enemy, her own family, that was bigger than life, and much more dangerous.

It was then that another thought struck Devon—Nevada's abusive first husband had been a *psi-cannon*. No wonder she held them in such low regard. And here he had boldly proclaimed himself to be one in front of everybody!

Devon felt his insides shrivel with regret. *Couldn't he do anything right?*

"Bai Lee?" Alya said quietly.

The telepath's gaze slid over to her. "Yeah?"

"I'd like to go next."

Say what?! Devon bolted upright, causing Alya's head to bump against his chest. "Alya, are you sure?"

She released a small sigh. "Yes, Devon. We all must take our turn at some point."

"But you're so weak."

Alya tilted her head back and gave Devon a reassuring smile. "Don't worry; I'll be fine."

"Yeah, but—" Devon couldn't say aloud what he really wanted to say, because it would only come out sounding stupid. He enjoyed feeling her heart beating against his chest when he held her in his arms. Her warmth made him smile; the scent of her hair made him delirious. And mostly, a part of him wondered when he'd ever be able to hold such a beautiful woman in his arms again. "Well, okay…"

Alya's smile brightened. "Don't look so sad." She planted a sweet kiss on Devon's cheek. "I promise I won't be long."

Devon's heart soared in anticipation of holding her again, and the kiss wasn't too shabby either. He just wished that it had been on his lips. But then again, everyone was staring at them, including Alya's twin, Alek, who would have no trouble punching Devon in the face the moment his sister's back was turned.

"Let me help you up, Alya," Alek said as he stood over them, his hand extended to his sister.

Alya hesitated a moment before taking her brother's hand, and Devon tensed up, readying himself to spring into action if things turned ugly. Alek was gentle as he helped her rise; however, it wasn't until Vahn stepped in and assisted that Alya was fully on her feet.

"Thank you, Vahn, Alek," Alya said as Devon popped up beside her. "But I think Devon can escort me the rest of the way."

"Yes'm," Vahn replied with a nod, and he stepped aside while Alya wrapped Devon's arm around her waist.

Alek, too, stepped back, allowing them to pass. Alya's twin appeared surprisingly calm…tranquil, even. As if he had never had an issue with Plant Boy wrapping his arms around his beautiful sister.

Devon, however, remained wary and made sure not to turn his back on Alek. It was always the trusting kids who got sucker-punched in the hallways. Then again, maybe Nevada's story had had some kind of effect on him. Either way, Devon wasn't about to get blindsided if he could avoid it.

Miguel helped Nevada sit down on the grass close to where they had previously been sitting. Nevada still looked out of it, though. Devon wondered what effect that kind of brain drain was going to have on Alya.

Devon nodded to Bai Lee as they approached. "Can you go easy on her when you do your voodoo this time?"

"My voodoo?"

"You know what I mean," Devon replied with a frown. "Alya's not feeling well."

"Devon," Alya said, with a wave of her hand. "It's fine."

"You saw how disoriented Vahn and Nevada were after they woke up from their replays…"

"The effects wore off pretty quickly for me," Vahn interjected.

"Yeah, but you're a super-soldier."

"Devon, please," said Alya. She smiled wearily at him. "It's my turn. We all made an agreement, and I mean to honor it."

Devon's shame twisted his guts into knots. His stupid plan was taking on a life of its own and proving much more complicated than he could have ever predicted. A part of him wanted to call a time-out, confess everything…but that would mean that he would never be allowed to escape with the others.

At a loss for words, Devon nodded and flashed Alya a tight little smile. He'd started this mess, and he'd have to see it through to its end. He just prayed that he could somehow be the last person to replay and, in that way, hold Alya in his arms just a bit longer before she saw what a complete and utter loser he was.

Vahn and Devon helped Alya lie down on the wooden lounge. As soon as her head touched the soft pile of leaves, Devon thought he heard the tree sigh. In a flutter of subtle motion, the tree's branches twisted around Alya, gently cradling her body. It reminded Devon of the time he compelled his mother's stubborn rosebushes to entangle their thorny stems around the lattice archway in her garden. Of course, he was fully aware that he was the only lame-o in the room who could achieve that kind of rapid plant growth in the real world.

But then again, this wasn't the real world. This was a world of Bai Lee's creation. Her grass didn't scream.

Devon watched the leaves silently sprouting around Alya's head as she gazed up at him. He hoped she was comfortable and that her replay wouldn't take too much out of her. "I'll be right here when you wake up."

Alya gave him a beautiful smile. "I know."

Though a part of him wanted to celebrate the fact that a gorgeous blonde was smiling at him, the worry tugging at his heart made that impossible.

"Is there anything you wish to tell us before we begin?" Bai Lee asked from her perch. Her expression was unreadable.

"Yes," Alya replied. She turned her head slightly to the others seated in the grass before her. "I was kidnapped from the Romanian Government Psionic Center by a powerful Russian mobster when I was five years old."

"But you were a princess," said Nevada. "Why were you at a government Psi-Center?"

"While it is true that I am of noble blood, I am not a princess," she replied.

"My sister's too much of a lady to tell you the truth of things," Alek interjected, rising to his feet. "Our birth was never officially recognized by the Romanian royal family. Our names were changed to keep up appearances, and we were given to a distant cousin to raise." He paused to scoff before continuing. "It was our dear cousin who placed us in the Psionic Center, which had once been a Soviet baby house. Complete with leaking pipes, soiled mattresses, and rats the size of small dogs."

"Alek, please," Alya said softly.

"You got off easy, dear sister," Alek sneered. "You got out of there within a year."

"I was kidnapped."

"You were spared the misery of that wretched place!"

"Alek!" Bai Lee shouted. "This is Alya's time to speak, so sit down and shut up."

Alek glowered at Bai Lee, but remained silent as he slowly sat back down. His anger was evident, however; Devon could feel it radiating off of him in waves. That Romanian psi facility must have been hell on earth for him.

"Alya," said Bai Lee in that husky tone of hers, "you were saying?"

"Yes…right." Alya paused to take a breath. "This mobster had a very sick son who was four years older than me. The boy, Viktor, had leukemia. And for the last ten years I have been keeping him alive. In a secluded mansion on Long Island, New York."

"You mean you've been held prisoner on Long Island for the last ten years?" Devon asked.

Alya looked up at him. "Darling, I've been a prisoner *all* my life. And because of what I can do, I probably always will be."

Devon brushed aside a stray lock of hair that had fallen across Alya's face. "I wish I could protect you from all that… you know, be more like Superman."

Turning her head, Alya rested her cheek against his hand. "Devon, you already are."

Huh? Devon wasn't sure what she meant by that, because he sure as heck wasn't Superman. But before he could reply, he heard Bai Lee politely cough.

"Alya," Bai Lee said. "Time's ticking away here. You ready, or what?"

Alya nodded. "Ready."

Devon was about to object when Alya closed her eyes and the world around them collapsed. With no time to shift gears, Devon was painfully ripped from this reality with a sensation that felt something like sandpaper furiously grinding away his every molecule.

He blinked out of existence with a mental scream.

Alya's Story

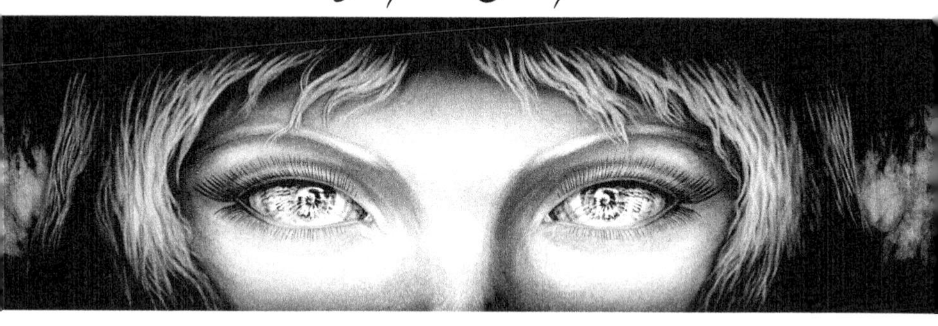

Chapter Thirteen

THE best evenings are the moonlit ones. I can see the shoreline from my tiny balcony and watch the waves crash upon the sand. I don't mind that it's chilly outside, because the rhythmic beating of the waves fills me with something so soothing—so primal—that I want to wrap my arms around it and press it deep into my soul. I want to carry within me this tiny measure of peace everywhere I go. Especially on the days I work with Viktor—acute myeloid leukemia is a vile disease and it takes me days to rid its effects from my body.

I shudder, and it's not just from the cold breeze off the water. It's because Viktor's disease continues to resist me. When he relapsed for a third time ten years ago, I was brought here to keep his leukemia at bay. I have been waging war with an intangible beast ever since. And I am frightened—because now the beast is winning.

And if Viktor dies… No. I can't go there. Worrying about the future is futile. There is only the here and now, and I must relish every moment I have alone in my comfortable little room. No one molests me or beats me here, unlike the horrors I left behind in Romania.

And the dear brother I was forced to leave behind, too.

Viktor emphatically assures me that Alek is no longer in that place, because the Romanian Government's Psionic Center was closed down seven years ago. He promises me he'll find him—somehow Viktor will find my dear brother and bring him back to me—but I have an unsettling feeling. I doubt that any psionic children ever made it out of that ghastly place alive.

I wrap my sweater tighter about me and take one last long look over the sea.

"May God protect you, Aleksei…wherever you are." I feel the warmth of my tears trailing down my cheeks. "May you be safe and well cared-for."

It is my prayer for him. The one I have said nightly since the day we were separated. Losing my twin was like losing a very dear part of myself. And I miss him.

Turning my back on the crashing waves, I return to the warmth of my room and slide closed the glass door to the balcony. A queen-sized bed with a soft down comforter and luxurious feather pillows takes up much of the room. The writing desk, bookshelves, and side tables are carved from sturdy Russian oak and stained a deep, majestic brown. They give weight to the room and add an old-world charm.

Viktor's father, Sergei Bogomolov, who I rarely see, spares no expense when it comes to my comfort. And for that, I am most grateful. It makes my long and painful recoveries all the more bearable.

The most used feature in this room, outside of my overstuffed reading chair, is the 52-inch flat screen television that hangs on the wall across from my bed. Recovering from a healing session can take up to a week. That television gives me access to the outside world. It's a way for me to seek freedom through the lives of others and imagine what kind of life I would have had, had I been born a baseline.

Fluffing the pillow on my reading chair, I'm startled by the unexpected knock on my door.

"Alya?"

It's Mrs. Mandelstam. What could she want at this impossible hour? "Yes, ma'am?"

"Are you decent, child?" she asks me in Russian. It is a strict rule that only Russian be spoken in this household. The one exception is during my sessions with Viktor. And that's only because his Russian is so terrible.

"Yes, ma'am. I'm dressed."

Mrs. Mandelstam opens my door, her reading glasses perched precariously on the tip of her nose; her salt-and-pepper hair has been hastily swept back into a bun. Though she has taken the time to pull on the black matron dress that is her uniform, I notice that she hasn't bothered with stockings. Heavy black work shoes adorn her feet.

"Alya, you're needed," she says urgently. "Come quickly."

My heart leaps into my throat. "Is it Viktor?"

Mrs. Mandelstam peers at me ominously over her glasses. "I'm afraid so."

"But it's not even been a week," I cry, as I rush about my room searching for my shoes. I only got out of bed yesterday from one of the most grueling healing sessions of my life. "How can this be?"

"Ach, child, if I had all the answers…" Mrs. Mandelstam shakes her head in frustration as she unmakes my bed during her search for my favorite pillow. "Just be thankful that the master isn't in. He pushes you too hard, you know."

"I push myself," I say absently, falling into the routine of familiar conversation. "Mr. Bogomolov has been very good to me."

I hear Mrs. Mandelstam snort in disagreement. "I know what drives you, child. Everyone in this household adores Viktor. We all wish he could be rid of his terrible disease. But—" Her voice trails away as she spots my pillow.

"But what?" I ask, looking at her pointedly, right shoe in hand.

"I've said too much already." She places my favorite pillow beneath her arm and plucks an afghan off a stool.

I stand stock-still, watching her. "No, tell me, please. What were you going to say?"

Mrs. Mandelstam stops fussing about and meets my gaze over the rim of her glasses. "You are a treasure, child. I've seen firsthand the miracles you perform."

"They're not miracles," I say softly. "I can't bring back the dead. I can't heal everybody."

Mrs. Mandelstam gazes pointedly at me. "But that won't stop you from trying, now, will it?"

"No, ma'am."

Mrs. Mandelstam's smile grows as she proudly gazes back at me in that grandmotherly way of hers. "And therein lies the miracle. It's you, child. Not your amazing power. Just simply…you."

My cheeks grow hot as Mrs. Mandelstam's compliment blossoms inside of me with a warmth that I know is genuine and heartfelt. But that doesn't make it any less difficult for me to accept. I am, after all, considered something less than human by my captor, Mr. Bogomolov. And I have no illusions that if I allow the leukemia to claim his most beloved son… he'll have no problem ending my life, too.

"We'd better get going," I say, cramming my feet into my tennis shoes without properly tying them. Conversations like the one I'm having with Mrs. Mandelstam make me nervous. I have no control over my fate, and acting otherwise could get me killed or, worse, sent back to another, even more horrible psi-facilty in Romania.

Mrs. Mandelstam holds open the door as I head into the hallway and press the call button for the elevator. My bedroom is on the third floor of the expansive, isolated mansion, but to find my room, one must know where the secret passage is located and have access to one of the three keys that power the elevator. It's real cloak-and-dagger stuff, I know. But it keeps me out of sight and well away from the small army of Russian henchmen who patrol the house and grounds. Sergei Bogomolov trusts nobody—not even his closest allies. And that philosophy alone is probably what has kept him alive and in power for over twenty-two years.

The elevator doors open and Mrs. Mandelstam and I get in. Without a word, she inserts her key and turns it once to the left. In an instant, the doors whisper closed and the elevator descends.

"Back there, what I said," says Mrs. Mandelstam, staring straight ahead at the door.

"Yes, ma'am?"

The elevator eases to a stop and Mrs. Mandelstam withdraws her key. She turns to me then, as the doors open, and offers me a sweet smile. "I meant every word of it."

Before I can reply, she steps out of the elevator and hurries down the short passage to the hidden door that opens into Viktor's closet. I'm right behind her, of course, but I find myself a bit puzzled by her behavior. Mrs. Mandelstam is not usually so chatty, let alone so emotional. Especially when Viktor's life is at stake.

Unless…

I step into Viktor's massive suite in time to see Mrs. Mandelstam exit through a door on the opposite side of the ornately decorated room. Strangely, the room is illuminated by candlelight, my pillow and afghan set neatly on an empty chair by the door. "Mrs. Mandelstam, where are you going? Mrs. Mandelstam?"

"She's off to the airport," I hear Viktor say in English. He may not speak Russian very well, but at least he understands it somewhat when he hears it.

"Airport?" I ask in heavily accented English as I turn toward the sound of his voice. I find him sitting propped up by pillows in his hospital bed, dressed to the nines in an elegant tuxedo, complete with crisp white gloves. His legs are covered by a thick comforter, but knowing Viktor, he's probably managed to pull on the pants as well. I am stunned by how handsome he appears before me, the candlelight softening his sunken features, making him look older than his nineteen years and much, much healthier. His dark chocolate eyes twinkle in the light from the massive candelabras that sit on tables scattered throughout the room. And I notice for the first time that he has become a nicer-looking version of his father. Which is saying a lot, because Mr. Bogomolov is not exactly an ugly man.

"Viktor?" I ask. "What's going on? Why are you dressed like that, and why is Mrs. Mandelstam going to the airport?"

He takes a deep breath, his eyes liquid and unreadable in the candlelight. "Because her services are no longer required."

"*What?!*" I gasp, not believing my ears.

"No, no, Alya. Wait," he adds, quickly. "It's not what you think."

"Then why did you fire her?"

"To protect her."

"From what? Your father?"

He looks away, staring pensively at the flickering candles on the bedstand. "You know, you and me… I'm not sure we were meant to endure our lives in this manner."

I step closer to his bed in an effort to assure him that I have no desire to be anywhere else but here. "I don't mind my life, Victor. It's comfortable."

"It's a prison."

Sitting on the edge of his bed, I give him an encouraging smile. "Not when I'm with you, it's not."

He lays his head back against the pillows and gives me a smile that almost overcomes the sadness in his eyes, but not quite. "Alya, you are my angel."

"No. I'm not." I'm shaking my head, but when he looks at me in that way, I find myself grinning like a bashful child. "I'm just a girl who wants to see you well again."

"I wish that could be so."

"Perhaps it will one day."

He smiles at me again, the candlelight dancing in his eyes. "I have something for you." He reaches for something on the tablestand and picks up a perfect rose. He holds it out to me. "I had all of the thorns removed. Mrs. Mandelstam told me you liked roses."

I take the rose and breathe in its rich fragrance. "Oh, Viktor, it's beautiful. Thank you." Touching the soft petals to my cheek, I find myself becoming suspicious of his overture. We are not lovers, nor am I in love with him. Viktor is my friend, my very dear friend, but our relationship is strictly platonic and I have never sensed anything from him other than brotherly devotion. So, then, why the tuxedoed presentation of a rose by candlelight?

"Viktor?"

"Yes?"

"Why did you let Mrs. Mandelstam go?"

"Because I adore her, Alya. She's been kinder to me than my biological mother ever was." He pauses, the orange glow of the candlelight reflecting in his eyes. "This last year has been a very rough year for me. But what has pained me more than the ache in my bones is watching you suffer for weeks at a time as you work harder and harder to rid yourself of my disease."

"But it's what I do. I have to take your disease into my body in order to repair you—that's how my power works."

"I'm not blind, Alya. I know this disease is killing you, too."

"No. I can handle it."

He takes my hands and gazes deeply into my eyes. "Alya, my most dear and perfect friend. You have given me ten long, wonderful years of life—life I could never have had without you. Your laughter has given me so much joy, and your faith in me has lifted me to stellar heights.

"But all I have to offer you now is pain and suffering and death. My disease is winning."

"No, don't say that—"

"Tonight, we must make our goodbyes."

The tears pour out of me, as a mixture of fear and loss blossoms inside my chest and quickly spreads to my extremities like a poisonous red tide. I have failed Viktor. And now both of our lives are forfeit. "Please, Viktor," I beg, my voice trembling. "Give me just a little more time. I promise I'll do better—try harder—I'll figure something out."

"But I'm killing you, Alya."

"No, no—I can do this! I must!" I reach down deep within myself in an effort to control my rising panic. "I am not going to allow you to kill yourself—you can't! I won't let you!" I reach out to him, psionic power tingling in my fingertips. All it will take is but one touch, one caress, and I will instantly know the state of his remission.

But Viktor takes my hand in his gloved ones and offers me a heartbreaking smile. "Alya, I never said anything about killing myself."

"Then why else would you make Mrs. Mandelstam leave?"

His voice drops to a whisper as he says, "Because you're leaving here, too. Tonight."

It takes me the breadth of a heartbeat to realize what he means, and the implication of his words will only mean a disastrous end for us both. "No! You can't! You'll die!"

"I was supposed to die ten years ago."

"And that's why I'm here. To help you get better—"

"But there is no getting better for me, Alya. All we're doing here is prolonging the inevitable."

"So? What's wrong with that?"

"Everything! I'm killing you!"

"No, it's not true! It's just not true!" But even as I speak these words, I know he's right. His disease cannot be healed. Not by me, anyway. I have failed him… I have failed myself.

I am terrified of what will become of me.

With tears rolling down my cheeks, my body trembling, I somehow manage to utter two little words. "I'm sorry."

Viktor's sweet smile is more comfort than I deserve as he wipes the moisture from my cheek with his gloved fingertips. "Alya, you have nothing to apologize for."

I shake my head in reply, because I fear the torrent of choking sobs that threaten to spill out of me if I try to speak. No matter what happens here tonight, there will be no going back to the fragile sense of security I had only minutes ago. Minutes I had squandered, unable to fathom that Mrs. Mandelstam's kind words to me were her way of saying goodbye.

"I've often wondered," Viktor continues with a faraway look in his eyes, "how many other people you could have healed out there in the world if you weren't stuck here with me."

"It doesn't matter," I reply weakly. "I like it here."

"There's no future for you here."

"But you can't just give up, Viktor. You have to go on living."

"And I will. Only without you to keep my disease at bay."

I lower my eyes. "Then you will die."

"Yes. I will die. But you won't." He gently tilts my face upward so that I am once again looking into his eyes. "You must leave here immediately, Alya."

The loss and fear inside me swirl together with the turbulent, gut-wrenching force of a whirlpool, which drains the fight right out of me, leaving me numb with fatigue. My death now certain, I embrace my fate. I knew this day was bound to come. I just had never expected it to arrive so soon.

"But, Viktor," I say softly, "I have nowhere to go."

"Yes, you do," he says, positively beaming at me. "There are people I have met who can help you. Good people, Alya. They are with the Psionic Underground Network, and they can protect you. Even from people like my father."

"Your father will kill me if I leave here, Viktor," I say in resignation. Surely, he already knows this, or he wouldn't have forced Mrs. Mandelstam to go.

"Not if he can't find you."

I audibly sigh and turn away from him, unable to meet his gaze any longer. "But what's the use of running? I have no one."

"Ah, but you do."

I shake my head in misery and allow my resignation to speak aloud what I have held secretly in my heart for years. "No, I don't. My brother is dead."

"Actually," Viktor replies, "he's not."

I can hardly believe my ears. It takes me a moment to organize my thoughts enough to speak. "B-but how? It's been so long."

"The Network found him. He was looking for you."

At that moment, Viktor's plan becomes crystal clear. He has kept his promise to me and found my brother, the only other person in the world I cherish as much as Viktor himself. *Viktor is sacrificing himself so that I may live.*

"Viktor," I say, turning back to him and taking in his sweet, caring smile. "You did all of this for me?"

"Yes."

I shake my head, overcome by his selflessness and feeling incredibly unworthy of his compassion. "Why?"

"Like I told you before, you're an angel—*my* angel." He reaches out to me, and I take his hand. "And it's time for you to fly away from here. I'm setting you free."

"Then come with me."

"I can't," he says, shaking his head. "This is your adventure, not mine."

I open my mouth to argue, but Viktor holds up a gloved hand. "No, no," he says. "No argument. Our time grows short. Now, you must listen to me very carefully."

I barely manage a nod, because it's such a struggle to keep it together. My eyes cloud with brimming tears. I lean in closer, lingering on his every word.

"You will meet up with Network freedom workers in Aberdeen, Texas, in three days' time."

"Aberdeen, Texas," I say breathlessly, my mind whirling with an endless tangle of questions. "But how am I supposed to get there? I have no money, no friends—I don't even know where Aberdeen, Texas is."

Viktor gives me a patient smile. "What? You think I'd send you into that big bad world out there without an escort?"

I feel my cheeks grow hot with embarrassment. I'm usually not one to jump to conclusions, let alone voice my fears. And this is definitely not how I want Viktor to remember me. "No, of course not," I say softly. "This is just all so—so—overwhelming right now."

Viktor's smile strains just a bit, as his eyes meet mine once again. "Mrs. Mandelstam told me once of a little prayer you say every night for your brother."

I nod, once again fighting back tears. I'm working overtime to be brave and not lose what little composure I have left in front of one of the most beautiful people I've ever known. "Y-yes."

"Would you say one for me from time to time?"

"Every night," I manage to say, choking back a sob.

He beams at me then. "That would be nice."

I put everything behind my smile. My love, my thankfulness, my friendship…my heart. And I hope—no, I pray—that in some small way, he can see it all in these final, heartbreaking moments. His supreme sacrifice will never be forgotten.

He glances behind me, looking deep into the shadows. "Are you there, my friend?"

"I'm here, Viktor," says a voice from the darkness, a voice that is much different than I remember…yet it is a voice I would recognize anywhere.

"Aleksei," I whisper in disbelief, my heart pounding. And suddenly, the room is tilting. The candlelight grows brighter and brighter until I am overcome by its brilliance. I feel as if I am falling down a terribly deep pit, straight through the heart of the sun. And I know deep in my bones that this is not how I remember it. This is not the truth of things.

This is—

Chapter Fourteen

IT was as if a monstrous black vortex had whipped Devon around and around like a spinning bola and then flung him at mind-warping speed across the universe. He thought for sure that the gray matter had liquefied between his ears by the time he arrived—screaming at the top of his lungs—back into his body. He was certain that something terrible had happened to Alya.

"ALYA!" The cry ripped from his throat even before he had full control of his senses. His heart pounded as he blinked his eyes and willed his body to move. Something had gone dreadfully wrong during her replay. And a million unanswered questions swirled around in his brain like an F5 tornado.

"Alya!" he said again, though far from the ear-splitting volume of his first savage outcry. This time, he found that he could move his arms, and the grass was once again tickling his feet through the fabric tears along the sides of his shoes. Yes! He was finally back and standing at the head of the wooden lounge just where he had been before Bai Lee had replayed her memories.

"Alya," he said softly this time, looking down at her still form. The branches of the tree were slowly uncoiling themselves from around Alya's body. Devon exhaled in frustration. He needed to find her wrist and check for a pulse. "Alya, please…stay with me."

Scooting around the wooden bench as the tree's tendrils further withdrew, Devon took her limp hand and felt for the soft rhythm of her heart. To his utter relief, it was there—faint, but apparent just the same.

"She's alive," said Bai Lee from behind him.

"No thanks to you," Devon snapped. "You assured me this wasn't going to happen. You said she'd be all right."

"And she is," Bai Lee replied matter-of-factly. "I think she just fainted or something."

"*Or something*?" Devon whirled on Bai Lee. "I told you she was too weak to handle this!"

Bai Lee didn't move. Only her frown lines deepened. "Then she must be too weak to escape with us. Is that what you're saying?"

The question shot straight through Devon and he felt his insides explode into a million useless pieces. This was his worst fear realized—the thing he had hoped to prevent. And all because of his stupid lies and bravado.

"No, no," he said quickly, the anger gone from his voice. "That's not what I meant." He lowered his gaze and turned back to Alya. "Is she going to be all right?" he asked weakly.

"I don't know," Bai Lee said. "She needs a doctor."

"It's Viktor's fault," said Alek, from somewhere behind Devon. "His disease has ravaged her. I knew I should have come for her sooner."

Devon brushed aside a stray lock of hair from Alya's face. "I don't think Alya or Viktor had a choice, Alek. You were there—Viktor gave up his life so that she could be free. There's no greater sacrifice than that."

"Devon?" said Vahn, as the big guy approached. "Is there anything I can do?"

Devon glanced over at him. "Yeah. Maybe you—"

"Devon?"

Devon leaned closer to the Romanian beauty. "Alya?"

Her eyes opened slightly as she smiled wearily up at him. "I'm still here."

"Well, that's a relief!" he said, a bit too exuberantly. And Alya's smile grew as she weakly chuckled.

"How could you ever think that I would leave you so soon?" Her voice was as soft as the flutter of butterfly wings, but it was the sparkling light in her eyes that calmed his fears. "I'm going to be fine. All I need is rest."

"Then we'll get you some," Devon said, and he knew he had to be beaming at her like a lovesick fool. But he didn't care, because Alya didn't seem to mind. And that was all the permission he needed to be himself around her.

He turned to Vahn. "Could you give me a hand?"

"Sure thing," the psi-blade replied.

As they helped Alya sit up, Devon noticed that the willow's branches were assisting them. With the tree's help, Alya scooted to the edge of the wooden lounge, and then the lounge lowered itself until she could comfortably place her feet on the ground. Once she managed to stand, leaning heavily on Devon for support, the wooden lounge returned to its original height.

Glancing at Bai Lee, Devon wasn't surprised to see her eyes closed in concentration as she manipulated the tree's actions. And he thought that maybe there was a small chance that Bai Lee would like Alya enough to allow her to escape with the rest of them, despite her apparent illness. At least, that was Devon's hope. He could accept any fate the baselines in Washington threw at him, as long as he knew that Alya was alive and free.

"Why don't I help you both to your seats?" Vahn suggested as he stood beside Alya, looking very tall and…concerned.

"That would be lovely," she replied. She allowed him to reach around her waist, while Devon supported her from the other side. They had no sooner taken three steps than Alya's knees buckled and she sank to the ground between them. "How about right here?" she said, joking about her obvious infirmity.

Vahn smiled. "Fine by me."

"Me too," echoed Devon. But he felt a tiny pang of jealousy as the buff psi-blade helped Alya sit comfortably on the grass. Dang, if only Devon could be cut like that! And his mind flashed to the images inside the arena—of what it had been like to *be* Vahn—along with the terrible responsibility and burden of authority that had accompanied his position. All in all, behind every sculpted bicep and chiseled ab, there had been a world of hurt.

And no loving family besides.

Vahn had Devon sit down on the grass behind Alya, and then he helped her sit closer to him so that she could lean back against Devon for support. It was exactly how they had been sitting before, and Devon was elated to find himself holding her once again. Even if it was only going to be for a little while longer.

"Thanks, Vahn," Devon said, and the psi-blade nodded.

"My pleasure."

"Well, now that we got that over with—who's next?" said Bai Lee, looking smug and defiant in her yellow robes. "Alek?" Bai Lee's gaze swept over to Devon. "Loverboy?"

"Me," said Miguel, rising from beside Nevada. "I will go next."

"Then get your ass up here." Bai Lee was already manipulating the wooden lounge as the branches withdrew to allow room for the untrained telepath to lie down.

"Miguel," Nevada said, her eyes bright with worry. When he turned to look at her, she added, "Good luck."

He smiled. "Thank you. I'll need it, where I've been."

Devon turned his attention back to the wooden lounge as Miguel made his way up front. It was then that he spotted Alek gazing back at his sister with a sad, conflicted look on his face. Devon wondered if he would ever be able to forgive Alya's seeming abandonment of him when they were children. It probably hadn't been easy to survive in that Romanian psi facility, let alone get out of there in one piece.

Growing up without a loving family was as foreign to Devon as speaking fluent Russian. Yet it was the reality that most psions faced. And Devon wondered if that lack of parental guidance and—dare he think it—*unconditional love* made the chasm he felt among his fellow psions that much wider.

Perhaps it wasn't simply his lame powers that had kept him forever on the outs with his peers. Perhaps it was something deeper than that. Something a bit more primal and far simpler.

He had a family who loved him.

As that insight swirled around in his brain, he felt Alya's heart lightly beating against his chest. Caught up in the intimacy of the moment, he gave her a little hug and breathed in the scent of her hair. To his surprise, he heard her pleasantly sigh and cling tighter to his protective arms wrapped around her.

Tilting her head up so that their eyes met, Alya smiled. "You know, when I said that I wish I could heal you?"

Devon grinned. "Yeah. Back in the real world, I think my arm's still pretty messed up."

Alya shook her head. "Nothing about you is messed up, Devon McWilliams. You're perfect just the way you are. Always remember that." She reached up then and pulled Devon's face down to her own. Her soft full lips touched his, and a joyous warmth blossomed inside his chest like a blooming rose. Was this what love felt like? He hadn't a clue, but it sure as heck felt amazing! He could have kept on kissing her for the rest of eternity, but he didn't dare push it when he felt Alya pull away with a bashful smile and a gleam in her eyes.

As she snuggled back into him, his spirit soared. He might not have had much longer to hold his lovely Romanian healer, but he promised himself that he would cherish these last minutes fully. And right now, not even the thought of his possible demise in a Washington, DC, prison could wipe the beaming grin off of his face.

"You have anything to tell us before we begin, Miguel?" Bai Lee asked as she took her seat on the edge of the wooden lounge.

Miguel's head was resting on the leafy pillow. The tree's serpentine branches had become downright ornate as they cradled Miguel's body with a strange, unearthly reverence. It reminded Devon of an intricate wooden sarcophagus, like something a mourning wood nymph would create for a forest king.

"Actually, yes, I would like to say something." He turned his head to face his peers and offered everyone a genuine smile. But his smile nervously faded just before he spoke.

"I know we hardly know one another, but our suffering is universal…because that is what life is. We endure for the beautiful moments in our lives—a child's smile, a glorious sunset, a lover's embrace. We live for fleeting periods of happiness and then we endure some more.

"But I must tell you, my friends, that I endured the best I could. Moments of peace have been far too few in my life. After the general shot my mother in the head, I stupidly lashed out with powers I could barely control and murdered not only the general, but all of his officers as well. It was a death sentence for my entire village. And I was the one to blame.

"But then something marvelous happened. The people in the village told me to run. 'Run to Father Gálvez,' they said. And they placed canteens of water around my neck and handed me a sack full of food. I was only five years old at the time…five years old and witness to my first miracle.

"My father looked me straight in the eyes and told me to say my prayers at night and to obey Father Gálvez. He told me not to worry about him, or my brothers and sisters, that they would be fine. I knew his words to me were far from the truth of things, but I chose to believe him and hoped that God would protect my family from the retaliation the Guatemalan Army was sure to send."

"So, what happened to them?" asked Nevada, rising to her knees. "Were they killed too?"

"Yes," Miguel replied softly. "Every last member of my village was gunned down the following week because of what I had done."

"And there wasn't an outcry?" asked Alek. "Baselines are killing baselines, and there's no demand for justice?"

Miguel shook his head. "No one cares about the poor, my friend. That is the way of things."

Devon could see Alek's scowl deepen as he considered Miguel's words, but instead of arguing, the Romanian settled back onto the grass without another word.

After several long moments, Miguel took a deep breath and slowly released it. "It took me two weeks of walking the back roads at night before I reached Father Gálvez's church in Chajul. Though I was an untrained telepath, I could use my powers to remain undetected in plain sight, and this worked against humans as well as hungry predators.

"Father Gálvez was a good and gentle man. He taught me to read and write and work numbers. He also taught me about God, and in his unfaltering devotion to my protection, he showed me what true bravery is." Miguel paused for a moment, a faraway look in his eyes.

"'Sister Mary Francis is coming for you from America,' Father Gálvez said to me when I was seven. 'She can take you to the people who can truly protect you.'

"After hearing this, I was so excited that I packed a small sack containing my few possessions. I was ready to leave for America at a moment's notice…only she never showed up. Three whole years passed, and still no sign of Sister Mary Francis. But Father Gálvez told me to be patient—that life ran on God's time, not man's, and that in the end everything works out as it should.

"Then one chilly winter's day, the army arrived. They had a telepath of their own, an older girl with hateful eyes who revealed my presence with a wave of her hand. The army was merciless. They murdered Farther Gálvez and took me back to Guatemala City with them.

"They told me that I would be their weapon. I was to torture their captives and read the minds of prominent people. I was to protect Guatemala from its true enemies."

Miguel sighed again and shook his head in disappointment. "But I resisted. I resisted because I was afraid of my telepathy. I knew I might kill the people whose minds I touched. But the government officials hardly cared. They beat me and starved me, but they could not force me to obey. I would rather die than willingly take a life.

"So, I prayed.

"I prayed for an end to my misery."

He looked over at Nevada and smiled warmly at her. "And then one day, the Lord answered my prayer."

Despite the tears brimming in her eyes, Devon saw a beautiful smile spreading across Nevada's face, but by the time he looked back at Miguel, it was only to see his eyes close. Oh, crap! A heartbeat later, Devon flashed out of existence, pulled along in the powerful wake of Miguel's replay.

Miquel's Story

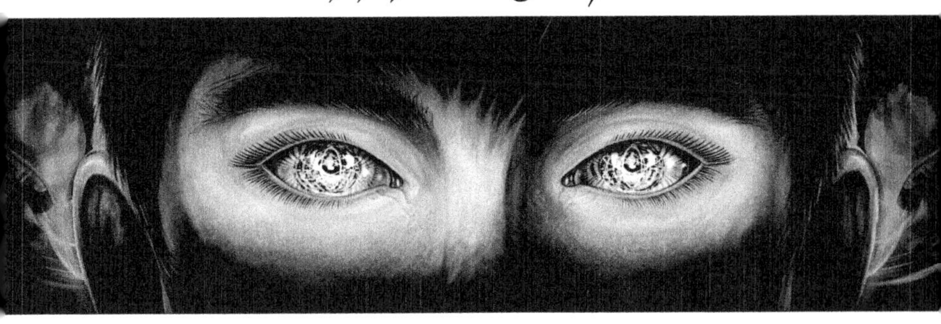

Chapter Fifteen

My cell smells like a sewer, because I have not been allowed to empty my latrine buckets in over a week. The guards find it amusing to torment me. Some of the less-religious ones have taken to calling me San Miguelito, or Little Saint Michael, because of my preference for prayer over torturing others. Baseline or psion, it makes no difference to me. I believe we are all God's children. And I refuse to knowingly harm another soul, let alone take someone's life.

And deep in my heart, I know that God has not forsaken me.

One way or another, He will answer my prayers.

Only, it will be in His way.

In His time.

The morning prayer tumbles from my cracked and bleeding lips as I sit on the cement floor, my voice barely a whisper. I hardly notice the damp chill in the room, or the rodents gorging on the rotten food the guards slide beneath my door twice a day.

As I recite the prayer, I open my mind and release my spirit to the rhythm of the words. I am transported away from my body, from this horrible little room, from the vermin that feast beside me. I become one with my prayer and I imagine my soul soaring toward the heavens, a loving tribute to all that is good in this world. I find myself no longer tethered to the fear and the physical hunger that consumes my body. I am free now, one with all creation. There is nothing in this world that can harm me as long as I hold the Lord God fully in my heart.

The cell door is thrown open with a terrible *bang*. The rats screech in alarm as they scurry back into the shadows.

"Get up," the captain orders. He steps into my cell, wearing a crisp, pressed uniform.

I look up at Captain Rivera, saddened that I have been disturbed, and meet his hardened gaze. "I—I don't think I can."

He scowls down at me, and then signals two of the guards standing outside of my cell door. "Get him up! Now!"

The men grab me roughly by the arms and haul me to my feet. My legs and bottom have gone numb from sitting so long, and the sharp, prickly sensation that follows makes me want to cry out in pain. But I bite my swollen lips instead, refusing to show the captain anything but a tranquil exterior. I will not allow my more human moments to lead to more beatings, torture, or manipulation for the captain's amusement. I could care less about my own welfare, but Captain Rivera is a persistent man. And, after weeks of interrogation, he has finally found my weakness.

I just pray that merciful death will come for me soon, before any more innocent lives are taken on my account.

"Come on," the captain says with a frown. And the two guards drag me out the door.

I squint in the bright hallway. My eyes are used to the velvet shadows of my dimly lit cell—a small window high on the far wall is its only source of light. I am disoriented by the twists and turns of the corridors that the guards take at a quick pace. They drag me up two long staircases and then past a security checkpoint. I have no idea where I am or where I am going within Guatemala City's new Justice Center.

We emerge in the enormous marble and glass lobby, where tall windows allow the sunlight to flood the entire room. I rapidly blink my eyes as they adjust to the bright light and colors. I'm surprised to see adults in business suits walking though the lobby. For the most part, they ignore my presence; however, I do catch one man stopping in his tracks at the sight of me. Judging by his expression, I'm not sure if he is more revolted by my dirty clothing or my starburst eyes.

We round a corner. The circulation has returned to my legs, but when I try to walk of my own accord, I find that the guards won't allow me to. Their grips become viselike around my arms and they hoist me up between them, making it impossible for my feet to touch the floor. Being half-dragged was better than this, but once again I divert my pain and frustration and let it go. I'm not about to give Captain Rivera any more ammunition than he already has.

The guards halt the moment we step through a set of imposing steel doors. The morgue. I was here once before, when Captain Rivera wished to prove to me that he had indeed murdered a young woman in front of me. Her name was Isabela. She was fourteen years old. Her only crime was poverty.

Throughout her torture, the captain had looked directly at me. "Just do what I ask and I will stop," he had said as he ripped out her fingernails one by one.

But I refused.

Because I am no murderer.

The captain steps up to a steel gurney where a body lay beneath a white sheet. "Look," he instructs, and he sweeps back the sheet to reveal the young woman underneath.

As soon as I see her face, I recognize her. Corina Castañeda. Captain Rivera's faithful fifteen-year-old telepath. The same person who helped capture me in Chajul. She has been shot once through the middle of her forehead. The small, circular wound is no bigger than a five-centavos quetzal coin. Apparently, someone else had a problem with the way Corina chose to use her talent.

May God bless her immortal soul.

"Estuardo Ramirez had her assassinated. Do you know who he is?" the captain asks me.

I shake my head.

"He's a Salvadorian drug czar who's been trafficking his goods through my territory. I won't be happy until he's either dead or rotting in one of my cells." And indeed, Captain Rivera does not look happy as he meets my gaze with his dark, penetrating eyes. "I need a new telepathic interrogator, and the only option I have right now is you."

My mouth falls open in stunned disbelief. After everything he has put me through—all of the suffering he has made me witness—he still believes that he can force me to use my powers to hurt and probably kill people.

"I—I won't do it," I say, my voice hoarse from thirst.

The captain's eyes harden. "We'll see about that."

He signals the guards, turns on his heel, and walks briskly out the door. I am again half-carried after him, my arms aching from the guards' grip.

We pass down a long, sterile corridor, and then I am whisked past yet another security checkpoint. Cutting to the right, I gasp when I recognize the interrogation block.

Oh, no, no, no, no, no...not this place! Please, God, no! I begin to silently recite the Prayer to St. Michael, when I am brutally shoved through an open doorway and thrown to the concrete floor.

A floor with a large drain in the middle of it—because a drain makes cleaning up all the blood after a grueling interrogation session that much easier.

I really do not want to be here. I don't think I can handle another interrogation session like Isabela's.

O my gracious and loving Father, I am but a simple young man, your humble servant. Please, do not ask this of me.

Captain Rivera stands before me, scowling. "I'll make this simple, Miguel." He points to a still form lying on the floor, not more than ten paces away. It is a woman with graying black hair, probably in her mid-fifties, wearing a tattered red skirt and a long-sleeved blouse. "That woman's a nun from America," he continues. "And she's been smuggling psions—*my psions*—across the border." He points a thick finger at me. "I need you to get me the names of her compatriots. Do it now, or I'll cut her to pieces before your very eyes."

I know that he means every word of what he says. He means to break me, no matter how many innocent people die in the process. But I'm not trained in my psionic discipline. I accidentally killed over a half-dozen armed guards the day the general shot my mother in the head. I don't want to hurt anyone else ever again—especially a nun.

But I don't want her tortured to death because of me, either.

It's an impossible choice.

My own death would be preferable.

"Well, go on!" the captain shouts. "Read her mind! I want those names!"

Rather than retreat into prayer, I somehow manage to rise to my feet and stagger over to the nun. I collapse beside her and look her over. It's only after I struggle to my knees that I notice the rise and fall of her chest. She's still breathing. Her hands cling to a small, worn Bible; a rosary is wound around her wrist.

"Um, Sister?" I say softly.

"Quit talking!" Captain Rivera shouts. "Just read her damn mind!"

The problem with that is, I'm not quite sure how to actually *read* minds. Sure, I can hide in plain sight from baselines, but that's not the same thing as actually trying to mentally reach out to someone's inner being. Just the thought that I might actually harm a nun by touching her mind makes me want to vomit...but then something occurs to me. I am wearing a disruptor band on my right wrist. It will have to be removed in order for me to access my psionic powers.

I turn to the captain. "Sir," I say holding up my banded wrist. "You'll have to remove this before I can begin."

The captain's scowl deepens as he gestures to one of his men. "Get it off him."

The guard doesn't hesitate. He approaches with a plastic key card and presses it to my disruptor band. The red light stops glowing as the metal band pops open. The guard pulls it roughly from my wrist and hurries back to his place by the door.

"Okay," says Captain Rivera. "Now get me those names."

"Forgive me, Sister," I say softly, before closing my eyes in an attempt to buy myself more time. I try to appear as if I am doing something psionic by contorting my face through a series of determined grimaces. When I hear the guards stir, I tentatively reach out my fingertips and place them on the woman's forehead, but I have no idea what I'm doing. It's useless.

I will not be forced to harm an innocent soul with my powers. I know I will kill this woman if I use my telepathy, just as surely as I know how to breathe.

My hand drops from the woman's flesh and I sit back on my heels and pray.

"Hail Mary, full of grace, the Lord is with thee."

"You little runt!" The captain bellows as I bow my head over my clasped hands. He marches over to me. "I ought to blow your head off for such insubordination!"

"Blessed art thou among women and blessed is the fruit of your womb, Jesus."

"Look at me! Look at me, you little worm!"

I do as he asks. And in that instant, I know I am not afraid to die. In fact, I would gladly embrace death if it was offered. *"Holy Mary, Mother of God, pray for us sinners now and at the hour of our death. Amen."*

Relief floods my soul the moment I find myself staring into the barrel of the captain's gun, and an unbidden grin erupts on my face.

"Forgive me, Father," I say just before the deafening blast.

"Ugh!" a girl's voice screams at me. "You are such an idiot! How could you just sit there while that fat bastard shot you? Aw, come on! Open your eyes, Miguel; I'm talking to you!"

Tentatively, I open one eye and then another…and I'm crestfallen to find that I am in my cell, once again choking on the foul stench of my own bodily waste. "No," I gasp, my mind reeling. "I was dead."

"No, you weren't. I hijacked your mind," I hear the girl say. I squint into the shadows to see Corina Castañeda, Captain Rivera's telepath, staring hard at me from a chair in the corner of the room.

"I only made you believe that the guards had you dragged out of here for another round of torture on the orders of Captain Rivera." She taps her temple twice with her index finger. "Telepathy is a hell of a thing once you know what you're doing. Though I have to admit you didn't need much convincing. Your fear did most of the work."

"*You* did all that?" I ask, stunned to still be breathing. "But why?"

"Here." She tosses a bottle of water to me and I catch it.

"What's this?" I ask, unsure of her intentions.

"It's called water. I suggest you drink it and shut up." She sounds more irritated than angry with me.

There's no use arguing, so I open the bottle of water. I don't even pause to breathe as I chug the cool liquid down. Water has never tasted as refreshing as it does at this moment. It takes me less than a minute to drain the bottle.

"You may want to ease up there, choirboy," Corina says, rising from her chair. "You're going to make yourself sick." I watch as she picks up her chair and sets it right next to me.

"The water tastes good," I say with a smile. "Thank you."

"You're welcome." She removes a second bottle of water from her satchel and hands it to me. "Just go easy on this one, okay?"

"I will," I say as I twist off the cap and take a sip. It takes a bit of willpower not to suck it all down at once. But I do my best to respect Corina's wishes. "How were you able to hijack my mind?"

Corina points to my right wrist. "Your disruptor band. Without access to your telepathy, you're as helpless as a baseline."

"Fair enough," I say. "But why would Captain Rivera have you do that?"

Corina's eyes harden. "I no longer work for Captain Rivera."

"But I thought—"

"Don't think. Just listen," she says sharply, and I fall silent.

She stares off into the darkness for several long moments before she continues. "Do you know why you fry people's minds whenever you use your telepathy?"

I shake my head.

"Because you're insanely powerful," she says. "More powerful than me, anyway. And I just thought—that maybe I could train you to use your telepathy, but I had to see for myself what you'd actually do with your powers when pushed." Corina pauses to stare off into the darkness again. "I had no idea you'd actually embrace death over the chance of harming someone else."

"I am not a murderer," I say softly.

"Yes. I see that now." Corina offers me a tiny smile, but it's a sad smile, full of pain and regret. "That's why instead of recruiting you, or killing you outright…I'm sending you to America."

"America!" I cry. "I don't know anyone in America!"

"Yes, you do." Corina tosses a worn Bible and a rosary onto my lap. "The nun from America was real. Her name was Sister Mary Francis. She wasn't smuggling psions out of Guatemala; she was here at Father Gálvez's request to smuggle *you* out of Guatemala. So that you could get the proper training you needed."

I hardly know what to say as I pick up the Holy Bible and run my fingers across the worn leather binding. "Then Sister Mary Francis is dead?"

Corina nods solemnly. "I'm sorry, Miguel."

I can feel the tears stinging my eyes, but I do my best to blink them back. The one that gets away, I wipe off my cheek with the back of my hand. I am heartbroken over the news that Sister Mary Francis is dead, and miserable with the thought that I have indirectly caused the death of yet another human being. "Were—were you there when she died?"

"Yes," she says with downcast eyes. "The name and address of your American contact are hidden beneath the cover of the Sister's Bible. I'm sure, with your ability to hide in plain sight, you'll be able to cross the border without assistance."

"I can't hide from cameras," I say miserably.

"Then cross in El Paso. Hop a tour bus, stick with a crowd of Americans."

I take a long drink of water, my mind stumbling over what Corina has just shared with me. But no matter how exciting the prospect of heading to America is, I am deeply troubled by Corina's actions, and I find myself compelled to question her intentions. "You told me that you no longer work for Captain Rivera," I say quietly and deliberately. "Why?"

"The only reason I ever worked for that beast was because he held my mother and brother hostage in Mixco. Well, yesterday, my disruptor band was left off for a fraction of a second longer than it should have been, and I saw into the guard's mind. He had taken part in my family's brutal murder. Once I saw their deaths in his mind, I shut him down by putting him in a catatonic state. Then I shut them all down, Captain Rivera included."

"You didn't kill them?" I ask, knowing that I am pushing for information that I may not like the answer to.

A deadly smile unfolds across her face. "No, not yet. But soon. I wanted to come and see if I could enlist your aid first."

"Me?" I say, startled by the revelation. "Why me?"

"Because I naively thought that you might help me start a little war. But one look inside your head and I knew that would never happen, San Miguelito." She says that last bit with reverence, as if she believes there is something to my saintly moniker. But I am merely a humble servant of the Lord God, nothing more. Though I sense that Corina means well, the reference to Saint Michael embarrasses me, so I change the subject.

"You could come with me," I offer, but Corina shakes her head.

"My place is here. With my family."

"But you said they were dead."

"That's right." Corina picks up her satchel and searches for something inside.

"But you cannot fight a war on your own," I say in an effort to convince her to reconsider her plans.

"I won't be alone," she states matter-of-factly as she removes a plastic key card from her bag. She takes my hand and touches the key card to my disruptor band. "I'll have the angels on my side."

The disruptor band falls to the floor between us with a metallic *clank*.

Corina levels her gaze at me. "Now would be a good time to disappear, Miguel. Before I change my mind."

"Is there anything I can say that will persuade you to set aside your revenge?"

"There is nothing more to say, Miguel. My mind is made up."

"This is a war that you cannot hope to win."

"Perhaps not," she says gravely. "But it is what I must do."

Looking deep into her eyes, I catch a glimpse of the loss that torments her soul. And I realize that, no matter how much I beg her to reconsider, she will not listen. She is determined to see her little war through to its conclusion.

There is only one last thing for me to say.

"May God be with you, Corina."

She wearily smiles at me. "You too, kid. Now get the hell out of here."

I gather my power around me like a shroud, and the moment her eyes blindly sweep the floor for my presence, I know that I have vanished before her eyes.

"Oh, by the way," she says over her shoulder as she heads to the open cell door. "I left you some money tucked inside the pages of that Bible. Try not to spend it all in one place."

As she disappears down the hallway, I open the holy book and gasp when I remove dozens of banknotes in large denominations—Guatemalan quetzals, Mexican pesos and American dollars—from between the pages. It is more money than I have seen in my entire life.

After drinking the rest of the water, I set the Bible carefully on the chair. Then I wrap Sister Mary Francis's rosary securely around my wrist before attempting to stand. I pray for strength from Saint Alban as I rise unsteadily to my feet, using Corina's chair for support.

Once I am standing, I am amazed by how much better I feel. And I suddenly cannot wait to get out of this horrible place and into the sunshine. I pick up the Bible and take a tentative first step toward the open door. When I don't immediately fall on my face, I take another step and then another, until I am well on my way down the hallway and headed for the outside.

It's bound to be a long walk all the way to America, but I know that God will see me though this like He does all things.

In His own way.

In His own time.

Chapter Sixteen

DEVON was surprised by the gentle return to his senses. There had been no extreme cycloning or stomach-churning cartwheels at warp speed, no painful molecular stretching or brain-seizing brightness. All in all, it was a most benign return to his body, one that left him wondering if his previous heave-worthy excursions were Bai Lee's little way of reminding him who was in charge.

But that was only a theory, and Devon wasn't about to bring it up. Especially with his own unavoidable replay drawing near. No, he'd have to assume that Miguel's fear of hurting others with his telepathy had something to do with Devon's ease of mental transportation.

After all, there weren't many people out there who would choose death for oneself over harming another. In that regard, the Guatemalan telepath had earned Devon's fullest respect. He had experienced firsthand how comfortable Miguel had been with his decision not to use his telepathy to torture others. Miguel's faith had filled his spirit to such a degree that the fourteen-year-old had never once felt abandoned and alone.

Devon wished that he had Miguel's inner peace, but without his family Devon found that he couldn't help feeling adrift and hollow. After all, wasn't that why he helped Colton form his escape plans in the first place? Devon desperately wanted his family back.

"Miguel, are you okay?" Nevada asked as she stood and made her way to the wooden lounge. Vahn, too, was on his feet and headed over to check on the waking telepath.

"Yes, Nevada," Miguel said softly. "I am fine."

Nevada grinned. "Thank God!"

Miguel looked over at her, a tranquil smile gracing his face. "But of course," he said, his eyes bright with mischief. "We should always give thanks to the Lord God."

Nevada rolled her eyes. "That wasn't exactly what I meant, and you know it."

Miguel chuckled. "Yes, I know."

The tree branches slowly untwined themselves from around Miguel's body. As the delicate tendrils retreated, Nevada and Vahn reached out to Miguel and helped him scoot to the edge of the wooden lounge and sit up.

Devon thought Miguel looked whipped as the young man set his feet on the ground. The Guatemalan telepath paused then and simply breathed, and Devon wondered how in the heck he had ever allowed Alya to partake in Bai Lee's little replay session. The process looked incredibly taxing.

"So, how long did it take you to get to America?" Alek asked.

"A little over two months," Miguel replied. "I stayed away from major cities, anywhere I felt another psion could detect me."

"So, how'd you end up captured by the feds?" Alek pressed. "Did Sister Mary Francis give you a bogus address, or what?"

Miguel shook his head. "It wasn't like that. I entered the US through Texas on an American tour bus. When I reached the safehouse, I was warmly greeted and made very comfortable. I lived there for two weeks before the feds raided the house and led me away in chains. It was just my bad luck to end up here."

Alek snorted in disbelief. "Yeah, sure it was."

"What's your problem?" Bai Lee asked Alek, narrowing her eyes. "You don't trust Holy Boy's word?"

"It's got nothing to do with trust," he replied, returning Bai Lee's critical gaze. "I just think that Miguel's perspective is a little naïve."

"Naïve?" echoed Miguel. "What do you—"

"You were set up!" Alek said explosively. "There! I said it! We were probably all set up!"

"What the heck are you talking about?" Devon asked, surprised by Alek's accusation.

"I'm talking about this whole Psionic Underground Network thing. What if it's not real? What if the government is just messing with us—you know, baiting us with ideas of freedom only to squash us one by one the moment we come scurrying out of our cells to find it?" Alek looked over at Devon. "Do you get what I'm saying? What if the Network is fake? What if it's all been one big flipping lie? And we're the patsies who fell for it."

The thought of the underground movement being a government front to round up fugitive psions sent Devon reeling like a kick to the groin. The Psionic Underground Network *had* to be real! Colton Weaver had staked his life on it—and so had Devon! How could it all be a government fabrication? That was impossible...wasn't it?

Too many good people had died during Devon's escape. And he wasn't about to believe something Alek proposed without a fight.

"You're lying," Devon said, and he was surprised by how menacing he sounded.

"Am I?" Alek crossed his arms, looking defiant. "Then by all means, prove me a liar. What is it you know that none of us here have seen for ourselves?"

"Too many of my classmates died breaking out of the North Central Psi Facility," Devon snarled.

"So?"

"*So?*" Devon echoed. "Colton Weaver was our leader, and my friend. He was receiving coded messages via snail mail from *somewhere*. He was too clever—too careful to have been killed over a government sting operation."

"Are you stupid?" Alek barked. "That doesn't prove anything!"

"Sure it does," Devon said, with a shrug. He desperately wanted to punch Alek in the face for calling him stupid. "A bunch of guards died that night, too. If the government had evidence against us—if they had indeed set us up—why not just arrest us while we slept in our rooms? Why risk the lives of so many baseline guards? Why risk *anyone's* life unnecessarily?"

Alek's gaze hardened as a sinister smile unfolded across his face. "Because they don't give a crap about any of us, that's why. It's all about power for them, and we psions have upset the natural balance of things."

"Aleksei," said Alya in a soft, chastising tone. "Please… don't do this."

"Don't do what, dear sister? What am I doing that is so very upsetting to you? I am merely pointing out to our friends a very likely reality."

"More like an *improbable* reality," said Devon, siding with Alya. "I saw a lot of the correspondences myself—I even helped decode a message once. The system was way too sophisticated to have all been a lie."

Alek scoffed. "Says you."

"Yeah, says me." The veins in Devon's temples throbbed as his blood pressure skyrocketed in rage. What the hell did Alek know about Colton Weaver or any of the psions who'd died back at North Central?

Alek's grin grew wider, softening his glare. "Well, then, my friend, why don't you just *show* us?" He paused then, tilting his head in interest. "Perhaps seeing things through your eyes will help me better understand a psi-cannon like yourself."

Devon froze. Alek had just called him out. Oh, crap! "Well…er, I—"

"Come on, Devon," Nevada said with an encouraging smile. "It's not that bad."

Oh, yes, it was! At least, for Devon McWilliams the *liar*, it was. But aloud he heard himself say, "Yeah, well…you see—"

"Nevada's right," Bai Lee chimed in from her perch at the foot of the wooden lounge. "Let's just get this over with, Devon. I have an escape to coordinate."

Head spinning, palms clammy with anxiety, Devon sat stupefied on the ground. He was having an out-of-body experience. His brain had shifted into high gear without any traction. Thoughts whirled inside his head as his chest swelled with apprehension. It was becoming harder to breathe, and Devon thought he just might pass out.

"Devon," Alya said urgently, her starburst eyes gazing up at him. "Look at me."

Her words took a moment to register, but Devon was able to pull himself out of his stupor just enough to focus on her face.

"That's right," she continued with a smile. "Now, Devon, I need you to take a deep breath for me."

Devon did as Alya instructed and drew in a cleansing breath through his nose.

"Now hold it—"

Devon held it.

"And…out again," she said, her eyes brimming with fears that her smile could not quite mask. "Feel any better?"

Devon nodded, anxiety shredding his insides. He didn't trust himself to speak right now.

"Can you stand?" Alya asked, pulling away from him.

Unwrapping his arms from around Alya's thin frame, Devon barely nodded while he joylessly rose to his feet. He hardly felt alive as he put one foot in front of the other, but he paused when he heard Alya call his name.

She flashed him a reassuring smile. "It's going to be all right."

He tried to return her smile, but it was impossible. Instead, he concentrated on moving his feet while he made his way over to the wooden lounge—that dreaded, brain-sucking wooden lounge.

Vahn walked over to him as Devon approached the position vacated by Miguel. "Hey, are you okay?" he asked.

Bobbing his head like a spastic rooster, Devon worked hard to keep it together, but he knew he was failing miserably. When he tripped over his own feet, Vahn managed to grab him before Devon crashed headlong into the wooden lounge.

"Th-thanks," he muttered.

"Don't worry about it," the big guy said. "It'll be over before you know it."

"Yeah—yeah," Devon replied vaguely. *Over* being the operative word. Soon, it would *all be over* for Devon McWilliams.

Glancing to his right, Devon saw that Bai Lee was studying him with an amused expression on her face. Was she—was she actually laughing at him? The look alone pissed him off enough to snap him out of his stupor.

"What's your problem?" he growled at her. And he was immensely satisfied when he saw the smile melt right off her face.

"I don't have a problem," she shot back with a scowl. "You're the one acting all jittery and freaked out." Her scowl deepened. "Not very psi-cannon-esque behavior, if you ask me."

"Yeah, well—no one asked you," Devon replied heatedly, his frustration overriding his common sense. Ninja Girl was the last person he should be picking a fight with. "And besides, I really don't care what you think."

"Is that so?" Bai Lee crossed her arms. "Then maybe I should just leave you here to rot in federal custody. I definitely don't need another psi-cannon to bust—"

"I'm not a psi-cannon!" Devon blurted, and he was surprised by the sudden lightness he felt within his chest. It was as if someone had punctured a hole in his ribcage and all of that horrible stress had instantly drained away.

"I *knew it*!" Nevada cried, jumping to her feet. "I just knew it! You're an elemental psion, aren't you?"

Devon leaned against the wooden lounge, not quite ready to actually sit on it yet, and dropped his gaze to the ground. "Well…kinda," he said softly. He didn't want to tell them the truth, because he was terrified of the laughter that was sure to follow.

"Are you a waterwielder?" Nevada guessed, looking perplexed. "No, that's not right… maybe a flamemaster?"

"I talk to plants…" Devon muttered.

"What?" Nevada said. "I'm deaf in that ear, remember?"

"I TALK TO PLANTS," Devon shouted, his head snapping up to look Nevada in the eyes. "I'm a total loser, okay? I get it! The useless Plant Boy. That's what everyone calls me."

Nevada stood patiently before him, studying him with wide, sympathetic eyes. "But Devon…you're not useless."

Devon scoffed. "Yes, I am. Even the scientists at North Central laughed at me. The guards laughed at me. Heck, *everyone* laughed at me!" Devon stopped himself then. He knew that what he said was a lie. And right now, he was sick of lying. "Actually, that's not entirely true. My family doesn't laugh at me… Colton Weaver never once laughed at me."

Devon's eyes teared up, and his voice caught in his throat at the thought of his friend. But he wasn't about to cry, not here, not now. He furiously wiped his eyes with the back of his sleeve as he sat heavily on the wooden lounge. He couldn't look at any of them right now; he was ashamed of his lies as much as he was of his truths. And that only served to make him even more angry and disgusted with himself.

"Devon," Nevada said sweetly as she placed her hand lightly on his shoulder. "No one here is going to laugh at you."

Devon miserably shook his head. "Well, they should."

"That is *not* going to happen." The clipped response had come from Bai Lee. "I knew you were hiding something from me, Devon McWilliams, but I never would have guessed in a million years that it all boiled down to a supreme lack of faith in yourself." She frowned then and shook her head. "You of all people."

"What the heck is that supposed to mean?" Devon asked indignantly.

"She means," said Alya, "that you have been the one to guide us here." Devon turned to Alya and saw that she was being supported between Vahn and Miguel as they guided her toward the wooden lounge. Even Alek had risen to his feet and joined them.

Devon went from face to face, searching for an answer as to what in the heck the girls were talking about. "I still don't—"

"You're a natural leader, Devon," explained Vahn. "You challenged every one of us to get over ourselves at the appropriate time."

Nevada nodded in agreement. "You encouraged us to work together, even when we didn't want to."

"You made sure to include everyone," said Miguel with a smile. "Even though not everyone here speaks English." His grin broadened then, and he laughed. "And by that, I mean only myself."

Devon felt his cheeks growing hot with embarrassment. Clearly, none of them had seen him for what he truly was.

"Yeah, well, it wasn't like I did any of it on purpose or anything."

"That's what I figured," said Alek. "You've been nothing but a whiny pain in the ass from the moment the feds locked you down on our transport—but I have to say, you've got balls, kid. I'll give you that. I, for one, never once took you for a plant geek."

It wasn't exactly a compliment, but it wasn't a punch in the face, either. So, Devon gave him a slight nod and a shrug. He'd never been called a plant geek before, and for some reason it didn't feel like an insult.

"I think he's called a tree shepherd," said Nevada. "Or plant enchanter, depending on how powerful a psion he is."

Devon did a double take. "You mean—you mean, there are more out there like me?"

Nevada laughed. "Are you kidding? You seriously haven't heard about that kid out in the Amazon rainforest somewhere—"

"Brazil," Bai Lee said dryly.

Nevada nodded at Bai Lee. "Yeah, right. Well, anyway, this kid caused an entire jungle full of ancient trees to rise up and literally shred this tree-cutting crew's encampment. People died. All of the machines were dragged into the ground by massive tree roots." Nevada flashed Devon a grin. "There's not much logging going on in the Amazon rainforest right now, I can tell you that much."

"You mean, that kid was like me?" asked Devon. He could hardly believe it.

"Why do you think you're the only one?" Bai Lee asked, looking him over critically.

Devon ran his fingers through his hair, unsure of how he should answer. "Actually, I guess—well, I guess I just couldn't imagine that anybody else out there would be stuck with the same lame powers as me."

"But Devon," said Alya, stepping closer to him, "don't you see? Your powers aren't lame."

"Perhaps not…but I am." Devon could hardly believe he had uttered those words, but they were the truth. So, he wasn't too surprised when he saw the sympathy in Alya's gaze.

"That's not how I see you," she said softly.

Anger swelled within Devon's chest, and he averted his eyes. He couldn't look at her any longer. He'd always known that he wasn't good enough for her, especially now that his plant-talking ability was out of the bag. He'd never wanted Alya's pity, and he simply couldn't stand himself for having to disappoint her. "Yeah, well, once you see what happened—how inept I was—you'll think differently about me," he said miserably.

Devon didn't wait for a reply as he scooted back onto the wooden lounge. The sooner he showed them his botched escape, the sooner they would understand what a complete and total loser they were dealing with. And he was confident they'd leave him behind once they experienced how utterly useless he had been when everything hit the fan.

Talking to plants did little when it came to deflecting bullets…or being able to save his only friend's life.

It was a regret he would harbor until the day he died.

Devon kept his eyes averted from the crowd as he laid his head on the leafy pillow. He stared up into the willow's massive canopy overhead, clinging to his anger, while the branches closest to him stretched and curled around his body. For an instant, he missed hearing the deep baritone of a *real* tree, its voice as strong and wise as the earth that nourished it.

And somewhere amidst that longing, he missed something else—his friend.

"I know you don't think much of psi-cannons, Nevada," Devon said while keeping his eyes fixed on the leafy canopy above. "But I think Colton Weaver was an exceptional one. He may have been stuck with me as a roommate, but he never complained. Not once." He paused to lick his lips and took one last deep breath. "I'm ready now, Bai Lee."

Devon's Story

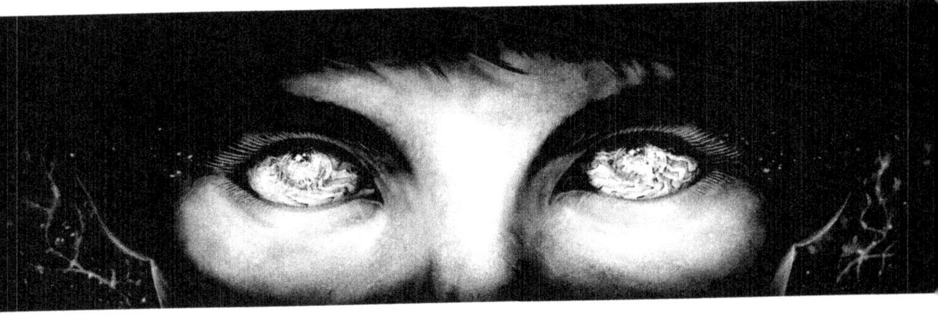

Chapter Seventeen

NEVER in my life have I had to deal with such plant drama! And now I'm probably going to be late to the rendezvous. I guess that's what I get for telling a bunch of self-centered house plants that I was escaping tonight.

The creeping charlies actually withheld the access code from me!

They were too upset, they said.

I was abandoning them, they said.

I glance at my watch and realize that I spent forty-five minutes in Headmistress Reeves's apartment helping her flora feel good about themselves before I was able to coax the access code out of the charlies.

I still can't believe I told them I was leaving. I mean, who does that?

Only a sap like me, that's who.

I pull the straps on my backpack tight as I step out of the headmistress' apartment. She's away for the weekend, which is why I'm able to be here so late. Over the last six months, I've had quite the all-access hall pass because she loves what I've done with her plants. If she had any idea that her creeping charlies had been giving me the facility's daily security codes, she'd have me sent to a Washington boot camp in a heartbeat.

Which would definitely not be a good thing.

And if people in general only knew how observant and *critical* their flora can be, they'd probably refrain from treating them like, well—stupid plants. They'd certainly take them out of their bathrooms and bedrooms, that's for sure.

I glance in both directions before taking off at a brisk walk down the sterile corridor. It's always dead silent in the administrators' hallway at this time of night, so I'm painfully aware of every slap and squeak my sneakers make as I hurry across the polished tiles toward the east wing parking structure's stairwell. My heart flutters with excitement in the back of my throat like an over-caffeinated hummingbird, so I clench my jaw in an effort to appear outwardly calm.

Okay, so I'm a little nervous. After all, I've never escaped from a high-security facility before. I just have to keep my head low and follow Colton's instructions. It's really quite simple, actually. Each of the six of us takes a different route to that stairwell without drawing attention to ourselves, and from there we make a break for it.

Lucky me, I get to cross the entire length of the administrators' floor, the route dotted with the most roving disruptor bots and patrolling hovercams in the entire facility.

Personally, I'd rather wade through a leech-infested swamp than take this route right now, but beggars can't be choosers—and I am most definitely the beggar of this crew.

After all, Braxton Miller has wanted me out since day one. Only Colton's insistence that I be included, and the fact that I have access to the daily security code, have kept me a part of this team. I just hope they're not too pissed off if they have to wait for me more than a couple of minutes in that damp, roach-infested stairwell. Though I'm pretty sure Braxton will make it a priority to slug me just for the hell of it the moment Colton's back is turned.

Keeping my eyes lowered, I walk as quickly as I can down the corridor. I can feel the textbooks bouncing around in my backpack as I move. Colton's supposed to bring my survival pack and my winter coat to the rendezvous point. He has to because there's no way that I would look anything *but* conspicuous wearing a bright-red down jacket through these corridors.

I keep walking, even though I hear the hum of a roving disruptor bot approaching. When I glance up, I can see the shiny metallic orb turning toward me a few meters ahead. They're about the size of egg cartons, and their entire purpose is to scan any living creature that crosses their path. The bots are looking for psions who have dismantled or taken off their disruptor bands. Me? Well, I'm so low on the psionic food chain that I don't qualify to wear a disruptor band, period.

Long story short—my powers are just too lame to be considered a security risk.

Which is probably another reason why Braxton Miller enjoys smacking the crap out of me every chance he gets. If I'm not careful, when we get out of here, he's going to toss me off a butte somewhere in the Badlands when Colton's not looking.

Eyes averted, I keep moving as the disruptor bot scans me. I can see the cherry-red light bouncing all around me, reflecting off the walls, but I know better than to stop. If I appear to be going somewhere with purpose, then chances are the bot won't hold me up once it matches my profile with the headmistress's approved hall-pass list.

At least, that's my hope.

I exhale as soon as I hear the disruptor bot chirp twice in approval and move on. As soon as I round a bend in the hallway, I pick up my pace just to be safe. Apparently, the bot didn't seem to notice that I was heading for the back stairwell and not the main lift station, which would take me back to my room on the tenth floor, so I had better be extra-cautious.

Like I always say, I wield the wimpiest of psionic disciplines. There's not much I can do without a plant around, and even then, talking to flora and fauna is about as exciting as watching the psychotic grass grow. Well, the grass family usually puts *me* on the brink of a psychotic break anyway, what with all of their constant screaming.

My family had to find out the hard way that too much of that kind of thing can make a summer picnic a downright certifiable event.

Glancing behind me, I check to make sure that the disruptor bot hasn't circled back before I open the stairwell door. Once inside, I quietly close the door behind me. Fluorescent lights flicker and hum, and the air smells of mildew and rotten garbage. It's dim, but I can see well enough as I take the stairs two at a time, launching myself down the steps flight by flight. I'm on the fifteenth floor, so I have quite a bit of ground to cover before I'll reach the garage level.

I hurry as fast as my legs will take me, only slowing when I find that the fluorescent lights on the eighth and seventh floors have burned out. I feel my way down two flights of stairs in near-darkness, then pick up the pace once I can see again on the sixth floor.

Breathing hard, I arrive on the first floor to the soft murmur of voices below and I know that I've made it. They haven't left without me!

My heart starts pounding as I barrel onward, but I stop cold when I find Braxton Miller glaring up at me from the bottom of the last flight of stairs.

"About time you showed up, runt." Braxton crosses his beefy arms, using his ample girth to block my way. "We've been waiting forever down here."

"No, we haven't," Colton says as he steps up with his own six-foot-plus athletic build, forcing Braxton to move over. "We just got here ourselves."

Despite Braxton's indignant glare, I watch Colton smoothly move the big guy aside further so that I can pass unhindered. It's times like this I find myself feeling a little bit envious of my cool-as-hell roommate. For one thing, Colton's a psi-cannon—which means he's a girl magnet. Secondly, he's probably one of the best-looking kids at the facility with his straight white teeth, flawless brown skin, and piercing starburst eyes, which again means that he has no trouble at all with the ladies. But third, and most importantly, he's simply a nice guy.

I mean, honestly, the guy's practically a saint when it comes to being kind to psions with marginal powers like mine. Well, actually, it's really *only* me, because the rest of the psions at North Central are all pretty kick-ass.

Sad but true.

Colton flashes me one of his running-for-homecoming-king-vote-for-me grins. "Come on, man, let's go. We have to keep moving."

I nod and hurry past Braxton, but I can still feel his intense glare following me. And I know that guy's just aching to get a punch in whenever he can.

I follow Colton to the keycode pad, which is located in the wall right next to a heavy steel door. "Okay, buddy," he says. "You're on."

"Right—oh, did you remember my pack?" I ask, as soon as I realize how outrageously cold it is down here.

Colton nods, pointing behind him. "You should know by now that I always got your back, Devon."

I glance at my overstuffed pack sitting against the wall and shrug. "I know you do, Colt. It's just been one of those days, is all."

"Tell us about it," Quincy chimes in. "I had a hell of a time getting our disruptor bands off." Quincy's a telekinetic like Braxton, which means they can move stuff with their minds. Unlike Braxton, Quincy's the same height as me, around five-foot-ten. We're considered the short guys of the crew.

Braxton scoffs from the stairs behind me. "Not like removing our bands did us any good—we're still unable to access our powers."

"That's because this keypad's emitting dozens of disruptor frequencies," I reply, and inside I'm rather pleased to see all of them gape at me in surprise. Guess Plant Boy's in the know about something after all.

Colton shakes his head, flashing me that grin of his. "Then let's shut this baby down."

"You got it," I say, my fingers hovering over the keypad. "You guys ready?"

When I see Quincy and Braxton strapping on their packs along with the other two guys in our group—Hector, a telepath, and Reece, a waterwielder—I punch in the code. As soon as I hit the last number, there is a loud *click* and the stairwell door pops open with a hiss.

"Let's go!" Colton cries as he shoulders his pack and races out the door. Quincy, Hector, and Reece are right on his heels.

I hurry over to my pack, but just as I'm about to grab it, I realize my mistake—I turned my back to Braxton Miller.

Braxton is on me in an instant. His beefy fist rams into my gut as soon as I turn to face him. The blow knocks the wind out of me and I double over as I crumple to the cold, hard floor.

Damn, that hurt!

"If you know what's good for you," he growls in my ear, "you'll sit this one out, Plant Boy."

Still reeling from the blow, I manage to draw air into my lungs, but little else. I'm doubled over in nauseating pain, my vision swimming, just barely holding myself off the ground with one arm. I'm about to call out to Colton for help, when I hear the *click* of the door locking closed.

"No!" I try to scream, but it comes out more like a wheeze.

Braxton has just completely screwed me over! *What the hell?!*

But there's no time to dwell on his motivation for leaving me behind, because if I don't get my ass up off this floor in a hurry, then I'll certainly never see my family again!

Fury alone gives me the strength to override my agony as I stagger to my feet. I throw myself at the metal door, but it won't budge. *Damn it!*

The moment I step over to the keypad, I hear the crackle of automatic gunfire from somewhere inside the parking garage. My heart leaps into my throat in panic just as the facility alarms go off.

From the stairwell above, I hear a door bang open and the sound of booted feet racing down the stairs. There's hardly time for me to duck behind a trio of empty steel drums beneath the staircase before an entire squad of armed guards, dressed in full riot armor, files into the room.

The squad leader steps up to the keypad and enters a series of numbers. The alarm in the room silences, but I can still hear others going off out in the parking garage and on the floors above me.

The squad leader turns to address his men. "You know the drill; take them alive if you can. But don't shoot the Miller kid; he's our mole."

My jaw falls open. How the heck did we miss that? Braxton Miller has been informing on us the whole time? I'm dead…I'm definitely dead.

"Hey, Captain," says a man by the door. "One of them left their pack."

"Take it upstairs to Lieutenant Baker. There may be something in there we can use to identify their Network contact."

"You got it," the guard replies as he bounds up the stairs with my pack slung over his shoulder.

Damn it! There goes my coat! Now what the flip am I supposed to do?

The captain enters a series of numbers on the keypad and the heavy door clicks open with a hiss, allowing the sound of gunfire and explosions to penetrate the room. It sounds like a war zone out there, and I'm terrified for Colton and the rest of the crew.

"Move out!" the captain yells. I watch in horror from beneath the metal staircase as the armed guards raise their weapons and, one after another, enter the fray.

There is a war being fought in the next room. I can clearly hear the patter of automatic gunfire followed by the sizzle and boom of an exploding psi-cannon burst. I cover my mouth and nose to keep from choking on the heavy black smoke that fills the stairwell through the open doorway, and I wait for my opportunity to move. If I'm going to do something to help my friends, I'm going to have to come up with a plan soon.

The squad leader is the last one to step up to the doorway, his gun poised at the ready. As he races into battle, he yanks the door shut behind him, and that's when I spring into action. Once the heavy steel door starts to fall closed, I launch myself at the doorway.

Somehow, I manage to wedge my foot inside the door frame just in time to stop the door from locking shut. Grabbing the door's edge, I cautiously peer into the parking structure.

Cars are on fire, huge piles of rubble litter the garage, and acrid smoke blankets everything amidst bursts of gunfire that echo through the massive concrete building. It's complete hell in there as the guards yell instructions to one another in an attempt to close in on the teenage escapees.

"He's behind that concrete pylon!" I hear Braxton Miller shout, and I'm surprised by how close he sounds.

I open the door wider and glance to my left. Low and behold, there is Braxton, looking every inch the evil son of a bitch that he is. He gestures at a billowing cloud of smoke several meters away in an effort to communicate with the three guards standing around him. "Just point your guns that way! He's over there!"

The guards aim their weapons at the smoke, and even I'm wondering why they're hesitating to shoot. It's then that I hear the sizzle of gathering psionic energy and I turn in time to see the neon blue glow of a psi-cannon shell streaking at them from the smoky darkness.

"Incoming!" Braxton screams, diving behind a concrete barrier. But the guards around him aren't as fortunate.

Colton's energy blast hits the ground in front of the three baselines and blows them off their feet. The men sail in all directions, and I'm forced to turn away as debris flies past me. When I look back at the scene, gunfire erupts from all directions. I cover my ears and watch helplessly as the guards empty their magazine clips, one after another, into the smoky darkness. After what seems like a heart-pounding, gut-wrenching eternity, the captain orders his men to stop shooting.

The silence that follows is weighted with anticipation. My entire body reverberates from the gunfire. I'm trembling, my eyes a watery mess from the dust in the air. As I slowly lower my hands from the sides of my head, the smoke clears long enough for me to see Colton stumble out from behind a pockmarked pylon.

I'm about to call out to him when I notice the confusion on his face—and the blood blossoming across the front of his white parka like an American Beauty rose coming into full bloom. Our eyes lock for an instant, and then, with the crack of a gunshot, a bullet catches Colton in the head and he flops backward onto the ground.

"NO!" The scream rips from my throat as I race full bore into the battle zone. I have no idea what I'm doing, but it only takes me a few strides to stumble headlong over a pile of rubble. I go down hard, the large chunks of concrete ripping the knees of my jeans. I'm about to scramble back to my feet when I realize that I am kneeling next to Quincy's lifeless body half-buried beneath a pile of rubble.

My mind spins as I struggle to come to terms with what I'm actually looking at. Quincy can't be dead! Colton can't be dead!

"They're all dead," Braxton says as he casually slaps the dust from the front of his parka. "So don't get any ideas, runt."

"Like what?" I growl, rising to my feet. "Punching your face in?"

Braxton chuckles. "Yeah, right." But the moment his eyes narrow, I know I'm in trouble. I sense more than I actually see the piece of rubble that he raises with his mind and flings at me. Instinctively, I hold up my arms for protection and turn my face away as the concrete block slams into me with a sickening *crack*. I crash to the floor, unable to breathe, but nothing consumes me more than the white-hot pain that emanates from my forearm and twists my guts, shattering my senses.

It's as if the entire world is upended. I can't see straight, my insides lurch with nausea, and it feels as if everything around me is violently shaking.

I open my eyes. And that's when I realize that everything around me *is* violently shaking!

The earthquake is seismically off the charts, and I watch in terror as the guards dodge falling debris while the very floor beneath their feet cracks and separates. Every car alarm in the place is screeching, and it's a cacophony of screams, sirens, and explosions amidst the chaos that surrounds me.

Cradling my arm, I look over to see how in the hell Braxton is doing this—when the roof above him gives way, sending a black SUV crashing down on top of him. In the blink of an eye, Braxton Miller vanishes beneath a pile of twisted steel and concrete. The SUV's horn angrily blares.

I gape in horror as the parking structure falls down around me. I have no idea what to do or where to go, and I'm about to totally lose it when some sort of survival instinct kicks in and I have an unmistakable urge to get the hell out of there. Ignoring the pain radiating from my forearm, I force myself to rise and stumble headlong toward the garage wall.

My heart's pounding by the time I reach the wall, but I manage to stay on my feet despite the earth buckling beneath me. I hurry as much as I can while the parking structure continues to send cars raining down on the ground floor through the rapidly vanishing ceiling.

Then, at last, I see it. The end of the garage! I can see the glow of the visitors' parking lot right outside, over a low wall that spans that side of the garage, allowing the chilly night breeze to flow through the building. I hardly notice the cold, the noise, or the pain once I step up to the wall and find myself literally shaken out of the building.

Without even the wherewithal to scream, I tumble out of the parking garage and into the tangled embrace of a row of golden potentilla.

We'll hold you…save you…help you!

It's a rush of voices in my head as the little plants struggle to hold me aloft. I can feel them bending the tips of their sharp branches in an effort to be as gentle with me as possible. Though I appreciate the gesture, I know that to linger, even in the presence of such well-meaning foliage, will mean my capture and quite possibly my death.

"Thank you—thank you all," I say, gritting my teeth in an effort to mask the all-out fear that consumes me. "But really, I gotta go."

Yes! Yes! Run! Run! the shrubs shout in unison. And then, with a mighty heave, the plants drop me to the ground on my feet.

My heart hammers so hard inside my chest that I can't tell if the earth has stopped moving or not as I stumble into the night. Amidst the cacophony of destruction behind me, I force myself to keep running, because there is no turning back for me. Many people have died tonight, and though I wasn't directly responsible for their deaths, I was a willing participant, and because of that, I alone will be blamed.

Me. The sole survivor.

There is a long, low rumble that builds behind me. With a sound somewhat akin to a thunderclap, the parking garage collapses, and I am knocked to the ground by the shock wave.

But it is utter terror that drives me now, and I am back on my feet and racing across the dusty badlands well before I hear the rescue sirens approaching in the distance.

I settle into the rhythm of my homework bouncing in my backpack as I hurry across the vast expanse of open land. There is a clear night sky above me with a host of glittering stars to keep me company on the long journey ahead.

I just pray that I will be able to remember all of Colton's instructions.

After all, he should be the one out here, not me.

He was our leader, the straight-A student, the nice guy—the one who mattered.

And who am I?

Just some kid who talks to plants.

I am probably going to die out here.

With that thought in mind, I quicken my pace.

Maybe, just maybe, I can find a safe place to rest before daybreak.

Chapter Eighteen

It was a struggle for Devon to rise to consciousness. He felt like he was mentally swimming through endless miles of gelatin. Somehow, he managed to will himself through the syrupy void until he broke the surface to a more perceptive state of mind.

At last, he was able to draw in a deep breath and release it. He could feel his heart pounding with the intensity of a tribal war drum, just the way it had the very night he'd fled in terror from the North Central Psi Facility.

The night he had fled from death like the ultimate coward he was.

With a pang of dread that resonated deep within his chest, Devon opened his eyes to the view of the willow's protective canopy overhead and the realization that he had just revealed his innermost demons to his peers.

And the one thing he feared more than anything was seeing the antipathy in their eyes.

Especially Alya's eyes.

Devon very much wanted to shrivel up and disappear.

"Devon?"

It was Alya's voice. He squeezed his eyes closed, unable to face her. Torture would be preferable to the shame that filled him.

"Devon, please. Look at me."

Alya's face was close to his. He could feel her warm breath against his cheek. Her soft, sweet voice eased the ache in his heart, but he would not open his eyes. He wanted only to remember her the way she used to look at him, with respect and a tiny bit of, *dare he say it?*...affection. To see himself diminished in her eyes would be unbearable.

"Devon," she said, her fingers lightly stroking the side of his face. "There's nothing to fear. You did everything you could for them."

"I did nothing for them," Devon groaned. "My powers were useless."

Alya continued to stroke his cheek. "You did everything you could to try and save them." And to Devon's consternation, her gentle touch and soothing voice began to melt his resolve.

"But it wasn't enough," he whispered through clenched teeth.

"No, it wasn't. But you were one against many. They intended for all of you to die." Alya leaned closer, until her lips brushed softly against the side of Devon's ear. "I am so thankful that you made it out alive."

Her words carried a sincerity that could not be faked, and Devon opened his eyes, ready to meet the reflection he hoped to find there.

He wasn't disappointed.

Her starburst eyes gazed lovingly down at him, devoid of the pity or rejection he feared he might find. Alya gave him a warm smile, her eyes brimming with tears. "I'm so sorry you lost your friends. What happened to you was horrible."

Devon reached up and wiped away a teardrop that had escaped from her eye. "No more so than anybody else here. I don't think any of us has had it easy."

"I wouldn't know," said Bai Lee, interrupting their private moment. The telepath was sitting less than two feet away, perched on the edge of the wooden lounge. "We have yet to hear from Alek."

Devon could feel his cheeks getting hot, as Bai Lee leveled her gaze at him. "Get off my couch, loverboy. It's Alek's turn."

Nodding like the embarrassed fool he was, Devon allowed Vahn and Miguel to help him off of the wooden lounge and onto his feet. He was stunned by how exhausted he felt. His rubbery legs gave out as soon as he stood, but Vahn and Miguel caught him and helped him get situated on the grass.

Nevada guided Alya to a spot beside Devon, and he was astonished by how quickly Alya reached for his hand. She looked radiant as she grinned at him, a grin so bright, in fact, that Devon felt himself blush all over again.

"Uh, thanks, guys," Devon said as Vahn and Miguel made ready to sit down themselves.

"No problem," Vahn replied. "But I've got to say that I'm going to be a lot happier once we're out of federal custody."

Devon nodded. "Tell me about it. I can't even tell how long we've been memory-surfing. Has it been minutes or hours?"

"Oh, please," Alek scoffed as he casually leaned against the wooden lounge with his arms crossed before his chest. "Bai Lee's good. But she's not that good."

Devon looked over at Bai Lee and was surprised to see that she had vacated her perch. She was actually standing quite a few feet away from her wooden lounge, looking uncomfortable, like she was struggling with a bad bout of gas. Devon wondered why she wasn't lashing out at Alek with a harsh quip of her own. She was just standing there, her expression unreadable as she quietly—uncomfortably—watched Alek.

"Okay," Devon said, when Bai Lee didn't speak up. "I'm not sure I understand what you're getting at there by insulting our hostess. Because I was only commenting on air transport time. You know, back in the real world."

Alek chuckled humorlessly, and Devon hadn't a clue as to what the heck the Romanian was laughing at. He sure wished that he felt stronger, because he would really love to wipe that smug look off of Alek's face.

"What's so funny?" Vahn asked.

"Nothing you would care to know about."

"Is that so?" Devon could hear the icy edge in Vahn's voice. The tension between them was rising. Yet Devon couldn't shake the feeling that Alek was purposely provoking a fight.

Devon sat up, shaking his head. "No, no, no, Alek—no more of this! We are not going to fight amongst ourselves! We have an escape to plan!"

"Do we?" Alek asked, his head cocked to the side as if he were talking to a simpleton. "Are you really so sure about that?"

Vahn went rigid beside him. "You mean we're not on an air transport bound for Washington?"

Alek stared hard at Vahn. "I'm betting that none of us were ever in federal custody in the first place."

"What?" Nevada cried. "That's impossible! I headbutted a guy in the nose—broke it, too! That sure as hell felt real!"

Alek shrugged. "Sure, it did." He gestured to everything around him. "Doesn't all of this feel real?"

Nevada frowned, looking warily at Alek. "Yeah, well, I know I bloodied some poor sap's nose. He looked like a federal agent to me."

"Mine too," said Miguel. "They had badges, the vehicles, guns too."

"I was taken by Army Special Forces," said Vahn. "I didn't get a good look at their faces."

"Me neither," Devon added, remembering his encounter with an involuntary shudder. "My captors were military too, and they didn't exactly shake my hand and offer me hot cocoa."

Alek smiled. "How do you know if they were friend or foe?"

"Most definitely foe," Nevada said, crossing her arms. "Because why the hell would the Network treat us like criminals? They're supposed to be on our side."

"Oh, of that I am quite certain," Alek quipped, looking quite pleased with himself. "But then again, perhaps the

Psionic Underground Network has something to fear from us as well…something none of you are taking into consideration."

Devon knew what Alek was referring to—a mole. Someone like Braxton Miller.

Vahn scowled. "So, we're not on an air transport, we aren't held by the feds, and now you—the person who tried to convince us that the Network doesn't even exist—are telling us that we need to worry about government infiltrators? How dare you even insinuate that a psion would turn on his own kind?"

"Oh, but my dear and noble psi-blade," Alek said in a menacing voice. "It happens all the time."

Devon caught a glimpse of the fury that Alek harbored behind his penetrating gaze. It was a dark and desperate look, one devoid of emotion. It was the gaze of a sociopath.

And suddenly, Devon was very afraid.

"Who are you?" Devon asked as he held tight to Alya's hand. "What do you want with us?"

Alya went rigid beside Devon. She cocked her head to the side as she looked at her brother with a strange expression on her face. "You were the one who altered my replay," she said breathlessly. "You were a beast from the shadows when I first glimpsed you."

Alek smiled at her but said nothing.

She pointed at him then, her voice only slightly above a whisper. "You are not my twin. You are a monster."

Alek's smile vanished. "No, my dear, dear sister, that's where you are most mistaken. I am the exact same monster you created the day you abandoned me in that hellhole!"

"He's a government spy!" Bai Lee cried, but Devon could tell it was taking her great effort to speak. "He's a para-psion! I'm releasing you! Get the hell out of here!"

Devon gaped at Alek as the Romanian's face contorted, and his starburst eyes turned a bottomless black. When next

Alek grinned, it was to reveal a mouth full of sharp, needle-like teeth. "What the—"

"Get the hell out of my head, Devon! Now!" Bai Lee's voice screamed inside his skull.

And all at once he was sucked into oblivion, traveling at the speed of thought down some mental drainpipe, hurtling toward his body somewhere. It was as if the floor of the world had opened and he had been tossed into the steepest, twistiest log plunge ride imaginable—only without the log.

Oh, yeah, this was insanity at its best. Especially if Scary Alek was correct about the entire federal arrest thing being a Network method for weeding out government moles. If that was true, then he prayed that his mind remembered where the Network had parked his carcass, because he sure as heck didn't have a clue.

Chapter Nineteen

DEVON opened his eyes and was knocked sideways by the sheer overload of his pain receptors. Hunger, pain, and nausea slammed into him like one big angry fist. His first instinct was to heave, but that would mean ruining the nice cross trainers of the person standing next to his hospital chair.

Hey, wait a minute. Where the heck was he?

"You're in a Network stronghold, Devon. There are no feds here," said a female voice beside him. "Just try and relax. I'll have you up and out of here in a jiffy."

Taking a deep breath, Devon clamped his jaws shut and willed the acid in his stomach to remain there. Once he was sure he wouldn't ruin anyone's footwear, he looked up into the face of a pretty female psion around his own age. She had skin the color of sweet melted chocolate and wide starburst eyes that would make her a head-turner no matter what Network cell she stepped into. She was tall and shapely in her blue jeans and white T-shirt. Devon couldn't believe his luck, but no matter how babe-a-licious this Florence Nightingale at his bedside was, his heart belonged solely to Alya.

Alya. Devon tried to turn his head to locate her, but he couldn't seem to move.

"Here. Let me get that," said the psion beside him. She reached above his head and retracted the metallic headgear that had been positioned over either side of his temples and attached firmly to the back of the chair. "Telepathic enhancer," she explained. "It's what enabled all of us to monitor you."

He was about to ask her what she meant by that, when he heard the unmistakable crack of gunfire.

"What's going on?" Devon asked.

"He's coming." She threw a worried glance past Devon to something happening on the other side of the room. Her fingers tugged two more restraining latches free before her eyes slid once again, warily, back to whatever was going on over there.

"Who? You mean Alek?" he asked, trying to follow her gaze, but he was too disoriented to do much of anything except gape at the elaborate bank of machines monitoring his vital signs. An IV line ran into his right hand, and his left arm was set in a cast. He welcomed the familiar ache that radiated up his arm; the pain anchored him. This was what real life felt like. And it was good to know that he was truly back inside his own messed-up body.

"Of course, that's who I mean," his attendant snapped, tugging with all her might on one last strap. "He'll be here any minute."

"Well, where is he?"

"Way back in the factory's old sewing room. Just him and his sister—"

An explosion resounded from the back of the building, followed a moment later by the sputter of gunfire and screams of agony.

Oh, no. That didn't sound good.

The girl worked even faster to free him.

Directly across from him, Devon spied Vahn with his black mop of hair sitting up on a medical reclining chair of his own. A psion and an adult baseline, both wearing black fatigues, were urging the psi-blade to get to his feet.

More gunfire echoed in the back of the building, along with the shouts of the Network freedom workers. Or at least, Devon *hoped* they were freedom workers.

Looking around the room, his eyes trailed across a long, rectangular window made up of at least a hundred square windowpanes. Each pane had been meticulously painted black at one time, but age and the elements had worn most of the paint away, allowing sunlight to stream into the large warehouse. He even caught a glimpse of a massive oak tree just outside, its mighty branches wending their way inside through a broken pane. The sight of the tree was enough to give Devon a bit of hope that he might actually, somehow, survive this.

Glancing around the brick building, he perceived that they were in the run-down storage area of a once-thriving production line. *McCallis Shirtworks* was emblazoned on many of the boxes and crates that remained stacked in orderly piles around the spacious room. The cement floor was well-lined with cracks and water stains, but otherwise the building appeared sound.

Devon was pulled from his thoughts by another explosion—one that caused the entire building to tremble. The fight was getting closer.

His attendant hovered over his remaining disruptor band, which, like the other two she had just removed, was attached to a thick chain that shackled him to the floor. She touched the plastic key card to the band, but nothing happened. Frowning, she grabbed a pair of crazy-looking glasses off a medical instrument stand behind her. As soon as she slid the glasses on, mechanized lenses whirled and clicked into position over her eyes, but she didn't appear to notice. Her attention was riveted to the plastic key card she held close to her face.

"There a problem?" Devon croaked. He couldn't believe how utterly toad-like he sounded. In front of a beautiful girl, no less.

"Shhh," she said, as she turned the plastic key card in her hand. "I just knew these mechanisms needed replacing. Ugh! I'm so stupid!"

They both jumped when a barrage of gunfire erupted nearby and a group of a dozen Network freedom workers—

psion and baseline alike—dressed in haphazard pieces of combat armor ran past them toward the back of the building.

"Oh, my God, I can't get you out of here until I remove this stupid disruptor band!" She appeared to be on the verge of losing it.

"Don't worry. We'll get it open," Devon said, in an attempt to calm her down. "But first, could you tell me your name?"

"Winifred. Winnie to my friends."

"As in the Pooh?"

She gave him a you've-got-to-be-kidding-me look above the rim of her funky glasses and abruptly jerked his IV line free.

"Ow!" Devon cried.

"You can call me Winifred," she said. She held up the key card and once again put it to Devon's disruptor band. This time, the device popped open and she tossed the metal band to the ground. "Come on, we gotta move! That para-psion's going to find his way back here soon enough, and we want to be long gone before he does."

"But what about the others?"

"What others?"

"You know—Alya, Nevada and Miguel?"

"Don't you go worrying. They've got lots of good people looking after them," she said as she tugged Devon off of the medical chair and to his feet. He winced when the jerking motion shot white-hot pain up and down his arm.

Winifred's eyes went wide when she glanced behind them. "Oh, boy! We gotta go—we gotta go now!"

She pushed him down to the ground just as a huge explosion rocked the building. Medical equipment and debris flew everywhere. Somewhere behind them, a fire started. Devon could smell the acrid stench of smoke filling the room.

Apparently, Alek knew how to make one heck of an entrance when he wanted to.

Favoring his good arm, Devon crawled to an overturned desk and helped Winifred around to the other side. The sound of gunfire crackled from all directions.

"Oh, boy, I knew this was going to be a bad one," she said catching her breath. "Government must have worked overtime on that poor kid."

"You mean Alek?"

Winifred nodded. "Recruiting isn't as hard as it used to be. The feds have a knack for finding some seriously sick puppies out there."

"You mean mentally disturbed," Devon said, trying to grasp what Winifred was getting at.

"You can call it what you like. But the fact is, Alek didn't become a genetically mutated sociopathic psychic cannibal overnight."

What did she just say? "A psychic cannibal?"

Winifred frowned. "Cannibal, vampire—whatever you want to call it. But just so you know, that dude out there doesn't just siphon off our psionic energy—he devours it. We're nothing but food to him."

"So, we're the Cheerios in his breakfast bowl."

"You got it."

"The beef in his stew."

"Uh…yeah." Winifred was frowning.

"The—"

She covered his mouth with her hand. "Will you get serious and focus here? We're in a world of trouble right now!"

There was the unmistakable sizzle of gathering psionic energy. Devon glanced at Winifred and threw his body over hers seconds before another enormous psi-cannon shell exploded a few yards away. Concrete, bricks, dirt, and debris rained down on them. Devon held her for a moment longer and then slowly looked around.

There was a gigantic hole in the floor where his medical chair had been a moment before. Holy crap! Apparently, Alek was a badass psi-cannon, too. Devon turned to Winifred as the enormity of what they were up against began to sink in. "What the hell else can he do?"

Winifred frowned. "It varies. Every para-psion is different. But the one thing about para-psions you need to know is that no matter how many psionic disciplines are at his or her disposal, they can only perform one discipline at a time. Their brains aren't wired for multitasking. Thank God."

"So, what's your discipline?" he asked as he scooted them both closer behind the overturned desk.

"Tech-head," she said pointing at her glasses. "But unlike a tree shepherd, such as yourself, I'm completely useless in this situation."

"Well, I'm hardly useful," Devon grumbled. "All I do is talk to plants."

Winifred raised an eyebrow. "Right. Like that earthquake that flattened a five-story parking structure just happened by accident."

"Well, I sure as hell didn't do it," he shot back heatedly.

"Oh, really? You sure about that?"

Winifred's words stopped Devon cold. *Was* he sure about that? Well, it wasn't like he was an earthmover who could command an earthquake to happen instantly. No, that night, he had been in too much pain to think about much of anything at all. He'd just assumed it was just one big natural coincidence that had caused the parking structure to collapse. Either that, or someone else had psionically contributed to his escape.

But there had been no one else alive to help him.

Unless...the trees surrounding the parking garage had thought to intervene on his behalf.

Once again, the sizzle of psionic energy filled the room, but this time, it came from the opposite direction. Grabbing Winifred with his good arm, Devon tossed her around the side of the desk. He dove in right behind her just as a large crimson energy shell came streaking toward them. It lit up the room in an eerie electric-red light before exploding fifteen meters away.

Devon covered Winifred's body with his own as more debris rained down on them. There were fires all over the building now, the windows were broken, and people were screaming and crying. The sound of gunfire had ceased.

"Devon McWilliams!" a thick, deep voice called.

Oh, great...Alek was looking for a fight. And with Devon, of all people!

"I think he's scared of you," Winifred said quietly.

"What? That's the stupidest thing I ever heard. He could squash me like a bug!"

Winifred shrugged. "Well, that's obviously not what *he* thinks."

Devon was about to disagree when he was struck by a thought. "Back in the badlands, the Network practically fried me. Why?"

"Because we were told there was a mole in your group, and after we heard about the nine point seven earthquake, we feared *you* might be a shadow walker. We had all kinds of gizmos monitoring you plus three disruptor bands chaining you to the floor because we were going to shut you down in an instant if we had to." Winifred shook her head in disgust. "We were so sure that you were the government spy that I didn't even strap Alek in with any kind of secondary disruptor frequencies. In short, I messed up." She hung her head and lowered her voice. "I'm the one who didn't contain the shadow walker."

"Shadow walker? Is that what you call them?"

"Yes. They can appear and disappear, using shadows as dimensional portals."

"Great. A guy you can't turn your back on. Literally."

"Oh, yeah, and a little ol' tech-head like me can't do squat to him. And he knows it, too."

"Devon McWilliams!" Alek's creepy voice boomed. "Face me now! Or I will start killing your friends one by one…starting with dear little Alison here."

Nevada! Devon's heart leapt to his throat. No! Not Nevada! Not any of them!

Devon scanned the bank of windows high above until he spotted the great oak's entwined branches. Without the disruptor bands on, he could feel the tree's presence—its thick roots nestled deep in the rich earth, its wide expansive canopy warm and impressive in the afternoon sunlight.

Opening his mind, he reached out beyond the oak and found a multitude of maples, ash, fir, and cottonwoods. An entire forest, in fact! All of them stirring at his mental touch.

We're here… the oak tree sighed as a breeze fluttered its magnificent canopy. *We feel you…*

"DEVON MCWILLIAMS!" thundered Alek. And Devon's heart stopped when he heard Nevada scream.

"Don't hurt them!" he cried as he bolted up from behind the overturned desk. He sidestepped Winifred's hand when she attempted to keep him from going out there.

"What the hell are you doing, McWilliams?" she urgently whispered.

"Heck if I know," he replied with a shrug. "But stay out of sight. This is probably going to get messy."

Holding his good hand up in surrender, Devon walked as far as he could toward the center of the room. He stopped at the rim of a humongous crater in the floor.

"Okay. I'm here," he said. The thought that his friends might die kept him focused on what he was about to do. "So, why don't you show your big bad self, Alek?"

Catching a glimmer from the shadows before him, Devon watched in awe as the darkness appeared to liquefy and then recede, leaving behind a thin, bald figure who crumpled lifelessly to the ground.

"Nevada!" Devon cried. He raced around the edge of the crater to her. It hurt like hell, but he managed to cradle her in his arms.

Relief rushed over him when he saw her eyelids flutter open.

"Nevada! Can you hear me?"

She gazed up at him, and Devon leaned in closer. "Hurt that little shithead good."

Devon nodded. "You rest while I go and see what he wants."

"What *I* want?" Alek cried in a mocking tone as the shadows liquefied around Devon. When they receded, the unconscious bodies of Vahn and Miguel lay on either side of him.

Vahn was the closest, so Devon grabbed his wrist and quickly found his pulse. But Miguel was simply too far away. "Hang on, buddy," Devon said, as he gently laid Nevada down and then hurried to Miguel's side. He took a deep breath when he found the telepath still breathing. Thank God.

"So then," said Devon as he stood, "where're Bai Lee and Alya?"

Alek's sinister laugh filled the room, and that's when Devon knew for certain that he was in way over his head.

Use us! We too shall fight! Darkness is no match for light! The oak tree's deep voice resonated majestically inside Devon's mind, its voice as strong and sturdy as its massive trunk.

Ignoring the pain in his arm, Devon stood straighter and addressed the darkness that ebbed and flowed before him. "I asked you a question, Alek! Where's—"

"Right here," he said, emerging from the darkness. But his face no longer resembled the handsome teen Devon had first met—when? Hours ago? Days ago? Devon couldn't be sure. The shadow walker's eyes were liquid night, his face contorted to make room for a set of evil-looking teeth that had no business being in a human mouth. What had the government done to him?

On Alek's right stood Bai Lee, still as a statue, her eyes wide open and unblinking, while Alek held her in a trance-like state. She was wearing black military fatigues like many of the freedom workers in this room, her face as lovely as ever. Their entire encounter on the air transport had been nothing but one incredible telepathic mirage. Even his vomit-encrusted face had smelled incredibly real.

On Alek's left, he clutched his sister by the throat. He held Alya so high that she was forced to balance on her tiptoes in order to breathe. She glanced over at Devon with wide, panicked eyes.

"Run, Devon!" she managed to cry before Alek tightened his grip.

"Alya!" Devon shouted. Then he looked directly at Alek. "Let them go! Now!"

That evil grin widened to reveal row upon row of saliva-coated needle-like teeth. "And to think I was ever concerned about you. You! A simpleton who talks to plants! The way you fretted so over the discovery of your pathetic little humiliations! Even Bai Lee here was impressed with your mental defenses! You fooled us both, while wearing multiple disruptors, no less!"

While Alek talked, Devon noticed that Vahn had partially activated his armor. The psi-blade was conscious and preparing for a last-ditch effort. That was reassuring to the tree shepherd, who only needed an opening to launch an attack of his own.

"You call me a simpleton," Devon shouted angrily at the creature standing across from him. "Yet you're the one who got so caught up with discovering who I was that you completely blew your mission!"

"I did not blow my mission!"

"Oh, really? Weren't you supposed to infiltrate the Psionic Underground and report back to your federal masters like some psychotic lapdog?"

Alek's face distorted as he struggled to contain his rage. "I am death!" he screamed.

"You are an abomination!" Devon shouted, and at that moment, he saw his opening. The minute Alek eased his grip around Alya's throat, Devon opened his mind full bore and called the entire forest to him.

SAVE HER! he psychically ordered his army of trees. The earth trembled as over fifty slumbering giants awoke to Devon's call.

Alek furiously locked eyes with him an instant before two thick roots burst from the ground, effectively separating the shadow walker from Alya and the unresponsive Bai Lee.

"No!" he screamed as Alya ran to the other side of the crater. Alek's eyes flashed and Devon saw him gather the darkness around him.

Don't allow him to escape! Devon ordered the trees.

Enormous tree limbs—maple, oak, pine, cottonwood—punctured the ceiling, and in one heave, they lifted off the entire roof. Sunlight flooded the chamber as Alek covered his eyes and screamed.

But the distraction didn't last long. The sizzle of gathering psionic energy filled the room. Alek was powering up a huge psi-cannon shell.

"I got this one!" Nevada yelled over the din of battle as the tree army continued its advancement. Around them, the ground trembled and the abandoned warehouse crumbled as the trees pulled it apart brick by brick.

Alya ran into Devon's arms at the same time Alek released his massive power burst. Together they watched the rotating ball of psionic energy fly toward them, only to be engulfed a moment later by Nevada's conjured tornado and sent skyward.

"NO!" Alek screamed, "I will not be defeated! I will not—"

Vahn's crimson blade appeared beneath the para-psion's sternum, effectively cleaving Alek's heart in two. Vahn flared his longsword before retracting his blade. The psi-blade then stepped back, shield up, wary of a counterattack.

Devon halted his tree army. The trembling ceased as Alek quietly fell to his knees. He looked over at Devon and Alya, the inky black draining from his starburst eyes.

"Alya," he whispered before tumbling headlong into the crater before him.

Alya gasped and buried her face in Devon's sweater as she sobbed. He could only guess that she wasn't crying for her twin's loss alone, but for the incredible amount of death, heartache, and destruction that he had caused.

Devon wrapped his arms around his Romanian princess and let her grieve, feeling her heartbeat flutter against his chest.

No one moved for several moments. Only Alya's muffled sobs filled the chamber. Slowly, Nevada set about helping Miguel to his feet, while Vahn and Winifred guided Bai Lee to a makeshift stretcher.

All around the building, soft cries and moans could be heard as the freedom workers began to gather. Soon, they would begin the task of searching for the wounded and the dead. Taking in the destruction around him, Devon knew that it was going to be one very long and somber day.

From high above, Devon heard a deep psychic murmuring, and he saw the trees sway. He understood instantly what they were doing, and he freely lent them his power as the trees moved in unison, their voices rising and falling in chorus; their powerful voices intoned a dirge as old and powerful as the earth itself.

As an ancient melody filled his mind, Devon hugged Alya a little bit tighter. He wanted so much to show her that she was by no means alone in her grief.

They had all lost so very much that even the trees were mourning.

But they were alive. And Devon was determined to face the next chapter of his life on his own terms.

He would always be a freak, but at least for today, with Alya in his arms and his friends safe and sound, he felt the tiniest bit kick-ass.

And that was a very good feeling indeed.

Epilogue

DEVON McWilliams hopped out of the back of the pickup truck, mindful of stray patches of grass that might have infiltrated the forest floor. It had only been two months since he had joined the Psionic Underground Network, but in that time he had learned how to wield his powers with an authority he had never known possible. Despite there being such an amazing support system of baselines and psions keeping him well-fed and out of federal custody, life as a member of the psionic freedom movement had proved challenging.

Devon was constantly on the move and exhausted from the travel. He journeyed from one secret hideout to another, and each new location took him farther and farther from home. Farther from home had been the last thing he'd wanted the day he begged Colton Weaver to include him in his escape from the North Central Psi Facility.

But, of course, those plans had gone horribly awry. And while Devon hadn't intentionally used his psionic abilities to harm anyone that night, he had unknowingly called the old maple trees surrounding the parking structure to rise up in his defense. Their thick roots had tunneled beneath the soil, while their great branches had smashed cars and punched their way through concrete walls.

Just like that kid in Brazil, Devon had used majestic, peaceful trees to bring about great destruction. It had been a shameful act that had killed not only humans, but the trees themselves. Without Devon's assistance, the maple trees had perished once the parking structure collapsed. The destruction had been so complete and devastating that the rescue teams had yet to find all of the bodies beneath the rubble. Devon McWilliams was listed as missing and presumed dead.

That was probably the only reason he had ever made it to the rendezvous point in the first place. No one from the North Central Psi Facility had pursued him into the badlands that fateful night. As far as they were concerned, he had been neutralized.

But his family thought he was dead, too, and that just added to his pain. It was yet another irreparable loss that he struggled to reconcile.

Thank God he had Alya. They were officially a couple now, and Devon still couldn't quite believe it. But at Alya's gentle urging, Devon was getting over himself a little bit more every day. It was hard not to think of himself as Plant Boy anymore. But as the days rolled by, his anxiety-riddled life before he met Alya became a distant memory.

Devon gazed at the noble redwoods that surrounded him as his companions walked leisurely up the trail. He stood in a redwood grove just off the California coastline. He had always wanted to visit a primeval forest of redwoods, and from the moment the truck had turned into the state park, he had felt their generous spirits stirring at his mere presence. He could feel the ancient forest dwellers watching him curiously, his psionic energy having pulled some of them from deep slumber. The oldest of the redwoods regarded him suspiciously; he could feel the weight of their mistrust hanging over him like a giant flyswatter ready to smash him to bits at the first sign of danger. With their Jurassic size and deep, almost godlike ties with the earth, these trees were practically alien creatures to Devon.

No matter what happened tonight, just being in their presence was already one of the most humbling and amazing experiences of his life.

"You ready?" Alya asked as she stepped up beside him beneath the canopy of trees.

Devon flashed her a nervous smile and took her hand. "I sure hope so."

Leaning forward, Alya kissed him on the cheek. "You're going to be magnificent. They're going to love you."

"Who? The trees, or my audience?"

"Both," she replied with a laugh.

"Devon! Hey, Devon!" called Winifred as she jogged toward them. "You got a sec? I've got something for you."

"Sure." Devon and Alya held hands and waited for Winifred to catch up to them.

Breathing heavy, she held a tiny box out to Devon. "Here. He arrived at my window this morning."

Devon looked at her dubiously, but opened the box as instructed. Inside was a tiny mechanical dragonfly, with delicate golden wings and large turquoise eyes. "It's beautiful, Winifred."

"Call me Winnie," she beamed. "Now, say 'playback.'"

When Devon hesitated, she fanned her hands at him in encouragement. "Go on, now—say it."

"Playback."

The dragonfly chirped and its delicate wings furiously beat the air. It rose from the box and hovered seven feet off the ground. Its green eyes flashed, and a tiny beam of light pooled on the ground before Devon and Alya.

"Honey? Devon, honey, can you hear me?" said a woman's voice.

"Mom?" Devon gasped.

"Oh, Ben, I think I might be doing this wrong," said his mother's voice. There was a click and a break in the beam of light, and suddenly, a full-sized three-dimensional image of Devon's mother was standing before him. She looked lovely in a bright summer dress, her thick brown hair perfectly styled, though she did look a lot thinner since he had last seen her.

"Oh, there! I think that's it, Ben." His mother looked to the right, listening to someone out of the projection range. "Oh, right, I almost forgot." His mom turned back to look at him. "Linny says to say hi, and she hasn't been in your room much since you left. You know, she misses you, honey. We all do. And yes, the FBI did tell us that you were missing and presumed dead, so you can imagine our relief when Linny found Winnie's dragonfly perched on one of my rose bushes. Isn't it just the perfect solution? Winnie Addleberry is an absolute dear—a bona fide genius. Tell her we said hello and thank you. We can't wait to see your first dragonfly hologram."

She paused then as she choked back a sob. Smiling through it, despite the tears held precariously in her eyes, his mother continued. "We know it's an uncertain time for you right now, honey, but one day, I know that we'll be together again as a family." She wiped a tear from the side of her face. "Oh, just look at me; I'm a mess. We love you, Devon. Be safe. And know that we'll be on the lookout for your golden dragonfly sparkling in my rose garden."

With a click, the hologram of his mother vanished.

Devon stood speechless, not even bothering to wipe away the tear that trailed down the side of his face.

"So, what do you think?" Winnie asked tentatively.

Slowly, he turned to her. "That was the most amazing thing anyone has ever done for me… Thank you, Winifred."

She looked at him pointedly. "I told you to call me Winnie. Only my granny calls me Winifred. Besides, it makes me sound like some old lady."

"Okay, Winnie it is, then." Devon reached out and pulled her into a hug. "Thank you."

"You're welcome, tree boy," she said, and then quickly pulled away from his embrace. "Speaking of trees, shouldn't you be making like one instead of slobbering all over me like some drool-challenged Saint Bernard?"

"We *should* get going," agreed Alya. She smiled at Winnie and waved. "See you at the afterparty, Winnie."

"You got it! I'll fill you in on how the dragonfly hologram recorder works later. Good luck tonight."

"Thanks again, Winnie!" Devon called as he and Alya raced down the forest path hand in hand, only to stop dead in their tracks at the top of a small rise.

"Oh, my," Alya gasped.

Devon wrapped an arm around her shoulders and took in the sight of hundreds of people, entire families even, sitting on picnic blankets beneath the trees, waiting for him. All of them were members of the Psionic Underground Network. And Devon was well aware that each and every one of them was risking their lives to be here this evening. "I thought this was supposed to be a small gathering."

"I thought so, too."

Devon could see people sitting in every direction encircling the three lounge chairs that were to be his stage. "Well, I guess word got out."

Alya laughed. "I guess it did."

Hand in hand, they strolled down the path, waving awkwardly at the large crowd that had gathered. An energized awareness flittered through the spectators as many of them sat up or stood to watch Devon and Alya pass.

"The Tree Shepherd," he heard an excited voice whisper in the crowd.

"Devon! Oh, my gawd!" cried Nevada, as she raced out from beneath the trees in greeting. Her hair was growing in, her psi-tat no longer visible on her scalp. "I'm so excited! I've totally invited, like, all of my new friends. I even recruited Jake's mom. She's working for the Network now. She came up from LA tonight to experience this."

Nevada threw her arms around Devon and Alya and hugged them both at the same time. "I totally miss you guys! Let's catch up at the celebration afterwards, okay?"

"See you there!" Devon said, beaming. Looking around, he couldn't believe the sheer number of people who had shown up. He had noticed both baseline and psionic faces in the crowd, all of them hoping for a chance to share in this once-in-a-lifetime experience.

Together, Devon and Alya walked toward Miguel, who was patiently waiting for them not too far from the lounge chairs. He was Devon's official road manager for tonight's demonstration. Miguel was in training to control his telepathy, but Devon still couldn't get over his rapid progress not only with the mastering of his powers, but the English language as well.

"There you are," Miguel said, clasping Devon warmly on the shoulder. "Where have you been?"

"We got held up. Sorry."

Flashing him a strained grin, Miguel stepped closer and gestured toward the Chinese beauty who was taking a seat on one of the loungers. "Please don't make her wait any longer. Waiting makes her extremely cranky."

"Thanks for the tip," Devon said with an apologetic shrug. He could only imagine what Miguel had had to endure in his absence.

"Don't mention it," Miguel replied with a wink. "Just get out there and do your thing."

"You got it." Devon turned to Alya. "You ready?"

Alya looked troubled. "Are you sure you want me to go out there with you? I mean, it's not like I'm going to be doing anything out there."

"Oh, yes, you are."

"I am?"

"Of course. You're my standby EMT."

Alya grinned. "Your what?"

"My on-site healer. You know, just in case."

"Just in case of what?"

Devon shrugged. "Who knows? It's not like I've been around ancient redwoods before. What if it's all too much for me and I need mouth-to-mouth resuscitation or something?"

Alya raised an eyebrow. "Mouth-to-mouth resuscitation?"

"Uh-huh."

"Because of a tree?"

"That's right."

Alya laughed. "Oh, Devon. If you want me to hold your hand through this, all you have to do is ask."

Devon sweetly kissed the back of her hand. "Then I am asking." He gave her his best Prince Charming smile. "Please?"

"You're impossible," she teased as she slipped her arm through his with a giggle. "Let's go, already."

Arm in arm, Devon and Alya walked toward the two empty lounge chairs. The third one was occupied by Bai Lee Chen. Oh, wait a minute, strike that—Bai Lee Chen wasn't her real name. That was the one she used for everyone's little replay head-trip—you know, to hide her true identity like the kick-ass freedom fighter that she was.

Her real name was Mae Sing Wong, and she was not a para-psion—just merely one heck of a powerful telepath. One with attitude to spare.

Devon nodded in greeting to Mae Sing, only to have her frown and tap her wristwatch.

Yup. One powerful telepath, one super-sized attitude.

But you had to love her.

Applause rose as Devon addressed the crowd, the sun sinking low on the horizon to his right. "Thank you for coming this evening," he said as loudly as he could, making sure to acknowledge those behind him as well. "Tonight is a very special night for me because it has always been my wish to share this experience with others. And I hope, after you hear what the trees have to say, that people worldwide will reconsider how we, as a species, treat our plant life.

"So, please, lie back, find a nice comfortable position, and open your minds. I guarantee you're going to be amazed at what you're about to experience here tonight.

"Thank you."

Polite applause broke out as Devon walked to the chairs. He helped Alya into her cushiony lounger, then lay back and got comfortable in his. As he swung his legs up onto the chair, he thought of Vahn and how he had first volunteered for Mae Sing's replay. He missed the quiet, noble psi-blade, but nothing was going to tie him down for long without his beloved Emily. Vahn had left three weeks ago to follow up on a promising lead. No one had heard from him since.

Devon prayed that the big guy was all right. If anyone in life deserved a happy ending, it was Vahn de Montague.

With one last look around, Devon reached over and took Alya's hand and gently squeezed it three times. That was their private code for "I love you."

He grinned to himself when she squeezed his hand three times in return.

She loved him, too.

Ah, this was one of those perfect life moments. He hoped that he wasn't about to mess it all up with what he was about to do.

Gazing up at the powerful redwoods that loomed above him, Devon relaxed his body and opened his mind.

Sing for us...the people are listening... Show them what it is to be...natural divinity...

He was not disappointed by the mental stirring he felt, as a solitary bass voice rose from a whisper and gathered strength in volume. One voice, then two, then five, then many, filled his head in song never intended for human ears.

Once the choir of trees began to hum, Devon pointed to Mae Sing beside him. It was her telepathy that enabled the crowd to experience what previously only Devon could hear. As the trees followed the rhythm of the warm ocean breeze, their chorus rose in a lovely melody that sprang from the natural world. The voices built upon the original tune with a series of delightful variations that filled his head with complicated runs infused with jubilant inflection. It was a vibrant, stirring sound that crescendoed until the voices united as one in a powerful series of chords that gripped Devon's heart in what could only be described as beauteous thunder.

When he heard the collective gasp from the audience, he knew that they had all just experienced it, too.

That was the natural world calling.

Voices once silent, now shared.

Devon had found a way to build his bridge, after all.

He was a tree shepherd.

Just one of the many beautiful freaks of nature.

Shhh.

Open your mind.

Listen.

The trees are singing.

Acknowledgements

I would like to thank some of the many people whose contributions made this book possible. First and foremost, a big warm thank-you goes out to my editor, Jennifer Carson, who saw potential in this manuscript and championed it all the way through to publication. Thanks too to Kate Kaynak, Jessica Porteous, and Raychelle Steele, and the many other wonderful and talented people at Spencer Hill Press who helped this strange little story out along the way. It's been a pleasure to work with you.

A very special thank you goes out to Chad Brigham, from the Leach Firm, LLC, who has graciously put up with my endless stream of questions and concerns and who has been absolutely invaluable in his ability to translate legalese. Thank you, Chad!

Deep in my heart, I know that this novel probably wouldn't have ever gotten off the ground if it weren't for the talented members of my writing group—Shellie Braeuner, Susan Shifay Cheung and Doan Phuong Nguyen. Thank you for your wisdom, friendship, and proofreading skills over the years. Your belief in me is humbling. I cherish you all.

Thanks also goes out to Mike Corriero, an extraordinarily gifted artist who has brought the Freaks of Nature universe to life through his creature, tech and character designs. It's such a pleasure to work with you, Mike. Your talent blows me away. Thank you! (Mike's work is on display in this book and at www.wendybrotherlin.com and www.mikecorriero.com. Check him out.)

I would also like to say a big think you to Dianne Ellenberger, my forever friend, whose encouragement and story editing skills are second to none. I couldn't have done this without your spot-on advice.

Thanks too, to my parents, Robert and Carol Brotherlin, who never doubted that one day I would be published.

Lastly, I would like to thank my husband and children for supplying me with ample amounts of hugs and laughter. Your support and encouragement are what inspires me.

About the Illustrator

MIKE Corriero lives in New Jersey and works as a freelance concept artist and illustrator for the video game, film and entertainment industries. Clients include: Applibot Inc., The Topps Company, Hasbro Inc., Paizo Publishing, Liquid Development, Radical Entertainment and Zynga among others.

MIKE specializes in Creature Design, Visual Development, Character Design and Environments. He has also taught as an online Instructor for the Academy of Art University in early 2012. Mike continues to pursue his passion and love of designing conceptual creatures as an independent contractor.

About the Author

WENDY Brotherlin is a screenwriter, music enthusiast and all around geek-goddess. She earned a Masters in Screenwriting at the University of Southern California and went on to write for children's television including Nickelodeon's *Are You Afraid of the Dark?*. Today, she lives in Manchester, Maine, with her husband and two little super-heroes-in-training. *Freaks of Nature* is her first novel.

CPSIA information can be obtained at www.ICGtesting.com
Printed in the USA
LVOW04s0554250615

443794LV00005B/10/P

9 781633 920064